DRIVE

The Volunteers Series

Book One

JOHN NUCKEL

First edition 2018

Published in the USA by *thewordverve inc.* (**www.thewordverve.com**) eBook

ISBN: 978-1-948225-05-2

Paperback ISBN: 978-1-082189-97-5

Library of Congress Control Number: 2017961523

~~~~~

Drive

A Book with Verve by *thewordverve inc.*

Cover design by
www.indiedesignz.com

Paperback and eBook formatting by Bob Houston
http://facebook.com/eBookFormatting/info

"It is not the critic who counts; not the man who points out how the strong man stumbles, or where the doer of deeds could have done better. The credit belongs to the man who is actually in the arena, whose face is marred by dust and sweat and blood; who strives valiantly; who errs, who comes short again and again, because there is no effort without error and shortcoming; but who does actually strive to do the deeds; who knows great enthusiasms, the great devotions; who spends himself in a worthy cause; who at the best knows in the end the triumph of high achievement, and who at the worst, if he fails, at least fails while daring greatly, so that his place shall never be with those cold and timid souls who neither know victory nor defeat."

-*Theodore Roosevelt.*

Chapter 1

October 18, 1899 – 3:00 a.m.
McSorley's Ole Ale House
7th Street, New York City

Captain Woodbury Kane waited outside of McSorley's Old Ale House. It was a particularly gloomy early morning, the sky shrouded in a cold mist. The moisture from his overcoat and hat seemed to seep into his bones. He shivered once and stepped out of his carriage.

He was waiting for Ward Boss Delvin Costello to exit the bar. Kane took position in front of the carriage and listened as the singing inside the establishment died down. It wouldn't be long. Kane stood erect, lifted his homburg from his head, and then put it back on, signaling to a man from a doorway to the left and another from the right to step out of the shadows onto East 7th Street. They walked slowly toward the entrance of the pub with sidearms drawn and held low at their sides.

As expected, Costello's hired men emerged from McSorley's first. Two Irish boxers, both drunk and bloated. Ten years past their fighting trim. They were no more than brawlers now, deputized by Tammany Hall to break the noses of Costello's late payers. Kane's men approached from either side and drew their guns to the brawlers' heads. Kane walked forward.

"We're here for Costello. We have no claim against you. Raise your hands, step to the side, and let him out."

The brawlers took a second to consider their situation. In unison, they raised their arms above their heads. The man on the right was so drunk the movement almost toppled him.

Costello swung the door open and stumbled forward in a drunken dance step, almost falling directly into Kane's arms. He righted himself and looked up at Kane.

"Do I know you?'

Kane squared his feet and prepared for confrontation.

"We've met. Last week at the beer hall on 22nd Street. You laughed at me."

Kane's face was rigid with disdain.Costello was full up with ale. He wavered on his feet.

"I don't remember."

"No matter. You're coming with me." Kane grabbed him by the arm and swung him around so his arm was locked up behind him. He pushed the arm upward, and Costello yelped in pain.

"Boys."

"Your boys can't help you, Costello. Can you, boys?"

Kane pushed the arm up farther. Not breaking it just yet. Although he felt a powerful urge to do so.

Costello sobered up quickly and shouted at his brawlers, "What are you doing?"

Kane looked at his men. "Let them go."

Kane's men dropped their guns and shoved the brawlers in the back.

Kane released Costello and turned to the brawlers.

"Go. Go ahead."

The men were confused.

Kane walked over to them, ignoring Costello for the moment.

"My name is Captain Woodbury Kane. First Volunteer Cavalry, Rough Riders unit. I'm remanding this man, Ward Boss Delvin Costello, for the crimes of rape and murder of two innocent young women. You can walk away or come with him. Makes no difference to me."

Costello made a move to run. Kane pulled a sap out of his pocket and, without turning fully, landed a blow squarely on his temple. Costello collapsed. His knees hit the sidewalk first, then he toppled over onto his right side.

One of the brawlers raised up. Kane's man lifted his gun, but Kane waved him away. He walked closer to the brawler. The man stunk of ale, onions, and eggs. Kane stared him down.

"I want you to tell your people about this. Tell them who I am."

The other brawler spoke.

"I know who you are. Captain Woodbury Kane. I know. Please, sir, we're only doing our job. I have a family."

Kane backed away from the confrontation. "Well, go then. Go. If I see you again, you'll be with this miscreant. That's not a place you want to be, believe me. Go!"

The man who spoke turned and sprinted down 7th Street. The man with the egg breath seemed confused and stood still. Kane's man shoved the brawler to get him started. After a stumble, he started trotting down 7th in the other direction. Kane's men walked over to Costello and lifted him into the carriage.

Chapter 2

October 20, 1899
J.P. Morgan Mansion
231 Madison Avenue
New York City

C aptain Woodbury Kane sat silently in the smoking room. Offered neither smoke nor drink, he was alone, waiting for the son of the great man.

It would be impossible to get an audience with John Pierpont Morgan himself, considering Kane's relationship with Teddy Roosevelt. He was scheduled to meet with his son, also named John—a serious man in his own right. Kane wondered if he was a proxy for his father. As did the rest of the New York business community.

John Morgan entered through ten-foot-tall double doors across the room. The exuberant pace of his step matched the smile on his face. Kane measured him immediately. He'd seen this many times since returning from the war. There were men, wealthy men, who seemed to come alive in Kane's presence. These men who have avoided conflict or action their entire lives considered a meeting with him as their brush with excitement. As if a handshake or a shared cocktail served as membership into the group of men, like Kane, who took action, took risks, for what they believed in. Rather than being offended, as some of his fellow Rough Riders had shared with him they were, Kane took this artificial comradery as an opportunity. A chance to imply complicity, to gain advantage in business—or in more delicate affairs, such as was his purpose today.

"Mr. Kane, Mr. Kane. What a pleasure to finally meet you."

Kane rose and shook Morgan's hand. "Mr. Kane is unnecessary."

"Oh, I'm sorry. Should it be Captain?"

"I would prefer Woody."

"Please, Woody, call me Jack."

Kane bowed his head slightly and said, "Jack it is."

Morgan's smile expanded, and his grip grew stronger. Kane thought to wink but avoided the over-the-top gesture, thinking Morgan malleable at this point.

"Please, excuse me. A drink?"

"Yes, please."

Morgan bellowed, "Charlotte!" and there was an immediate knock on the door. "Come."

The door opened, and a young woman entered and bowed her head. Morgan turned to Kane.

"I have a sublime burgundy set aside for the evening. Would you mind if I had my sommelier open it for us?"

"No, of course not. It sounds perfect."

Morgan turned to the girl. "Please have it brought."

"Yes sir." She smiled, then looked over at Kane and smiled again. As young women tended to do.

Morgan walked over to the chair opposite Kane, and they sat in unison. Morgan crossed his legs and pulled out a handkerchief. He wiped his brow with it, then placed the hanky on his knee. Kane was surprised— John Morgan was far from a dandy. He dismissed the act since he had seen far more foppish gestures in his time among the gilded set.

Morgan spoke. "John D. has recommended that I meet with you."

"Yes, Mr. Rockefeller was most kind when we met. And your father, will he be joining us?"

"Well, Captain," Morgan said in deference to his new "friend," speaking as if he were a Rough Rider himself, "you must know of the strain between my father and Mr. Roosevelt."

Kane did not want Morgan to feel too chummy—after all, men gave a lot of themselves for the right to call him Captain. He cringed when anyone other than the men under his command referred to him as such. "Please, call me Woody. We should be aware that Mr. Roosevelt, Teddy, is the governor of our state now."

Morgan shifted in his chair. "Yes, he is. And my father is J.P. Morgan."

The room fell silent. Kane smiled but didn't respond. After a moment, there was a knock on the door.

The sommelier came in and went through an elaborate ritual serving the wine. Morgan sniffed and twirled and sipped, finally nodding his approval. Kane smiled and waited as his glass was filled.

The sommelier bowed, folded a monogramed towel over his arm and departed, leaving the rolling tray behind. Morgan took a sip without ritual. Kane followed. The wine was excellent. Morgan rested the base of his wine glass on the handkerchief on his crossed knee. Kane smiled, realizing the purpose of the hanky and noticing the lack of a table in the entire room.

"My wife is using a new decorator. Minimalism, they call it. Seems like balderdash to me. Then, we do want the missus to be happy. You, Woody, a married man?"

"No, not yet, Jack."

"Why should you, a man like yourself? War hero and what else? Yachtsman? No, no need for marriage. It will do you good, though. I've had my bon vivant days. A man does need to settle to accomplish his goals, I have found. You have time yet."

Morgan, a younger man giving out fatherly advice. Not a bad thought, Kane had to admit. It wasn't until two that afternoon that Kane had risen to meet the day. The tasks ahead of him would require a clearer mind. He sipped again, then reached into his pocket for a hanky. He made a point to slowly place the hanky over his knee and smiled, resting his glass on it. Morgan leaned in and got to the point.

"You know how my father feels about Mr. Roosevelt, but I thought that I should give you an audience. A man of your accomplishments. You see, Woody, unlike my father, I can see a time where the name J.P. or, for that matter, Jack Morgan, won't be enough to bully our way through the world. Mr. Roosevelt has taught us some hard lessons. My father won't change at this point in his life, but I'm looking to the future. Besides, if we only did business with people we agreed with, we wouldn't have much success, would we?"

He raised his glass and sipped. Kane did the same, nodding in agreement and also in recognition that the son was not a man to be trifled with. The thought gave him confidence that his request that evening would be granted. The favor he would ask was not one granted by the faint of heart. Morgan spoke again.

"I am in fact very much like my father in one respect. I have no patience for idle chatter. To business, please. Why is the man who ran into gunfire up San Juan Hill with only a pistol in his hand in my smoking room drinking wine with me?"

Kane placed his wine glass on the floor beside him and pocketed his hanky. He stood and walked toward the center of the room, knowing the sentiment, the emotion with which he would speak, could not be expressed while seated. He turned to Morgan and addressed him the same way he'd addressed his men in the past.

"A little over two years ago we came home and disbanded. The Rough Riders. Yes, we were victorious; there were parades, parties, and much revelry. I'm sure you've heard of the celebrations. I went back to my life as did the others. But I found that it wasn't enough. You see, the true name of the Riders is the First Volunteer Cavalry. *Volunteers*. It is a spirit, a desire to give, to help in a way that can make a difference. This life, this entitlement you and I live with every day, is no longer enough for me. I met with Mr. Rockefeller because I read how he wants to dedicate the rest of his life to helping mankind. Building museums, institutions of learning, giving back. I know you and your father have heard the same call to serve in your own way. I applaud you for it. But, Jack, there is so much more that can ... no, *should* be done. People in this very city, within blocks of this magnificent home, are living under the boot of tyranny. I volunteered to oust the Spanish from an island ninety miles from our shores. Donating art or building institutions of learning are vital, no doubt, but I have come to realize there are more insidious forces at work within our own borders, within our own city. I've dedicated myself in the spirit of the original volunteer cavalry to make a difference, to right these injustices within my city. To cast out the tyrants."

Morgan leaned forward in his chair, hand on his glass.

"Very stirring, Mr. Kane. I see why you are a leader of men, but I don't know what it is that you are asking."

Kane continued without addressing the question.

"Shortly after the celebrations ended, I started an organization. We call ourselves the Volunteers. I contacted many of the men who served under me and have put together a group of skilled, dedicated men. We are dedicated to fairness. That is our only guiding principle. No politics, no religion—we serve no master but our guiding principle. We seek only members of the highest caliber. Men who have succeeded on their own, long before joining us. No man seeking fortune or notoriety is considered. Indeed, we prefer anonymity to publicity. The Volunteers have been assembled in a way that individual members don't know the identity of the others. Each man brings with him a special set of skills."

Morgan then stood as well. He seemed both intrigued and a little concerned as he walked parallel to Kane with his glass in hand. He took a long, contemplative sip.

"What type of men, what skills?"

"We have gunmen, swordsmen, lawyers, bankers, and merchants. A man I *can* name, since he is one of the founders of the Volunteers, is the journalist Jacob Riis."

"Riis. He published that book about the Five Points. The one with the photographs. The squalor of the tenements down there. Yes?"

"Yes, Jacob is a dedicated man. As an objective journalist, he isn't interested in politics or religion. He also has the power of the press behind him. Read the tabs; he has been exposing the type of thing we want to stamp out of this city."

"What exactly is it that you do, Woody, and why are you discussing this with me?"

"We endeavor to make things right. Simple as that. The details of how we get things done may be better left unspoken."

"Are you going up against Tammany Hall? The cabal that has been running roughshod over the city for decades? Is this what this is about? My father and I have made peace with that group of criminals. They are vile in every way, but they do get the votes. A necessary evil, I think."

"An evil, yes. Necessary, no. Which leads me to why I'm speaking to you. The First Volunteer Cavalry had the government's backing. We had

Colonel Leonard Wood, a. lifelong military man, with the full faith and confidence of the United States behind him. We had Teddy, with all of his political muscle. Right now, we have Jacob and me. I have the full faith and confidence of the men, the Volunteers. Jacob has influence within political factions, more than you may imagine. We need our own colonels, and we need political and financial power. John Rockefeller has pledged his support if he doesn't have to stand alone. We need you."

Morgan walked over to the rolling tray. He refilled his wineglass and sipped. He went to his seat and extended his arm. "Please sit, Mr. Kane."

Kane went to his chair.

"Mr. Kane, I have had countless men come to me with ideas or proposals. All kinds of schemes. I have to admit, this is the most outrageous thing I have heard in years. Truly, this must be some type of amusement for yourself and John D."

Kane stared into Morgan's eyes with the intensity that inspired men to run into danger, a piercing glare that made men face the horrors of battle with enthusiasm and determination. He was not insulted or angry; he was hardened.

"Mr. Morgan, there is a Tammany Hall ward boss who has killed two showgirls in the last nine months. One of them seventeen, the other nineteen. Raped and strangled. Midwest girls who came to the city not a year ago. Jacob Riis has confirmed this with his police sources. I confirmed it by speaking to the miscreant personally. He laughed at my inquiries as his men escorted me from the beer hall where we spoke."

Kane leaned in closer, still furious at the indignity, not a foot from Morgan's nose.

"I won't name the man, for your protection. He is currently on a merchant ship headed toward Ireland. He will be jailed at Derry Goal in Londonderry. I put him on it personally. I and two other Volunteers took him into custody the night before last. I would imagine that word of it may get around to you shortly. There will be considerable fallout from this action. We need your influence to keep this matter private. Jacob will see that it stays out of the papers. I know you can speak to the right people or pad the right pocket to help our cause. I took this action to protect our city and the citizens who live in it. The police would have never gone after a

Tammany ward boss. I'm sure you know this. Do I have your support?"

"Two young girls?"

"Yes, both suffered a horrible fate before dying. The man took a knife to them after his sexual assault. They were defiled and tortured. This is a man who would have most certainly struck again."

Morgan looked into his glass. He swirled the wine, and it clung to the sides of the glass before slowly gliding down. He stood.

"You have my support."

Kane practically jumped from his seat and shook his hand. Seizing the moment.

"There is work to be done. I must leave now. Et Omnia Recta." He kept hold of Morgan's hand.

Morgan smiled. "I know my Latin, Woody. You go make this thing right. We'll speak after."

Kane let go of his hand and clapped Morgan on the shoulder.

"Welcome to the Volunteers."

Chapter 3

October 22, 1899 – 7:00 p.m.

They were to enter Delmonico's separately. Jacob Riis arrived first. A noted journalist, his presence was met with respectful nods from the maître d' and a number of the staff, but those of the bar men who noticed him were not about to offer any kindness. Riis was seen as a thorn in the side of Tammany but hardly a threat. Most of the patrons were members of the party or beholden to Tammany in some way. Jacob Riis was not a man to be met with much enthusiasm in the vaunted tap room of Delmonico's.

He thought it best to go directly to the private dining room reserved in his name for dinner.

His entrance was quickly forgotten because, not long after he left the room, Woodbury Kane strode into the bar. Kane did not stop at the podium of the maître d'. He simply threw his hat and coat over the hat stand near the door, walked right up to the bar, and ordered whiskey. "Irish please."

When the tumbler was placed in front of him, he turned his back to the bar and looked out at the bustling bar tables. There was a near roar from the men in the room. Kane stood and looked at them all, catching the daggers from the Tammany cronies. They knew what he had done: Costello, one of the most powerful ward bosses, sent out on a prison ship to Australia. Kane had no doubt that the version of events from the confrontation at McSorley's had been embellished by the two Irish mugs.

All the better, he thought. A fright was good for these criminals. He raised his glass in defiance to the group, the gold hue of the Jameson his liberty torch. The toast went unanswered. Kane drank the whiskey in one long gulp and headed to the stairway to the private room. As he descended the stairs, he heard a collective withdrawal of breath from the barroom, then the rumble of outrage accompanied by slammed fists on tables. He smiled and entered the room.

Riis was seated, hidden behind the enormous menu. Kane stood at the table head.

"Jacob, my friend."

Riis was having none of it.

"A rooster, that's what you are. A strutting rooster. We don't need this raucous. None of it. We must stay calm. Measured. Deliberate. Remember? That was my last word. Deliberate."

Kane smiled and sat. Riis was the only man who had ever spoken to him in such a way. In truth, the only man to speak that way twice. Any others in the past had been put in their places with Kane's wit or clenched fist. Riis was different, of course. Kane respected him perhaps more than Teddy himself.

They couldn't be more different, Kane and Riis. Kane learned of Riis's past from Teddy, who had equal admiration. Roosevelt held a peerless ability of measuring a man. On his recommendation alone, Kane committed himself to Riis as a friend and confidant.

"Yes, Jacob. You're right. There are times when I can't control my vigor. I know, I know, I must try to maintain my decorum. I couldn't possibly outshine Teddy in that department, anyway. I don't know why I continue to try."

Riis responded with a scolding smirk.

"Now, Jacob, go easy on me, old man."

"No more antics, Woody. This is too important."

Kane settled in and picked up his menu. Their relationship had been strained from the start, and Kane assumed it would continue that way. They didn't get on well without Roosevelt in their presence. Perhaps they were just too dissimilar to ever get along.

Kane was born into great wealth and privilege. Riis came to America with fifty dollars and a revolver. He worked the mines of Pennsylvania and the steel mills of Pittsburgh. Kane knew there were times Riis had slept in the streets or in the basements of municipal buildings. Although he was a successful journalist now and had access to money and the highest seats of power, Riis still had that edge. As if he expected it all to be taken away at any moment. It was this fear, Kane knew, that drove him, made him the man he was.

Until Kane met Riis, he'd never questioned his wealth or the place that he occupied in the world. Teddy was a brother in arms but also a man of privilege himself. Kane understood Teddy, since they were alike in many ways, but Jacob Riis was a puzzle to him. A puzzle he feared he would never solve.

Kane had come to the determination that Riis was a better man then he, perhaps better than Roosevelt himself. Unlike Riis, Teddy and Kane knew nothing of hardship.They were too well ensconced in a life of luxury.Yes, they sacrificed for the greater good, risked their lives even, but neither of them gave up any of the trappings of high society.

Kane could never imagine himself sleeping in the tenements of the Five Points to get a story as Riis had done many times. Or even walking those streets late at night as Teddy himself had done with Riis on one of their many secret ramblings. As Kane scanned the menu he came to the realization that he was the least of them. It was no slight. They were the two greatest men of New York.

A side door opened, and a waiter rolled a table into the small dining room. He was followed by a sommelier and James, the head waiter and floor manager.

James made a formal announcement. "Your third party has arrived. He is making his way to the room through a private entrance. It won't be but a minute. He has taken the time to call ahead to order for the party."

On cue, the waiter lifted the cover from a large silver tray to display the first course. Oysters on ice with lemon wedges lining the tray. There must have been fifty of them. *Oh yes*, Kane thought, *Teddy has ordered.* It would be a long night.

Riis and Kane heard the stomping of his shoes before he came to the door. They stood to greet him. Theodore Roosevelt burst through the doorway as he had been doing his entire life. He was not a man who knocked. He went directly to Riis and bear-hugged him without a word. Finally, he spoke. "Jacob, my friend."

Kane sidled over, and Roosevelt grabbed his hand without releasing Riis, his thick arm over Riis's shoulder.

"Captain. You have been busy, haven't you? Costello, I hear. Bully. Yes, bully indeed."

With those words, he released Riis, who let out a breath of relief upon his escape from the big bear.

Roosevelt, wearing a full tuxedo and top hat, clapped his hands together then spread them wide.

"My men, my good men of New York. I've missed the city so. I'm not in Albany a year and the dreariness of it has me worn. I've longed for a meal at Delmonico's and the companionship of hearty men. Yes, yes, fine food and company."

He shooed Kane and Riis with his hands, then turned and placed his top hat on a vacant chair. He peeled off his gloves and dropped them into the hat.

"Sit, sit. Eat. Drink. We toast the captain's action tonight." He turned and spun a half-turn around the room. James and the sommelier had left when he entered. "James, James. Where in dickens have you gone to?"

James hustled back through the door.

"Sorry, sir, I assumed you wanted privacy. What can I do?"

"Drinks, my man. Wine, whiskey. We have much to celebrate. Stay alert, my man. Mr. Kane here will keep you busy with his orders. In fact, bring a bottle of rye whiskey for me, Irish whiskey for Mr. Kane, and open the bottle of wine I ordered for Mr. Riis. Bring them straight away, then leave us to enjoy our cocktails and oysters. Do you have the Delmonico steaks at the ready?"

"Yes, of course, sir."

"Very good, very good. Drinks now. Straight away."

James scampered from the room. The men engaged in small talk until the bottles were presented and the drinks served. Teddy waited for the staff to leave the room, then stood.

"A toast to my friend, Woodbury Kane. The unforgivable crime is soft hitting. Do not hit at all if it can be avoided. But never hit softly. You've taken them at the core. I salute your brass."

He raised his glass, and they all drank.

"Tell me everything, Kane," Teddy all but hollered. The basement room echoed with Roosevelt's booming timber.

Kane recounted the apprehension of Ward Boss Costello. Teddy asked for every detail, not allowing Kane to skip a word.

"To Australia he goes then. Jolly, jolly. A stout man, Kane. A stout man you are."

Riis did not act as impressed. "There may be consequences to follow. I fear this may have been a bit too aggressive for our first attempt."

"No, no, Jacob," Roosevelt admonished. "I support Woody's decision. A strong first impression was the right thing. Now it's time to think more tactically. This is why we dine. But no, Jacob, we support our men. There is no sense in questioning a tactic after it has been implemented. No sense at all to it. We move on. Now come, sit."

He put an arm on Jacob's lower back and steered him toward the table. Kane sensed that Riis felt the sting of Roosevelt's reprimand. He was right, though; it was not wise to question his aggressiveness. Not after the fact. He turned to Riis before sitting.

Riis extended his hand and Kane shook it. "Woodbury, my friend. You acted with decisiveness and valor. I mean no offense."

"No offense at all, Jacob," Kane replied. He turned to Roosevelt. "Can a man get a decent cut of meat in this place?"

The three laughed, knowing that the Delmonico steak was the prized meal of New York. It was Kane's attempt at humor, not one of his strong suits, to keep the mood light.

'Yes, you can, Mr. Kane," Roosevelt replied. He turned toward the open door and bellowed, "James, where are my Delmonico steaks?"

During the course of that very long meal, three of the most important men in the history of New York set an agenda that would affect thousands of people for over a hundred years. The rules of the Volunteers were set, the first being that Teddy could never be known as a part of them. His ambitions were clear, having stated to each of them on numerous occasions, "I will be president one day." It was decided that Riis and Kane would run the operation and Jack Morgan and John D. Rockefeller would provide financial and political support. Teddy would only be contacted in extreme cases. Unless, of course, he wanted a report. Riis and Kane agreed to all. In fact, they had no choice in the matter. It was Teddy Roosevelt's will. There was no turning away from that. Their cause was just and had the approval of Teddy. That was enough of a contract for the two of them.

With the agenda set and the last of the food eaten, Roosevelt rose from his seat. On the table in front of him was an empty bottle of rye whiskey and the T-bone of a two-pound steak. He turned and grabbed his top hat. He was as bright-eyed as a school boy. Even Kane, the drinker that he was, having gone through two thirds of his Jameson, was bleary and slow-witted. Riis had his head on the table, snoring, having not lasted through dessert.

"I'm off, my friend."

Kane looked up with a quizzical smile. "The top hat and tails. You never did explain."

"And these," Roosevelt said as he pulled white gloves out of the hat. "I'm at the opera, don't you know." He smiled. Put on the hat and tipped it. "Et Omnia Recta."

Kane smiled as Roosevelt slipped out the door.

Chapter 4

Present Day
Edgartown, Massachusetts

Jim looked down at the fitness app on his phone. The jostling from his moderate running pace was enough to make it difficult to read. Holding the phone in his left hand, with the Stones blaring through the earbuds, he finally got a bead on it. A mile and three quarters. *Jesus*, he thought. It seemed more like a half-marathon. It would've helped if he had stretched a little before taking off. It would help more if he wasn't fifty-two. No changing that. He needed a distraction, time to fast-forward. He landed on a Marvin Gaye song and picked up the pace, thinking about the cold beer waiting for him when he returned to the resort.

He was on Edgartown Bay Road in the blazing sun. Not halfway done with his goal of four miles. He'd reached the four-mile milestone last week. Before leaving this morning, he had to mouth off to his wife. "Four is the new three," he'd bragged. Even though he was far removed from his athletic youth and there was no training goal to reach, Jim didn't want to take a step backward. He had to do the four miles, maybe a couple of yards more. He was down ten pounds and counting. Ten more to go. Needed to drop twenty to keep the doctors and his wife off his back, but a cold beer right now ... man, that would be nice.

Ahead there was a wooden sign. He ran up to it and read: "Huckleberry Barrens." The sign was at the base of a trail. He turned in. *Huckleberry! Should be a nice path*, he thought.

It was nice. Jim didn't know what the hell a huckleberry was, but the path was pretty damn beautiful. A winding dirt trail surrounded by waist-high flowered brush. Within a few yards, he was cut off from the road and engulfed in greenery.

He picked up his pace and forgot about the distance he had run and how far he had to go. He thought that he would tell his wife about it and they could come back for a walk later. He turned a corner and smelled the flowers. The trail was longer than he'd imagined, and he looked ahead of him, trying to see around a bend, taking his eyes off the path.

Suddenly he was falling forward. He heard a branch snap as he landed face-first onto the dirt path and slid into the brush. A small branch nub stuck in his cheek. "Shit, shit, shit." Damn, it hurt. He put his hand up to his face, wrapped his fingers around the small branch, and pulled himself back. He felt his face for blood, but there was only a small drop on his finger. Not a large cut. Then the pain in his leg hit, shooting through him. *God! What the hell?* He felt a chill rush up his body from his legs. With it came goose bumps, then more pain. A blanket of agony was pulled up over him. It was unlike anything he had ever felt playing ball in college with all the turned ankles and broken fingers.

He rolled onto his back and managed to sit up leaning on his left elbow. He looked down at the source of the pain. His stomach came up at the sight. He burped up a little of his pancakes from this morning's breakfast. His lower leg, a few inches above his ankle, was hanging limply. The snapping sound hadn't been a branch. It was bone when he'd come down on it awkwardly. It was clear the bone was broken straight through, and it seemed like the only thing keeping his foot from hitting the ground was the skin.

His phone was still in his hand. He looked down at it to get away from the sight of his leg, then thought that it might be a good idea to call for help. He pressed on the contacts icon. Luckily, his wife's number popped up; he must have called her last. He started getting lightheaded as he pressed the button. She picked up. "I'm hurt bad. Edgartown Bay Road, a trail marked Huckleberry Barrens. Come quick; it's bad."

"Jim, Jim. What? Is that you? Huckleberry?"

"Yes, get someone. It's bad."

Jim started to lose consciousness. Before he went out, he looked down the path to see what he had fallen over. It looked like a machine of some sort, a small helicopter or something. It didn't make sense. A helicopter? Here?

He blacked out.

Chapter 5

Pap Martinez has been dead for over two years. Nine million people had downloaded the amateur video and watched him die on YouTube. Lying on the sidewalk outside of a New York City tenement after a police raid. Foaming at the mouth then turning blue and passing out, his eyes still open, rolled up in his head.

Two years gone. Along with fifty million dollars to finance the CIA and the Justice Department's greatest production: *The Death of Pap Martinez, Internet Mogul.* He was in fact dead at the time of the taping. The team sent to rescue him had been ordered to film every step of the raid. They stopped after he was loaded into the back of the van. No one saw the paramedics revive him. The mouth-to-mouth and the frantic pressing on his chest.

It was Pap who had put the idea together after seeing the video, once he'd regained his bearings at the hospital. One of the cops who helped wheel him into the hospital showed it to him shortly after he was in a private room. Pap didn't remember exactly what the cop said. Something to the effect of, "You were pretty fucked up, man."

Pap, half dead, still had the foresight to have the captain of the team confiscate the video and download it to a patrolman's phone. He knew his audience. Who wouldn't want to log in to see the great Pap Martinez writhe in pain on a filthy New York sidewalk? What theater!

Before drifting off from the sedatives, he knew who was behind his kidnapping. Sheng. Had to be. Only three men in the world at the time of the kidnapping knew his identity. Three men whom he trusted with his life.

Sheng was the only man, other than those three, who had the ability to find him.

It was a brilliant plan. The video was perfect because it was real. He did die on camera. It was Pap's idea to post it. Have one of the cops do it, lose his job over it. That was the first payoff. There were many to follow. It had to be done. Sheng wouldn't give up. Pap knew something that threatened Sheng. He didn't know what it was, but then, Pap knew an awful lot. It could have been anything.

The video was the start. The revealing. Pap Martinez, the brilliant shadowy figure of the tech world. Rumored to have written the code for just about every great innovation in the last fifteen years—the Amazon algorithm, Google's search engine, Facebook, and Twitter—dying on a grubby Manhattan street. Pap did none of those things, athough he did train a few of the men who did. He was a legend in the elite coding world, but outside that small community no one had any idea who he was or what he looked like. He had to fabricate his death to a select group——the people who could spot a fake video or clunky data better than any cop or government agent. He had to fool the people who invented the tools he would use to fool them. Most importantly, he had to fool Sheng. His idea was to spin the story of a reclusive genius who spiraled down in a world of drugs.

The dying part was easy. The CIA had a protocol for that.

It was the new life that was difficult and costly. It started with Pap being removed from the hospital in a zipped body bag. A hospital employee tipping the press. Under the flashing lights, the body in the bag put into a hearse, never to be seen again. The funeral was private. A cadaver burned to ashes. Pap's father, his only living relative, not understanding how he wasn't allowed a few minutes with his dead son. Security reasons, he was told. They said the cremation was accidently administered before he could get to the funeral home. Pap knew how this would break his father. Through everything, all the secretive work he did, the years of collecting sensitive data, the changing identities and the months and sometimes years apart, Pap always kept his dad close at hand and closer to his heart. Pap knew that this time his father would have to be convinced of his death, like the rest of the world.

The will was executed. His father getting close to seven hundred million from the dissolution of Pap's tech firm. Pap was left with a hundred million which he managed to hide away in case of such an emergency. Money he would gladly set aflame for an afternoon drinking beer and bullshitting with his old man.

The new life was what cost. It was one of Pap's greatest undertakings. From his research, he knew what made people do what they do. All the data he had collected over the years was put into the charade. The last thing he'd been working on before the kidnapping was a program that would allow him to know where a person would be on any given day at any given time. Gathering data about an individual's life, past, present, the way they were raised, religion, family structure, and over a thousand other factors had enabled Pap to predict to a 93-percent accuracy where a person would be in the future. Not just predict, but to know what they would do, what they would purchase. He was on the cusp of not just *predicting* behavior but *influencing* behavior. The logic was pure. If he knew how a person would act in the future, why would it be difficult to make a person act in a certain way? Pap had the means and the data to move forward with his groundbreaking work when the kidnapping happened.

All of his research had to be destroyed as part of the new life he'd made for himself. Pap knew he could get it up and running again within a year or so, but it all had to be shelved for his survival.

That very research is what he used to create his new life. Henry "Hank" Suarez, retired video game designer.

The fact was, most of Pap's fortune was made from writing gaming code. It was easy enough to play the part. The money, and his genius, was put to work to create this person. Hank.

Hank's family, dead in a fire, the news reports created, the fire department logs, the reporter standing in front of the burning house, the funeral, scratchy film from a lost family member. High-school yearbooks, old dear friends, CIA operatives playing the roles.

The public information was easy enough. The detailed work was creating an online footprint. There were thousands of pages of data that needed to be invented. A lot of the money went to the government agencies which were the source of most of the information before anyone had ever heard the word "Google." From elementary school attendance records to a Stanford diploma. Pap created it all. He built Hank Suarez from the ground up. In a way, after months of creating him, Pap himself started to blend the identities together. Pap had to remind himself that it was Hank, not Pap, who had fallen on the bleachers and needed twelve stitches in sixth grade.

Two years of his life, most of his fortune, and most heartbreakingly, time with his father had been wasted now. Pap's sense of loss and disappointment was as dark as the lights of the police car in front of his house were bright. Pap, Hank now, watched the officer get back into his patrol car and cut the lights.

A drone had been found across the street from his home. The cop read from a report that it looked like a model 3DR Spektre industrial inspection drone. No markings. Still warm, it must have crashed the night before it was found. Some poor tourist ran over it, fucked up his leg.

Hank knew. He had to run soon. Pull up stakes, get on the move again.

Sheng, fucking Sheng. The top hacker for the Chinese government. Hank had known him back when he was still Pap, at MIT. He was a little commie prick even then. Brilliant, Pap's match in many ways, but he lacked imagination. Sheng had no equal in terms of technology, but he couldn't create. So he stole.

As the cop car pulled out, Hank had put it together. Sheng, the thief, was after Pap. He wondered if he could be after his program, the work he was forced to shut down two years ago. It would be foolish to ask himself how Sheng could know. Sheng could find out anything. Hank shuddered at the thought of Sheng having the ability to influence people's behavior. *Jesus*, he thought, *that prick has done enough damage to America already, hacking into just about every government agency and commercial business.* Hank knew that almost every online security breach in the last ten years led back to that little bastard.

The realization was frightening, but it did have a positive spin to it. No one was going to kill him. They needed his mind. Sheng had no interest in Pap Martinez or Hank Suarez. He was after the program. Hank or Pap ... didn't matter to Sheng.

Hank had a brief moment of fear. Could Sheng know about his work for the government? Did he know about the data that he planted into the Chinese military? That the misinformation Pap created led to executions of a half dozen of the Red Army's top officials. He wondered now if it wasn't Sheng at all. Perhaps it was Chinese agents following Sheng's orders. Hank shuddered at the thought but soon gathered himself. He was panicking. The one man who knew Hank Suarez was actually Pap Martinez—Pap's lone contact—had briefed him that Sheng had gone missing months ago. It was assumed that he ran afoul of the government in some way. From what Hank knew of Sheng, he assumed he had done something so greedy or stupid or egotistical that he became more of a burden than an asset. Sheng was on the run, and he wanted Hank for some reason.

From this moment on, Hank had to assume that all communications had been breached. Time to implement his exit strategy. He would go down to the post office tomorrow and mail a handwritten letter. Drop it in the box himself.

Send it to the one man who knew he was alive. That was until tonight, before Sheng. The letter would go to a drop box at Penn Station in New York and be picked up by an agent, the man who checked the box every day on his way down to Wall Street. It would be delivered by hand to Hank's lone contact—Frank McGinley, whom Pap served with on the executive committee of the Volunteers.

Chapter 6

D inner used to be once a week. Every Sunday, for years. At the house. Lately, Annie Falcone and her father had only been able to meet once a month, if they were lucky. It was because of his job— chief as chief of detectives for the New York Police Department. She was on the job too, ten years now. She was still a grunt, and he was practically running the force.

Since her mom passed, Annie had made a point of pinning him down when she could. Getting him in a room so she could take a look at him. She thought he drank a bit too much lately, too much wine since the funeral, but overall he was holding up.

Anthony Falcone. The upper echelon of the force called him "The Hawk" because of his name and aggressive demeanor; but Tony knew that not a little of it was because of his prominent Roman nose.

He sat at a table at Babbo and held out his hands to his daughter. Annie thought it strange; the man had barely kissed her on the forehead since she'd turned twenty-five and joined the force. Pushing thirty-two now, she guiltily thought that at least he wasn't going to ask her about a man or marriage like her mother would have. Annie knew he had something to say; he'd seemed uncomfortable all evening.

Annie took his hands and asked, "What's the trouble, Pop? You seem a little off tonight. Is it Mom? You thinking about her? You okay?"

"Yeah, yeah. I'm good. I have to talk to you about something, though."

He pulled back his hands. Annie released; the moment passed. They both took the last sips of their wine. Tony toyed with his glass, delaying.

"I have to tell you something that can never be repeated. Before you get worried, it's work-related, nothing about the family or health or anything. We've had enough of that this year."

"Yes, we have."

He leaned in, as he always did, a man adept at telling secrets.

"I want to tell you about an organization that I've been a part of for years."

Annie smiled, a little unnerved by his tone. "I hope it's AA, with the way you been putting away the wine lately."

He frowned. The look that had shut her up her whole life.

'No, this is serious. I want you to listen very carefully. This is a very important night."

"C'mon, Pop, you're scaring me."

"Nothing to be scared of. I waited. Waited to tell you until I thought you were ready. With the way you've been handling yourself, with your mom and all, the job you've been doing ... you're ready."

"Okay. What?'

He leaned in a little more. For a second, she thought back to when she was a little girl and he would sing silly songs in her ear. It was the closest she'd felt to him since her mom died. He broke the spell.

"I've been a member of a private organization for over twenty years. I'm on the executive committee now. It's a high honor. One of the committee members left two years ago, which led to my promotion."

"What is it, like the Knights of Columbus, the PBA or something?" Annie was confused, but from the look he shot back at her, she got it. This was important. She immediately felt stupid for what she'd just said. This had to be bigger; she could tell from his tone.

He sat back but kept eye contact.

"You can't repeat this conversation. Ever. On your life, you can't repeat this."

"Holy shit, Pop, I'm officially spooked now."

"Nothing to be scared of. It is a high honor to be told. You've earned it. The name of the organization is the Volunteers."

She went to speak, but he held up a hand to stop her.

"Let me finish, then you can question. There's a lot."

"Okay."

"The Volunteers were started right here in New York City in 1900. A man named Woodbury Kane was the founder. There were others, but since no one kept records, their names are lost. Kane was a Rough Rider, a captain, friend of Teddy Roosevelt.

"We believe he got backing from J.P. Morgan and maybe Rockefeller, but there's no way to confirm this. The purpose of the organization—well, at least the phrase passed down—is to endeavor to make things right. "Et Omnia Recta" in Latin. We look at it as a group of influential people who care about fairness. I don't mean the law. We're both cops; we believe in the law, but there are times when things need to be done outside the normal protocols. You see this a lot yourself, the things that slip through. The bad guys who walk every day because of politics or money or circumstance. Timing, politics, bullshit mostly."

"Are you vigilantes? God, Pop, that doesn't sound like you."

Tony shook his head. "No, no. It's not like that at all. I'm not talking about street crime or even the local graft that goes down on a regular basis in this city. I'm talking about terrorists, hackers, mass murderers with asylum. Right here. In this city. The United Nations is a magnet for them. There are henchmen for dictators and warlords sitting in embassies on the Upper East Side while their citizens are getting hacked to death. There are terrorists in our city right now plotting to blow up a bridge or building whom we can't arrest without a warrant. You know, we stopped a guy from gassing the number seven train in Times Square just two years ago. Remember that FBI bust?"

"Yeah, of course. You had a hand in that?"

The Hawk didn't answer. He kept on.

"We're even bigger than that, though. We go back. The Volunteers thwarted a Nazi plot in the early forties to blow up a synagogue on the Upper West Side. Nazis working right out of the Empire State Building. Can you imagine?"

He stopped to take a breath and sip his water.

Annie was mesmerized. "It sounds like you're talking about a movie you saw. This sounds crazy."

"It's no movie. There was sarin gas in that terrorist's apartment in Sunnyside, Queens. The guy who was after the seven train. That's no movie. This is real. We are real. It's an honor to be called to serve. The executive committee is made up of men and one woman who are some of the most influential and recognizable people in the country. We serve no politician, follow no religion; we only follow our purpose. We endeavor to make things right. Et Omnia Recta."

"Wow, Pop. Nazis, terrorists."

"Yes. No bullshit. It's what we do. When the group started, it was to root out Tammany Hall around the turn of the century. You can research it. Things were pretty dire in New York if you weren't from a certain class. That's what makes Kane, our founder, such an inspiration. He was very wealthy. He volunteered to join the Rough Riders. Can you imagine that now? A millionaire's kid—well, he was related to John Jacob Astor, so maybe he was a billionaire's kid, in today's dollars—volunteering to go to war? It's that kind of spirit that is our founding principal. Established, successful people who want to do what is right. For our city, and our country now. We've had a West Coast branch since the eighties."

Annie was tingling. She hadn't seen her father this excited, this passionate, in years. She could barely stay seated. "I have to get out of here. This is too much to listen to, sitting here silently. I can't believe this. Pop, what the hell? This is ... I don't know. Let's walk." She stood. "C'mon."

Tony smiled up at her. His girl. "I have to pay first."

She grabbed her bag. "I'll wait outside."

"So I guess it's on me tonight?"

"Damn right it is." She turned and walked out.

It was a perfect early summer evening. Tony came out of the restaurant, up the stairs. Annie had her back to him, turned right and started to walk along Waverly toward Washington Square. He caught up.

"Jesus, I buy you dinner, and now I have to chase you down the street."

"C'mon, Pop. This has me freaked. A secret society or something. This organization. How come you never told me this?"

He took her by the shoulder and turned her to face him. "Honey, you're the first person that I have ever told this to. Not even your mom. It's that important. Hey, you know I told her everything." He gazed off for a second, but only one. "This is the most important night of your life. You've been called to join the most prestigious group in New York, probably the country. Only the absolute top people in their fields are asked, and only if the time is right. The time is right for you, and you are one hell of a cop. I don't say it enough, I know, but you're damn good."

She stared back at him, not knowing what to say. She smiled and hugged him.

"Thanks." She was touched deeply because it wasn't that he didn't say it enough; this was the first time he'd *ever* said it. Although she was sure he thought he had. "So this is why you took me to such a fancy restaurant tonight?" She pulled back and saw that he was tearing up a little. "Pop, you okay?"

"Yeah, yeah. I was just thinking that now it's just you and me. You know?"

"Yeah, I know."

She put her arm around him, and they started walking east toward the arch at the base of Fifth Avenue. To her surprise, he didn't pull away.

He asked, "Are you attached to anyone at the moment?"

"*Attached.* What do you mean? Do I have a boyfriend? I thought it was Mom's job to worry about that stuff."

"Oh no. You'll be fine. Any guy would be lucky. I'm asking because you are about to meet with another member of the executive committee, and you're going to have a decision to make. It could have lasting repercussions. You may be away for a while."

She stopped walking. He continued a few steps then turned to her. She stomped her foot slightly. That foot on the ground was Annie's demand for more information or she would stay in that spot for the rest of the night. As a petulant child, Annie had once held her breath until she passed out.

Her footstomp reminded Tony of the bad days. The days when a dinner alone with Annie would have been unthinkable. It seemed like forever ago. Angry Annie they would call her. He would sit with Rose at the kitchen table after one of her fits. The fits that had Tony holding the doorknob of her room. The "timeout" a battle. Annie would ram against the door of her room. Tony had to stand there holding on until she calmed down. Sometimes it would take hours.

Afterward they would sit together and wonder why she was so angry so often. It completely confused Tony. Annie grew up in a stable household. A happy family. Good house, nice neighborhood, friends. It didn't make any sense to him. He removed himself from her life for quite a while during her teenage years. He was absorbed in work, and frankly, Annie was too difficult to deal with. It wasn't until later in her life, her mid-twenties, that they started communicating again. It was because of Rose, like all that was good in his life, that they started talking. Over dinner, a meal that Annie would make with her mom. Every Sunday.

It wasn't until she was older that he started to understand what made her tick. Maybe it was because she was better able to express herself as an adult; more likely, it was because Tony took the time to listen. He came to realize that she was unhappy. He could see it in her smile of all things. She had a sad smile. It would fade a little faster than the moment of happiness that brought it on deserved. Annie was always the first one to stop smiling.

A couple of years ago Tony finally figured out his daughter. She was unfulfilled. It was so clear to him that he beat himself up for not seeing it sooner. Annie was an exceptional person living an ordinary life. She was a thoroughbred locked in a pen, a poet in remedial English. She needed to do great things. She needed to be part of a worthy cause. Something bigger than herself. It was this realization that led Tony to believe that Annie was the right person for what he was recommending. It would be dangerous, he knew, but it would be cruel to allow her to keep living a smaller life than she deserved.

"Pop, are you with me here?"

Tony came back to Waverly Place. "Yeah, sorry. I was thinking."

"We have to do this tonight? Now?"

"Yes, in a few minutes. He's waiting for you down the street. In McGreevy's Tavern. Just past University Place."

She looked up to see that they were right under the arch at Washington Square Park. The place where Sally had dropped off Harry in the movie. She remembered Sally's line before Harry walked away: *"You're the only one I know in New York."*

"So you're asking me to join something? This man I'm meeting——he has a job for me and I may be away for a while?"

"Yes. You see, even I don't know what the task is. We have to maintain anonymity. It's the way we have survived for so long. No one man or woman knows everything. I'm putting you in the hands of a trusted committee member, just as he has sent others to me. I trust this man with my life ... I guess your life now. I wish I could tell you more. I really do. All I can say is that you should trust your judgment when you meet with this man. It's a lot to take in, I know. But you're ready, I know this. You're ready."

"Can I still be a cop?"

"I don't know, honey, I don't know. Your life will change after this evening. That I'm sure of."

Annie braced her back and stood tall. "Shit, why not? Let's do this."

Tony took hold of her by the arms and held tight. He put his finger to the side of his head and said the same words he used before the prom, a hundred basketball games, the day she graduated the police academy, and so many other times. He tapped twice on his temple.

"Be smart."

"I will, Pop."

Chapter 7

Edgartown, Massachussells

Shizi brought the man in. Sheng stared at him over his soup. He lifted the bowl, drank the last bit with a loud slurp.

"Tell me now, why were you unable to retrieve my device?"

Gaspar took off his hat and bowed. He looked at the little man in front of him. He wore what looked like gray pajamas and was barefoot. It looked like he hadn't washed or combed his hair, ever. "The spot isn't on the GPS. I couldn't find it."

"But Mr. Gaspar, you were told the location. Why would this be?"

"I couldn't find it. I put it in the phone like your man here said, but when I turned on the map, the place your machine crashed didn't show. What is the word? It's not on the map, uh, the grid, that's it. The grid. It's not on the grid."

Gaspar was nervous. These two Chinamen frightened him, but there was something about this little one that was off-kilter. The big one, Shizi, called him and picked him up this morning. Gaspar had been asked to wait on the road between Edgartown Bay and South Beach. For a little over a year now, he had lived on the island, having fallen out of favor back in Boston, with the drinking and all. The fucking Southies drove him out. He fell in with the locals soon enough. It seemed his reputation for slipping into a window undetected preceded him.

When the big guy picked him up, he'd slipped two grand in hundreds into Gaspar's palm. Like he was tipping the coat check. Said he got his number from someone in Boston. That should have tipped him off that this would all go to shit. The guy gave him an address, told him to get a truck, go to a park off Edgartown Bay Road, and pick up one of those drones they were fucking around with, then call him. Gaspar had the number, the cash, and the place to make the pickup. It should have been easy.

Should have been, except for the fact that Gaspar didn't have a truck, or a license, or many friends he could count on. He got the big guy to drop him off at a garage. He figured that Matz would have something for him. Matz took care of him all right. To the tune of five hundred bucks.

When he hopped in the truck, Gaspar checked around, knowing that Matz liked his whiskey as much as he did. There was a half-bottle of Old Grand-Dad in the glove box. Since the cheap fuck squeezed him for half a grand for one day, Gaspar felt he was entitled to the bottle.

This turn of events had led to Gaspar getting to the spot a little later than he would have liked. He finished the bottle as fast as he could, knowing he was on the job, but it was a delay. Besides, the place wasn't on his phone. He knew the spot, but these Chinese didn't have to know that. By the time he'd arrived, the place was swarming with cops.

He'd returned the truck to the garage, and when he got there, this big motherfucker was waiting for him.

Now here he was, with two Chinamen. In deep shit. Again.

Sheng turned and put his bowl in the sink behind him. He walked around the kitchen island. There was a board covering the surface of the island with eight laptops in a semicircle. The power lines ran down into a larger cable which snaked across the floor down through a hole in the kitchen floor. Sheng walked around the island, glancing down at the screens, and came around to face Gaspar, who was sitting now.

"The police have my property now. How do you plan on replacing it?"

"Replacing it? Hey, your man here didn't tell me the right directions. It's not my fucking problem. This is bullshit."

Sheng smiled at Gaspar. He turned to Shizi and slowly walked toward him. Gaspar could tell the little guy scared the shit out of the big dude. He couldn't figure it out.

Sheng slapped Shizi hard. "You bring me this shit? This shit man.

Stinking of liquor. You know what I can do. You know. If we were home, what would be done? You bring this man in front of me. A thief. A foul thief, to me. You bring this here?"

Shizi answered with his head bowed. "Sir, I—"

Gaspar stood. "Hey, what the fuck do you think—"

Shizi looked at Gaspar. "Sit, now," he hollered. Gaspar looked over at him, ready to go at this guy who was fucking around with him. Take out the big guy first. Then he'd make this little prick feel some pain. Then he heard the little man yell from his right.

"Thief."

He turned and briefly saw a gun in the little man's hand, not six inches from his face. The gun went off, and Gaspar felt a flash of heat, then nothing.

———

Sheng walked over to Shizi and stood close. His eyes were level with Shizi's chin, so he looked up at him. Shizi knew better than to look down. He faced forward, knowing now that Sheng would start one of his rants. His rants were famous back home. Shizi had seen him go for hours, getting into such a frenzy that he would come close to passing out. It could be about anything and come at any time. Once Sheng spent half a day ranting about the quality of his tea. Another time about not being able to break Goldman Sachs's high-frequency trading algorithm. Both were delivered with equal ferocity. This time Sheng had a gun in his hand. He waved it like a toy, turned away and walked over to his laptops. Then turned back. To Shizi's surprise, he spoke calmly.

"One hundred men. I had one hundred men under me at one time. The people I served turned on me. Not my men, though. No, they were loyal, skilled. Yes, one hundred skilled men. We did great things, served our dear leaders well. No one could stop us. You know that. No one. These fucking Americans, so fucking smart. So fucking smart. These fucking Americans. They were helpless before me. Helpless. Children. Fat, lazy, stupid children."

Sheng slowly started closing the lids of the laptops. His nightly ritual. To Shizi's relief, he put the gun on the counter.

"Now I have you. Only you. My security man. The man who dispatches the unworthy, the unreliable. How many men have you killed, Shizi? How many?"

"Seventeen, sir."

"Seventeen. How do you feel? How do you feel after, I mean?

"Not much to be honest. Not much at all."

"This thief here, this thief, was my first. I don't feel anything. Nothing."

He paused and rested his hand atop one of the laptops.

"You fled with me because they would surely have killed you. I know. I know. Please don't say anything. I know it's true. There is no loyalty anymore. I understand. They turned on me, on us. You see, I know too much. I know everything. I'm a danger to them now. They really believe that the men I trained could take over? The men I trained? Do they think I am stupid enough to tell them everything? The back doors to the programs. They didn't realize that I could shut most of the operations down remotely. I have done it, you know. They no longer have access to the American's military codes. The banks. The IRS. Citibank, Chase, Goldman, UBS. Nothing—they have nothing now. Without Sheng, they have nothing. I have the codes. I have the bank access. I am redirecting a million dollars a day to my private accounts. Your million for this month is in your account, as you have seen. You see? I am loyal. You got me out. You will be paid a million a month for as long as I am alive. I have the codes up here."

He tapped his temple.

"I have everything up here. What I do not have is peace of mind. I will not until my former masters are appeased. They will continue to hunt me until they are satisfied. That can only be done two ways. They get me back to give them access to what they want, but I am sure they will kill me afterward. Or I can give them my replacement. That is why I must get this man. Pap Martinez. He is the only man in the world who could replace me. I must deliver him to them. The Party. I must have him alive. I can give him the codes. He is the only one who would understand them. You see, the codes I have are just the start. The entry to the algorithms I have created. It is a puzzle. You know how I love puzzles. The code is but one of the pieces. Martinez could solve this puzzle I have created. It will take him time; he's clearly not as skilled as I. But he will get it. They know this. The Party. They know him. He has done great damage to our country. As much or more than I have done to this country. Like me, he is a spy. Yes, a spy. You see, I thought I was a patriot, but I see it now. Just as this Martinez sees it. He is in hiding. His own country does not know he is alive. We are spies hiding from our own countries. They will not get me. We will have this man. I have been working, researching, but I cannot know what is waiting for me if we approach this man. I must stay removed, protected. Martinez will know of my presence by now. There were police cars, yes?"

"Yes sir. I believe a tourist was hurt. There was an ambulance."

"Yes. He will know. He will at least suspect something, and that is enough. Soon he will move. We do not have much time. Did you study the profile I sent of the police officer?"

"Yes, of course, every word."

"Good. We will move with him. Go see the Boston gangster tomorrow, the brown one. I want his people here and ready for tomorrow night. I will go into the policeman's bank accounts in the morning. Call the pilot tonight. Have him prepare for our departure. When we leave, it will be without much notice. He must be ready. I must rest now. I will see you in the morning. Six."

Shizi bowed and headed to the door.

Chapter 8

Shizi returned from dumping the body around 3:00 a.m. He sat in the car deep in thought. He would have to be up in three hours, but it didn't matter—there would be no sleep tonight. After watching Sheng kill the man, he was convinced. He had to kill Sheng.

He was hoping Sheng would stabilize. That his anger and rants would decrease now that he was out of the country. He cursed himself now in the driveway. He should have known better. As the lead officer of the diplomatic guard, he had seen this with the operatives under his command in the past. The stress of covert work could make good men lose control, and Sheng was half-crazed to begin with. Most fell into depression, alcohol, drugs, or other lifelines for the weak.

He had witnessed the beginning of Sheng's downfall in China. The violent episodes, the purposeful disrespect of his superiors. Shizi knew they would come for him. As the man assigned to Sheng by the Red Army chief of staff, Shizi knew all the loopholes in the government bureaucracy. He was uniquely qualified to arrange covert travel, so he set up Sheng's and his escape through his diplomatic contacts well in advance. Shizi convinced Sheng of the inevitable. They would come for him. Sheng saw how they were training men to replace him. He knew as well.

It was easy enough for Sheng to create diplomatic passports. Shizi knew whom to bribe, and Sheng transferred the millions into the man's account. They'd strolled onto a plane headed to Spain as easy as an American tourist. From Spain, they'd traveled extensively, each step an opportunity to establish a new identity. They'd jumped from continent to continent, name to name, until Sheng figured out the permanent solution for them. Their path to freedom. For a while, Shizi believed in him, but slowly, Sheng's madness began to reassert itself. Shizi knew now that there was no permanent solution as long as Sheng was alive, but he could make it on his own with Sheng dead.

There was a more compelling reason, a more urgent need to kill Sheng. He would kill again, and the next bullet would be for Shizi. He had seen it before. Bloodlust. He saw Sheng's face after he pulled the trigger. The passion for the act. The satisfied grimace.

Killing Sheng had to be planned carefully. There was the money, of course. None of this works without the money. The money was real. It was there in his account; he had access to it and it was clean. It was over seven million now. Shizi needed more in order to live off the grid for an extended period, but he may not have much time. Shizi decided to wait and watch. See if Sheng's plan worked. Sheng needed Shizi to do the grunt work to pull it off, so it gave Shizi more time and maybe another million. It was clear, though—whether the plan worked or not, Sheng would not leave this island.

Chapter 9

McGreevy's was a college bar. New York University kids. Annie worked her way through the crowd clogging up the front half of the joint. *Damn, they all talk so loud,* she thought. She headed to the back booth on the right as her father had instructed.

The last three booths along the wall were empty. In the third, the last booth, she saw who every cop in New York knew as the most powerful man in New York——Frank McGinley.

He was wearing a black suit jacket and blue shirt. Both looked like they cost more than her entire wardrobe. Annie had seen him once before. A year or so ago at the Al Smith dinner at the Waldorf. That night, he had been sitting on the dais between Cardinal Dolan and the police commissioner. Annie knew he was the biggest supporter of the NYPD in the city. He ran numerous charities that helped families of fallen officers, 9/11 families, and a half dozen others. Most important to Annie was the way her father spoke of him. She couldn't think of anyone else whom Pop spoke of with such reverence. Tonight he was looking up at her from a bar booth that smelled like Pabst Blue Ribbon. From a distance that night at the Waldorf, he had looked handsome. Not now, though. Not in this light. He was damaged. He had the face of a guy who used to be attractive. Someone had broken that face. It was patched together. Annie thought he looked to be somewhere between Clooney and Mickey Rourke without looking like either one of them.

He sat up formally as she approached but didn't bother to attempt to stand. It was a business meeting. Social graces weren't needed or expected. He waved a hand toward the booth bench across from him.

"Annie, please sit."

The table was bare except for his drink. It looked to be a club soda with lime. Annie was aware of his drinking past. Being a cop in New York, there were things you just knew. Then, knowing McGinley was a drinker was like knowing Derek Jeter liked the ladies. It was a New York thing. Annie's father called McGinley one of the great New York drunks. Whatever the hell that meant.

Annie slid into the booth. She thought about how she was dressed for the first time all evening. Something about this guy made her do a mental check that all was in place. She was wearing one of her nice dresses from Theory, because of the dinner with her dad. *Thank goodness*, she thought.

He stared into her eyes. "Would you like anything? A drink perhaps?"

Annie did want a drink. Before she could respond, McGinley waved his right arm and a man, not a waiter or even an employee of the bar, stepped up out of nowhere.

"Your father says you recommend all of his wines. You're just out of Babbo. Nice meal, huh?"

Annie sensed that McGinley was attempting to order on her behalf. That was something she could not tolerate. Not from her father and certainly not from Frank McGinley. It is why she had learned so much about wine. Her father had taught her that if she wanted to do the ordering she would have to know what she was doing. Before he could go further, she interjected, "What are you having?" It was said with a bite.

McGinley was unfazed. "Club soda for me."

Annie turned to the man. "What reds do they have here?"

The man turned to Frank, not sure to whom he should respond.

McGinley nodded in Annie's direction with an eyebrow cocked and said to the man, "Well, tell Ms. Falcone."

"The bartender said they have two types of wine, red and white."

Since the battle of the drink order had been turned to farce, Annie chuckled. "I'll take the red."

The man turned, took the two steps to the bar, and shouted, "Red." He came back with the ten-dollar wine in a two-dollar glass and placed it on a napkin in front of Annie. The process took less than fifteen seconds. The man faded into the background.

Frank waited for Annie to sip. A gentleman. He smiled.

"Your father told you about us, yes?"

"Yes." Annie leaned back but kept hold of her glass on the table. *Keep hold of something.* "I must admit it's a little surprising, this secret society thing." She smiled and chuckled nervously.

Frank didn't smile back. "Did your father tell you about Woodbury Kane?"

"Yes, he mentioned the name."

"Kane's occupation was described as yachtsman and bon vivant. Imagine that. Bon vivant, and he goes off to war. Volunteers. Runs up San Juan Hill into gunfire. For a cause. For what he believed in. His life story is the motivation for everything we do. We are the Volunteers; we are not a society or a secret group. We're an organization of professional men and women who strive to make things right. Plain and simple. We have the means, and more importantly, the will to do what needs to be done to protect the innocent and punish the guilty. As you know, there are times when the usual procedures of our justice system come up short. Too often, bad actors are not held up to the law. The rich and connected tend to get away with it. The Volunteers were created around the turn of the century to break up Tammany Hall. I would advise you to research New York City history to learn how devastating Tammany was to the common man of this city."

He paused to allow Annie to ask a question.

"So the Volunteers have been around for all these years? What have you done; what do you do exactly?"

"It's not our way to speak much about the things we do. I will say that my role since volunteering has been to root out Wall Street crime and corruption. The latest fine—you know, the five-billion-dollar settlement that was in the paper yesterday—that was us. I ran that operation. It was about money laundering for terrorist groups."

"I thought it was about mortgages or something."

"Well, don't always believe what you read in the papers."

"I guess." Annie relaxed and settled into her seat. Took a sip of her wine. Frank spun his glass one rotation then lifted it and sipped. He put down his glass and looked straight into her eyes.

"It is likely that men will die as a result of this conversation. I need to know that you are okay with that and you understand the gravity of what is about to be explained to you."

Annie didn't look away. "Yes I do. I'm here because of my father. There is no man on earth whom I respect or love more. If he asked me to see you, then I'm in, all the way."

"Great. There is one formality that we must get out of the way. Do you mind?"

"No, sure, go ahead."

"Do you volunteer to join us?"

"Yes, of course."

Frank extended his hand, and she took it and shook firmly. He smiled for the first time. "Welcome to the Volunteers."

"Thanks."

"Et Omnia Recta."

"My father said that also. It's Latin, right? What exactly does it mean?"

"It's the motto of the Volunteers. Passed down all these years. A loose translation is to make things right. To make right." He tapped both of his hands lightly on the table. "To business. The word I hear about you is that you're a bad cop."

Annie started to interject, but Frank held up both his hands to fend her off.

"I don't mean to insult you, but this is what I've heard from your station. I asked around. You're not very popular with the higher-ups. That's okay, though; actually, it's a good thing. We don't take on volunteers who fit into a mold. We want free thinkers. I tend to recruit people that don't play nice, don't get along with others. I know your history with the force. Seven partners in eleven years. More arrests than anyone in your precinct, yet no promotion. And you're still in blue with your record, with your father who he is? No, you don't play the game, do you?"

"There shouldn't be a game."

"I agree. You see, you're right for this kind of work. The job I have for you. We're not, you and I ... we're not the kind of people that work well within a large organization. You want to get shit done. I get it. Hey, I've been a pain in the ass my whole life. Look how far I've come."

He smiled warmly, and for the first time since she'd sat down, Annie felt at ease.

She returned the smile. "Okay, okay. I forgive you for the 'bad cop' crack."

It was unusual for him to be so relaxed this soon into a recruitment, but she made him feel comfortable. It was likely because she reminded him of her old man. Accomplished, yet a regular guy. The kind of guy Frank got along with. She was the same. Even before he'd met her, he figured he would like her. That might make it a little more difficult, what he was going to ask of her. The danger she could be in. But that was the way it was. She volunteered.

"We need you to protect a very important man." He paused, watching her reaction. There was none, only that she eyed him in return with equal intensity. "His name is Hank Suarez. He is in Martha's Vineyard. You know, the island off Massachusetts."

A slight smirk from her. "Yeah, I know it."

"He's been in hiding for two years now. There is a threat, and we need to protect him."

"Who is this guy?"

"Hank Suarez is the single most important asset to our country's national security. He is a gifted man. The source of many of our country's technological advantages over the last ten years."

Annie scooched forward in her seat. 'Is that his real name?'

"His name is Hank Suarez; that is all you need to know. Listen, there's a lot to go over. Let me get through it and you can ask questions after."

"Sure, but I get the feeling that you won't answer any of them."

"I won't answer many, but don't ask till I'm done."

No smiles or pleasantries from this point on, Annie knew.

"Hank went into hiding two years ago after he was abducted by Chinese agents, and he barely escaped with his neck. They just about killed him. The man behind that abduction is a Chinese hacker, *the* Chinese hacker, who goes by the name of Sheng. That's all I can give you on him. Deep, deep national security clearance would be needed for me to go further. Be advised that Sheng is one of the most dangerous men in the world. When I say *the* Chinese hacker, I'm not exaggerating. He is behind almost all the security breaches of our government and most of the business hacks in the last ten years. I believe that Suarez and Sheng have a personal history, but I'm not sure about that.

"Two days ago, an industrial drone was found in a park across the road from Hank Suarez's property. This is the type of drone used for military surveillance. They don't sell these at Best Buy. It wasn't long ago that the CIA received an alert that Sheng had gone missing. We have known for years about increasing tension between Sheng and the Party. He has gotten too big. He's also become increasingly unstable recently. Our agents are confident that Sheng would never be killed—he knows too much—but, hey, we're talking about the Chinese. Our intelligence led us to believe that Sheng would have been put away somewhere. The Chinese government would try to milk him for information. Our agents have already started working their assets to figure out his successor. Not that he could be replaced. He's truly one of the smartest men on earth. No joke.

"The thing is, Hank Suarez is *the* smartest. Which brings us to you. We don't think that Hank's life is in danger. No one wants him dead; he's too valuable. I think that Sheng is here. Likely close by. No, I don't think it; I'm sure of this. Sheng is here, and he wants to grab Suarez and offer him up to the Chinese as his replacement. It's the only way Sheng can save himself. Suarez is the only man that could replace Sheng, and he would be such a prize that it is likely the Chinese would let Sheng walk. If someone like Sheng is able to roam free ... well, we're talking about a major clusterfuck. Bond villain shit.'

He finally took a breath to take a sip of his drink. Annie sat motionless. Too many questions in her head to pick one, not that she would dare to ask at this point.

Frank continued, "There are many moving parts to this. It is best that you only know about your role. You will be the body man for Hank Suarez. The one that stays glued to his side. You will be armed but only use force if it is absolutely necessary. We will also have an FBI team on sight. One of them will contact you when they see fit. They will act when the time comes. Your sole job is to protect Hank Suarez. The major complication to this job is that since Sheng is the man we're after, we must assume that any and all communication has been, or will be, breached. I'm talking about everything. Whatever you do online or on your phone once you leave this bar should be assumed to have been breached. In fact, I received notice from Hank through the US mail. He closed all possible access points immediately upon his going into hiding. You should maintain your use, but you cannot contact me until the job is completed. You can call or text your father. Communicate like you always have. No more, no less. I've already discarded my electronic devices. We will be off the grid on this.

"You will meet Hank Suarez tomorrow morning at his CrossFit class on the Vineyard. You'll introduce yourself and mention my name. I can't emphasize how important it is to not let anyone hear my name during this entire operation. Not the FBI, the CIA, or anyone other than Hank. Tell me you understand."

"Yes. I understand."

"Good. Hank will take it from there. Do not leave his side. Go back with him to his house. Get to work on the detail as soon as you arrive. Use your police instincts. Protect that home and that man. His life is far more valuable than yours or mine or your father's. Shit, he knows more about national security than our president."

Closing her eyes, Annie inhaled then exhaled slowly. Finally, she looked at him again, leaning forward. "Can I say something?"

"Sure, go ahead."

"Who else is involved in this? It can't be just your group."

"No, this is a big one. We have Homeland Security, the FBI, and the CIA. My job is to keep these blowhards from stepping all over each other. We have to be very stealth on this; like I said, no cell phones. That even goes for the agencies. Sheng is that good. We're going on the assumption that he has already hacked into most of the agencies involved. Your entire mission is to keep Hank out of trouble until you can hand him over to the

FBI team that will be sent to support you. Make sure he stays in the house for the duration. I know Hank. He's not going to want to sit around. I'm giving you the authority to use force to keep him out of harm's way. By any means necessary. Got it?"

"Yes."

Annie was intrigued, like she was listening to a movie plot. It still was hard to believe it was all happening, but here she was with Frank McGinley telling her national security secrets. She sipped her wine. "Why me?"

Frank didn't respond, and she guessed he was waiting for her to expand on the thought. So she did.

"Why me? I mean, I'm just a cop. Like you said, not much experience above the street. You're talking to me about national security and Chinese hackers. C'mon, man. This doesn't add up to me."

"There are two reasons. The first is that no one outside of the agencies I mentioned know that the man who is posing as Hank Suarez is alive. His death was staged two years ago, after his abduction. Officially, he was drugged by his captors and died of an overdose during the raid to release him. At least, that's what the records show. Furthermore, rumors were planted, indicating the kidnapping was a lie and he died of a drug overdose on his own. Nothing like a conspiracy theory to increase attention to the lie. Of course, it didn't matter much to the overall public, since most never knew who he was. Still, the deception is important; there are more Shengs in this world. The only way to keep Hank safe and productive to our agencies is to keep the illusion alive. The big agencies ... they're in it for Sheng. They don't know about the original identity of Hank. Sheng or the Chinese government will be aware if a major operation has been rolled out. Remember, we're running on the suspicion that everything has been hacked. We need a no-name for this task. So there you have the first reason for your involvement.

"The second reason is that you fit the profile for this job. You don't have a lot of experience, but you're not going to be doing much. Just sit on the guy for a few days. Also ... well, I'll be straight with you. You're a good looking woman about the same age as Hank. The way this has to play is that Sheng, who will have eyes on Hank again in some way soon enough, will have to believe that Hank took you home and you stayed for a few days. That's it. Sorry if it rubs you the wrong way, but we all have to start somewhere."

Annie wasn't offended from a feminist viewpoint. She wasn't too far removed from being an undercover hooker. In fact, that was about a month ago. It was policework, she knew. It was a letdown, though. For some reason, she'd thought she was being elevated in some way. Called to a higher purpose. Maybe it was McGinley and his elegant manner, the thousand-dollar suit.

She smiled to herself and came back to earth, to reality. Hell, she was a cop, a street cop, no more. She looked up at McGinley as she took her last sip of wine.

"So I'm here because I'm a chick and you can trust my father. Is that it?"

McGinley wasn't affected at all by the question. Either he did not sense her disappointment or he did not care. She figured it was the latter.

"Not totally. We think we can count on you, but this is entry level, and yes, your father was the biggest deciding factor. After meeting you, I think you can handle it, if that means anything to you. It doesn't matter much now, though. You volunteered, and you have too much information to walk now. So you're on the job."

"Yeah, I'm on the job."

"Good. There is a car waiting outside. There is a change of clothes and instructions on where to meet Hank. As I mentioned, he doesn't know you're coming. You're signed into his CrossFit class. After the class, go over and introduce yourself. Use my name as a reference but make sure no one hears you. No one!"

She did have another question and came out with it quickly since she sensed her time was short.

"Why not send in the troops? I mean, if this Suarez is so important, why not have a dozen Feds come and take him away?"

"That's one of those questions that I'm not going to answer."

She nodded.

"Hank will want to take over once you meet," he continued. "Do not let him go anywhere but back home. No bullshit on this. The FBI team is on their way now, but they will need a day to set up their operation. We don't want the locals in the loop on this, so you will be solo for about four or five hours. Those hours should be spent indoors. Got it?'

"Yeah. How about a weapon, other clothes, money?"

"All in a kit in the car. The driver will take you directly to the ferry at Woods Hole. You'll go over to the island like any other tourist. Be discreet. You're on vacation, getting away from the city for a while."

"I'm going now?"

"Yes. Everything you need to know is in the kit in the back seat. Read what is on the agenda, memorize it, then rip it up and throw it out the window. Tell me you will rip it up."

"Yes, of course, I'll rip it up."

McGinley rose. He buttoned the middle button of his jacket and started walking. Annie barely had time to move in her seat before his back was to her. He turned. "Good luck."

Frank stepped out of the bar and gave a nod to the driver, who walked past him and into McGreevy's to retrieve Annie and take her up to the Vineyard. He turned up his collar and allowed himself a moment to feel like the scumbag that he was.

He couldn't tell her the truth. He thought back to when his mentor, the man who became like a father to him, William Brogan, had recruited him. Frank remembered how he was manipulated for the greater good. Damn it, he had been pissed him off to be used like that. Tonight he realized how Brogan must have felt. It was worse from this end of the lie.

There was no FBI team on the job. Only the top brass of the CIA knew that Hank Suarez was Pap Martinez, but Frank wasn't sure of their intentions, so he kept them out of this. They might be happy if Pap Martinez never surfaced again. The other agencies ... they didn't know who Hank Suarez was. The world knew that Pap Martinez was dead as of two years ago. It had to stay that way. For Pap's protection and for the security of all the secrets Pap had in his head, and for the good of the Volunteers.

Frank turned west on Waverly and silently asked the God he long ago stopped believing in for forgiveness for lying to Tony and Annie Falcone. He'd sent two men ahead this afternoon. A sniper and spotter. They would pose as the FBI team. It would be the two of them and Annie against how many, he didn't know. Annie couldn't know the details of the mission. She wasn't experienced enough to execute it. The mission was twofold: to make sure Pap Martinez wasn't taken by the Chinese, and to kill Sheng. The decision to abort was in the hands of the sniper. His task was clear. Get Pap Martinez back to New York, to Frank's townhouse. If there was any chance at all that Pap could not be freed, his duty was to take them all out—Sheng, his agents, Annie, the spotter, and Pap Martinez. The final shot would a suicide shot; the sniper would kill himself.

Frank had looked into the man's eyes just this afternoon when he gave him the order.

"Kill 'em all if you have to."

He had no doubt the man would execute the task.

Chapter 10

Edgartown, Massachussetts

J oe Riggins had been a Boston cop for twenty-three years. He left his chief detective role two years before his twenty-five-year anniversary and with a three-quarter pension. It wasn't the stress, or the pressure, or the grit and crime. It wasn't even the head in the dumpster from 1999 that used to haunt him. He'd received a lead on this job—chief of the Edgartown Police—at the right time is all. He didn't leave for this job or to get away from his old one. He didn't even do it for the kids. He left to get out of that fucking house. He couldn't take it anymore.

Every night when he got home, he would look up at those stairs. For years—five years—he had come home and looked up at those stairs. The kids, Matty and Stephanie, only three and five at the time, barely remembered that day. He was able to keep them away until the ambulance had gone.

They were older now. They would be in the family room when he got home, playing video games or watching TV. They didn't run to greet him anymore. Before going in to them, he would stand at the foot of those stairs. He saw it every night. His wife, Linda, falling. Rolling over with a laundry basket in her arms and the phone tucked under her chin. She had stretched forward when the phone rolled out from the grip of her neck and shoulder, and her head lodged in the railing, the forward momentum snapping her neck like a branch.

He had stood there and watched it all. Smiling at first, thinking how silly she looked and how they would have a good laugh over it. Then her neck had snapped.

All the shit he had seen over the years, the most horrific things people did to each other. Murder, deception, all of it. And that's how she died? The love of his life, an amazing woman. His everything. He relived the scene every night. Her legs splayed awkwardly. Her neck, her face. He couldn't recall exactly how she looked soon after the accident. The shrink said it was a defense mechanism. *Thank God for small favors*, he thought. He didn't want to remember her that way. But he came home to it, to that house. Every night.

Joe sipped the coffee from his Styrofoam cup. It was cold and bitter. He cursed himself for letting his mind go back to that house. Shit. It was bad enough at night; did he have to fight off the demons at work now?

He was distracted, he knew. The drone. That fucking drone had his head screwed up. It didn't sit with him. He rose from his desk and went around to the door.

"Get me that file on Suarez again," he hollered to no one in particular. They still weren't used to him. Those Vineyarders. He knew they bristled at his harsh manner. For the most part, he'd adapted to the surroundings, the gentler side of life. Hey, it snowed and was plenty cold in the winter, but it was still an island. People thought differently here than in a precinct house in Boston. Still, when he didn't take the time to think about it, he hollered.

He went back to the desk and looked up Hank Suarez again on Google. Jesus, this guy was perfect. Maybe that was what stuck in his craw. Perfect. No such thing. Perfect credentials, clean financials, great bio. The references for his cash purchase on the Edgartown Bay Road house right across from Huckleberry Cove Park were a Who's Who of the technology world. He was perfect. Joe's assistant walked into his office after a quick rap on the door frame. She dropped the file on his desk like she was slapping his face. She turned and walked out without speaking.

He sat down with a groan, folding his six-foot-six frame into the undersized chair. He hunched over the file but didn't open it. He gazed down at it and made up his mind. This guy was dirty somehow. He was bent. Cash purchase of twelve point three million. Direct sale. No broker.

Owner in the wind. Touring Europe, the file said. The cop in Joe Riggins told him something wasn't right. He'd been a cynic for twenty-five years, and more often than not, he was proven right. He'd been profiling for years. The dirty secret of most police forces. It worked. Shit, the husband almost always did it. The guy shot after 2:00 a.m. was involved in drugs. Very few good guys out and about at that hour. A new man in town buys a house worth over twelve million with cash, no broker, no lawyer to be found. This was bullshit.

Joe's guess was money laundering. Converting dirty cash to hard assets. He'd read the alerts. It was happening all over New York City. Russians and Chinese buying real estate to get cash out of a volatile country. In the FBI reports he read, the purchases were all done through brokers. Sure, there was some cash under the table—hey, it was New York—but not many direct sales between buyer and owner. Not many at all.

Add the drone to the mix, and he knew something wasn't right. Joe went over the files, the sales record, everything for the last couple of days. There was nothing illegal he could see, but he didn't like what he did see.

He vowed to make things difficult for this Suarez guy. Drive him out of town like the sheriff in an old Western, hassling the gunslinger until he thought it better to move along. Old-fashioned police work was what it was.

Chapter 11

Annie Falcone arrived in plenty of time to catch the 6:00 a.m. ferry. The drive there had taken four and half hours, but the driver, who didn't speak the whole trip, let her sleep in the back of the Town Car. He had nudged her awake around five o'clock, and she had changed in the bathroom of the ferry station, doing a quick check from head to toe. Her weight, her looks as a whole, had never been a great concern of hers. She just didn't have the time for it. This certainly wasn't the time for mirror-gazing. She was on the job.

When she'd exited the bathroom, she saw the Town Car pull away. She slung her bag over her shoulder and headed over to the ferry.

The trip was short and bracing. For a few minutes, Annie let herself believe she was on vacation. She stood at the head of the ship, like on the *Titanic*. Only it was cold and so windy she had to hold on to the rail. No perfect hair and makeup, just wind and sea mist. Annie loved it.

As they approached the dock at Vineyard Haven, Annie went through the one sheet of instructions from the pack. She ripped that thing into a hundred pieces and gradually tossed the crumpled pieces into the waters over the course of an hour or so during the ferry ride. She was pretty sure she had it all memorized.

When the ferry docked, she went down the gray, metal staircase to the front of the ship. As she decended, her feet stuck a bit on each step. The moisture in the air made the gray paint feel wet. Annie had been to the island twice in high school. A summer vacation with a childhood friend's family was one trip; the other was a weekend with her mom.

They'd visited someone, but she couldn't recall whom. She remembered her mom on that ferry. Wearing a scarf around her head. Like Jackie O, but much prettier. There were moments like this in which the memory of her was almost crippling. The idea that she would never see her mother again was too large to imagine. Annie wiped the tears from her cheek and turned her attention back to the job. The plan was for her to go straight to the hotel, check in, and change into her workout gear. She thought it would be best to bring her big bag with all her toiletries and clothes to the gym where she would meet Suarez since, if things went according to plan, she wouldn't be returning to the hotel.

As she walked off the ferry and onto the wooden pier, the temperature rose about ten degrees. It would be a nice, early-summer day. Annie looked at her watch and saw that she had about a half hour to check in, change, and get to the gym. She picked up her pace. Rushing past the people who were waving to friends and family at the dock, she headed straight to the hotel on Main Street.

The girl at the front desk was blond, young, and nauseatingly chipper. Annie did her best to keep her "New York" to a minimum, but the girl was just moving too slowly.

She turned to Annie and smiled. "Would you like me to send up coffee or tea?"

"No thank you."

"Would you like a spa appointment?"

"No thank you."

"A spa schedule? There are wonderful group classes in our exercise room."

'No thank you. Just my room key."

"We have tea in the afternoon, complimentary beach towels, there's a lobster bake at ..."

"Just give me my key."

Annie snatched the key out of the girl's hand and turned to go up the stairs. She knew she fit the stereotype, but she was in a hurry. The room was just okay. Didn't matter to Annie. She dropped her bag on the bed, pulled out her workout gear, and changed clothes in half a minute. She dumped the contents of her bag onto the bed to see what else was packed. She took inventory. Three pairs of underwear, a couple of bras, two pairs of jeans, another pair of yoga pants, a few t-shirts, and a travel makeup bag.

She looked down at the stuff on the bed. No other shoes. The bag was obviously packed by a man. The only shoes were the Nikes she just changed into. There were the shoes she'd worn last night, but strappy heels didn't seem to be the thing for this job.

Annie looked at her watch. She had three minutes to get to the class. She scooped up the remains of the clothing, held them in her arms, and stuffed all of it back into the bag. The bag was overstuffed with the her more formal clothing replacing stretch pants and a T-shirt. Time was getting short so she pushed down on the clothes to jam it all in. She heard a snap and knew it was a heel. *Damn,* she thought. Those were my best shoes. She zipped it up and threw it over her shoulder.

As she headed to the door, Annie did a mental inventory. Keys, purse, clothes, toiletries, makeup, underwear, gun. She was set.

Chapter 12

Boston, Massachussells

Hector Gomes was doing God's work and making a nice score from it. Every one of his jobs was a molesting priest. Every one.

The guy who did him was dead. Hector saw to that when he put the bullet between his eyes.

Hector recognized the money-making angle at his first support-group meeting. He didn't go because of the long-ago abuse or because of any feelings of guilt about killing the pervert. No, he went for research. Hector had heard about how they talked at these meetings. Boy, did they talk. They dropped names and locations of parishes. Hector would get everything but an invitation to the rectory. He had the good sense to keep his mouth shut about his molester, for fear that someone would put the pieces together. He never mentioned it, and no one was the wiser. There had been a big story in the *Boston Globe* years ago but not much since. No one wanted to hear about that shit.

In the first meeting, he had picked up the names and addresses of two more priests. Still walking around. Working with altar boys. His first thought was to kill them like he had the first one. Then he had an idea. Why not grab these pigs and threaten to expose them? Let the church know that he would bring it to the press. The *Globe* would run a big story if they knew these guys were still out there. Fucking these kids up. He knew this.

The first job went perfectly. Hector and the Murdock brothers picked the priest up right out of the rectory. Just knocked on the door. An old broad let them in when they said they had an appointment with Father Degnan.

Billy Murdock punched him in the face, and they brought Degnan to the office of the carting company that Hector worked for. The company had gone under a couple of weeks earlier, but Hector kept his set of keys.

They'd tied the priest to a chair and called the main line of the diocese. A couple of transfers later and the voice of Degnan pleading for the Murdocks to let up on him, arrangements were made for a hundred grand to be dropped into a dumpster that Hector had scouted out earlier.

The deal was that the priest would not be killed but was to be transferred out of town, and Hector and the Murdocks got the cash.

Hector hadn't been sure it would work, but it had. One day's work and he was eighty grand richer. He gave the Murdocks ten grand each. They were stupid fucks and didn't care much about the money. It was enough to keep them in beer and women for a few months. Hector had picked the right guys. He knew that both brothers had been bent over by the priests plenty of times. It had turned them to the street. Mad as hornets. No, they just wanted to beat on a priest for a day or two. That was enough for the Murdocks.

Hector had other ideas. He started going to meetings all over Boston. Then a few in Rhode Island. These pricks were everywhere. When he was a kid, he thought it was only him. Now he realized that it was happening all over.

No, this was the right thing to do. Some of the stories he heard were enough to make you want to kill the motherfuckers. He didn't kill them, though; he just handed them over to the Murdocks. They took care of the rest.

He was up to five priests for the money and three who were so fucking perverted that he left them to the Murdocks. Eight hundred grand so far. Shit, he had dozens on the back burner. Hector realized he needed to start keeping track. Set up some kind of filing system or some shit. He also realized that if this was going to be an ongoing enterprise, the Murdocks would have to go. They drank too much and talked more. Word was starting to get around about the kidnapped priests.

It was perfect timing when the Chinaman—Shizi, he'd said his name was—had called him, asked to meet. Dropped the name of a New York wiseguy Hector knew from way back. Said he had a job for him. The guy hinted at Hector's kidnapping expertise. He figured it may be a big payday. Besides, it would be best to back off from the priests for a while. Hector still had access to the old carting office, so he set up the meet with Shizi there. He was thinking about getting a new place when the Chinaman walked through the door like he owned the fucking place. He said his boss knew all about Hector's operation and had great admiration for his work.

Hector, of course, said he didn't know what the fuck he was talking about. The Chinaman proceeded to rattle off the details of every kidnapping and even had papers that showed the bank transactions of the church to raise cash for the payoffs.

It was all like a magic trick to Hector.

"How the hell did you find all this?"

"I work for a very powerful man. He sees everything, and he likes your work."

"Well, I don't know what the fuck you want from me."

"Of course you don't. I haven't told you yet."

Shizi was a serious man. Hector knew he was no match for the Chinaman, and if he didn't show some respect, he might get himself killed. He also knew this guy had enough on him to put him away for a long time.

"So what do you want?"

"We would like you to send your men, William and Caleb Murdock, to kidnap a man for us."

"That's funny. You think I'm going to work for you just like that?" Hector was trying to maintain a little air of importance, Hey, they were in his office.

"Oh, we will pay."

He lifted the bag he was holding at his side and placed it on the metal table in front of them. Shizi unzipped the duffle and started taking out stacks of twenties. All wrapped in thick rubber bands. The bills were crumpled and weathered. This guy knew what he was doing. Not a crisp bill in the lot. The stacks kept coming. The duffle was like that cartoon cat's magic bag. More came out than seemed reasonable to expect to fit inside. When he finished stacking, there was a small fort of money on the table. It stood a foot high.

"That's a lot of scratch."

"Yes. Five hundred thousand. All used and unmarked. An equal amount will be paid upon completion of the task."

"Whaddya you plan to buy with that?"

Shizi closed his eyes, as if he were trying to maintain patience. "You will send your men, the Murdocks, to the location in the plans I will soon text to you. They will attempt a kidnapping according to the instructions. They will be shot and killed by a police officer. Do you understand?'

The shooting of the Murdocks wasn't what bothered Hector. It was the text.

"What text? You have my number?"

"Of course."

Shizi pulled out his phone and tapped a few times. Hector's phone pinged. He took it out of his pocket and looked. A series of emojis.

"What is this?"

"Type the number 6321 as a response."

Hector did, and the word "TEST" appeared where the emojis had been. Hector stared at the phone. Witnessing another magic trick.

Shizi broke the silence. "Every communication will be encrypted. If you don't respond within thirty seconds, the message goes away. Your number will be 6321. There will be two messages. The first will be shortly after I leave. It will tell you where to send your men. The second will be to tell you the task has been completed and that our business is done."

"And where to pick up the rest of my money?" The Chinaman was moving too fast for Hector. He wasn't used to being told what to do.

"Yes, along with a location to pick up the rest of the money. If you speak to anyone or if the task is not carried out to our specifications, we will send the information we have to the police and you will be arrested. The police suspect you as it is. The Murdocks talk too much, as you must know, since you seem receptive to our offer. We need a plausible kidnapping scenario, and you need the police to get their men. It's what you Americans call a win-win."

Hector didn't like having this guy setting terms. "What if I pull the gun in my pocket, shoot you, and take off with the cash?'

Shizi smiled. "Mr. Gomes, I'm a highly trained professional. You will not get to your gun before I get to mine. Take the money as a gesture of our goodwill. As I mentioned, my employer admires your work. It is a good thing that you do. Be assured that we will keep our end of the bargain. One more thing. You are going to have to leave this area of the country and find another line of work. The police are indeed on to you, and we will not tolerate you getting arrested. I'm afraid we can't allow you to speak to the authorities. Do I make myself clear?"

"Yeah, yeah. You're going to pop me if I get picked up. I throw you the Murdocks, and I walk with some cash to help me get the fuck away from the heat, and you can go on with whatever kind of bullshit you're involved with."

"You're a wise man, Mr. Gomes. That sums up our agreement perfectly."

Shizi smiled and bowed slightly.

Hector didn't know if it was a gesture of respect or if Shizi was mocking him. It didn't matter much either way. He was still puzzled. "How do you know all this? You had this all orchestrated before you walked in the door. How?"

"The answer is in your hand."

Gomes looked down at his phone.

"We're in your phone. We know everything. Good day."

Shizi turned and walked out as Gomes placed his phone face down on the table and looked over the cash.

Chapter 13

Vineyard Haven, Massachussetts

Annie had worked out her whole life. She was All-City in high school basketball and played on the NYPD women's team until two years ago, but she'd never felt anything like this.

This was crazy. It was her first CrossFit class. Flipping a gigantic tractor tire. Climbing ropes. Burpees!

The class was coming to an end, although it wasn't really much of a class. Everyone went off on their own in the gym, the box they called it, and worked on their own thing. The instructor, a super-fit twentysomething with abs like an Olympian, strolled around, barking at everyone. The woman seemed to relish busting on the new member, Annie, the most.

Maybe Annie was a couple of pounds over perfect, but she knew she was in shape. The sideways glances of the men in the class confirmed it. Maybe it was the glances that set the skinny bitch off.

Annie ignored her and thought about her approach. She spotted Hank Suarez right away. The photo she memorized in the car on the way up didn't do him justice. He was fucking beautiful. *A pretty boy*, she thought. *No, worse. A rich, pretty boy.* She knew he was forty, but he didn't have an ounce of fat on him. He looked like soccer star Ronaldo's better-looking older brother.

She sensed this guy was going to be a pain in the ass. He was the exact type she couldn't stomach. She mentally prepared for his inevitable attempt to get her into bed. No doubt he smelled of cologne and privilege.

It was going to be a long day.

The skinny bitch rang a bell by pulling on a big rope at the far end of the box, signaling the end of the class. The first thing Annie did was fall on the floor after finishing what felt like her hundredth squat with a kettlebell held over her head. She didn't stay there long, though; she didn't want Suarez to leave without her.

He was toweling off next to the water fountain. She walked up behind him and waited as he bent down for a long drink. She was happy to see he was breathing more heavily than she. Maybe he wasn't perfect. He stood and stepped aside and let her get a drink. He waited there as if he wanted to speak. Since she was new, he may have been anticipating her approach. She hoped he wasn't going to try to hit on her. When she stood up from the fountain, he made eye contact and walked away toward a quiet corner of the box. Annie forgot what her opening line was going to be, so she moved in close and simply whispered, "Frank McGinley."

Suarez nodded. "Let's go."

He headed straight toward the exit, picking up his gym bag near the door. Annie had left her bag across the box, so she had to trot over to retrieve it. Her legs almost buckled from fatigue; she went halfway down with one of her strides. She righted herself but felt a twinge in her hamstring. She limped to her bag and then went back across to the door with a hitch in her giddyup.

Suarez was waiting inside a five-year-old Jeep Cherokee. It was muddy and had a half-dozen local bumper stickers on it. Annie had no doubt it was staged to blend in.

She got in the passenger side, and he threw it into reverse before she could buckle up. They didn't speak until they hit the open road.

He spoke first without turning to her. "Do you know any Latin?"

The question seemed to come from out of left field. Annie didn't know what the hell he was talking about. He pulled over, hard, to the side of the road. She had to brace herself on the dashboard from the sudden stop. He turned and faced her. His voice raised, threatening. He didn't look so pretty anymore. "Do you know any Latin?"

It came to her. The phrase both McGinley and her father had used.

"Et Omnia Recta."

His response was to put the Jeep back into drive and pull out to the road. After a moment, he spoke again. "Sorry for being so harsh. This is my first time out of the house in few days. I knew that I needed to get out to make contact. This is the protocol if I were found. Tell me everything you've been told."

"McGinley said that ..."

Suarez raised his hand. "Never say that name again. Got it?"

Annie nodded. She was starting to feel a little intimidated. This guy was nothing like she thought he would be. He was wired, for sure. Annie had seen it before. Guys on the run. She had sat on a federal witness once. He had been in the city under protection before testifying against some West Coast crew.

She would have to be delicate if she wanted to control him. She had to take the upper hand soon enough to keep him settled until the FBI relieved her. She decided to play nice for now. Later she would set him straight.

She took a deep breath and turned to him. The Atlantic was beyond him, out the driver's-side window, and she could hear the surf in the silent car.

"He told me that an important man from China is nearby—'

He interrupted. "Sheng, yes. You can say it. Just no names from our end." He attempted a grin, but it came off like a smirk. Too much tension in his cheeks.

"Okay. Sheng is here," she said. "It has been confirmed that he left China. All I know is that our mutual friend thinks that Sheng wants to take you back to China to secure his freedom. It seems that he was getting a little too smart for his own good, so he ran and wants to offer you up in exchange. Our friend didn't share this, but I'm assuming the Chinese are not too fond of you either. He made it very clear your security is essential. I'm only here to sit on you until the FBI gets here to relieve me. I go home tomorrow, and I'm done. I don't know the big picture. I'm just here until the cavalry arrives."

He answered with a grunt. They drove a while in silence. She glanced over at him and could see he was deep in thought. She felt something stir inside of her and cursed herself immediately. He looked better to her now that she knew he was in trouble. She smiled and looked out her window and thought, *What a schmuck you are. The troubled-guy thing again? Jesus.* She steeled herself and put her mind back to the job. Get him back home. Lock his ass down and sit in the living room until someone arrives. She prepared herself to be up all night. She had begun a mental checklist of all the tasks ahead when he spoke.

"You have a gun?"

She was surprised by the question. "Yes. Glock police special."

He paused as if he pondering how much to say. "I don't know if you have been told, but I have a history with Sheng. He was behind my kidnapping a few years ago. I died as a result."

Annie didn't fully understand what he meant, but she waited for him to continue.

"They grabbed me right outside my office. Right in the middle of Manhattan. I was drugged to keep me quiet. They pumped so much shit into my veins that when the SWAT team finally got me out of there, I was dying. I actually died on the street, but they revived me in the ambulance. This is some serious shit going on. You keep that gun close until we get to my house. It wouldn't surprise me if we were ambushed anywhere along the route."

Annie took the pistol out of her bag and locked the chamber. She looked over at him and could tell he was spooked. Her police training kicked in.

"How far to your house? Do you have a security system in place? Is there access from the water, the woods, anywhere other than the road?"

He didn't turn back to her. He answered with a clenched jaw. "Mile or so. Water and road access only. I have a proprietary security system that I'm sure even Sheng can't hack. Once we get on the grounds, we'll be safe."

Annie tried to soothe him. Talk him down a bit. "Good. Let's go straight in and wait. We should be fine."

He turned left onto Edgartown Bay Road. The water side of the street was lined with stately beach houses, one of which Annie figured was his, since these homes had both water and road access.

He clicked a remote attached to the rearview mirror, and Annie saw a gate in front of the house swing open about fifty yards ahead. He didn't slow down much, and she worried that the Jeep might flip when he turned in. She looked at the house as it came fully into view. It was a mansion, not a house. Suarez cut a sharp left, tapping the breaks slightly as they started the turn. Annie was thrust up against the side door, but the Jeep didn't flip. He timed it perfectly. The Jeep barely made it between the still-opening iron gate. He reached up and clicked the remote again. They came to a stop under a portico adjacent to a side door of the house. Annie looked out her side window and watched as the gate closed. Suarez was about to jump out of the Jeep, but she put her hand on his arm and held it a second to be sure the gate had fully closed. When she heard the loud clack of metal against metal, the grinding of the gate's motor, and what sounded like bolts locking in place, she let go.

He looked out the rearview and let out a sigh of relief. "That's fortified steel bolted into six feet of cement. A tank couldn't get through that gate."

He stepped out of the Jeep, and she immediately did the same. Keeping a quick pace, he pulled out a device from his pocket and pressed a button. The side door of the house unlatched. He spoke as he trotted the ten feet to the door with Annie close behind. "This is a universal remote. The entire security system is managed by a server in the basemant. No one gets in."

He held the door for her while looking past her to the yard. She entered the mudroom. There weren't many mudrooms in Brooklyn, but she'd read about them in a magazine. He closed the door and bolted it behind them. There was another door that led to the interior of the house, but he didn't make a move for it.

He took a deep breath and closed his eyes for a second, opened them, and said, "There is no FBI. No cavalry is coming. The strategy for this type of operation is to send a sniper and spotter. That's it. I'm guessing they're on the scene now. Maybe with eyes on us. We're bait. The job is to kill Sheng. He's too great a security risk to our country. Yeah, I can see it. The man who sent you is a great friend of mine. We've worked together many times, but this is bigger than friendship or either one of our lives. The job is Sheng. Sorry to say, but you're expendable. You're here to get me to sit in this house until Sheng or his agents reveal themselves. You're the human shield in this operation. I'm valuable to our country, and they want me alive, but killing Sheng is more important. I have no doubt they would take me out if it meant a way to get to him. It's smart. I would play it the same way."

Annie looked back at him, astonished. He had spoken quickly, but it was sinking in. *McGinley lied to me. That fucking scumbag. Now I'm stuck here waiting for a sniper's bullet. Shit, my father's friend.*

She had to put it out of her mind, though. She was on the job. Suarez was clearly spooked, and she had to take control. "Let's get you in the house, and we'll talk this through."

Suarez clicked the remote again, and the inner door opened a few inches on its own. He walked through first without holding the door for her. She followed and immediately sized up the place. There was a lot to take in.

The room they were in seemed to be the entire footprint of the house. She didn't get a very good look from the outside, since they had come in fast and at a sharp angle, but this had to be the entire bottom floor. There was an open stairway off to her right that climbed along the wall up to a hole in the ceiling twenty feet above. She wondered if the second floor was laid out the same.

This was the largest single room she had seen in a private residence. Annie knew next to nothing about architecture, but the room had to be fifty feet by forty. Or maybe it was sixty or seventy. The distance between the walls made it hard to get a perspective. The kitchen was as far away as first to third base on a baseball diamond. The full-length glass sliding doors at the back of the room were a similar distance away, but in a different direction. The room was bright from the reflection of the sun on the ocean outside the glass doors. The furniture was sparse and white. The kitchen was mostly stainless steel with a long white table between the appliances and the sunken living room. There were barstools along the table and not a pot or pan in sight.

He must be very neat or he eats out a lot.

Suarez walked toward the kitchen. "Let me make you a smoothie."

His voiced echoed slightly in the open space.

Annie answered, hoping to hear her own echo like when she was a kid in the old Fort Hamilton High School gym. "That would be good." It did echo, and she couldn't help but smile.

Annie walked toward the glass doors. She heard a cabinet open and looked over her shoulder to see him removing a blender, which had been neatly tucked away. He was a neat guy.

He half-shouted from across the diamond. "You allergic to anything?"

"No. Make what you want."

She was at the windows now. The view was amazing. Straight ahead was the Atlantic and to the left was Edgartown. Annie could see half of the town through the yachts docked in her sight line. The church steeple rose above it all. She was looking at a postcard. The cop in her kicked in. "What kind of security do you have out here?"

In the middle of the sentence, the blender started. Turning toward him, she waited. The machine stopped, and he popped the top and poured two glasses. She spoke again when he started walking toward her, a glass of green goop in each hand.

She asked again. "What kind of security do you have?"

Suarez took a sip and a small shadow of green stuck to his upper lip.

"Like I mentioned, it's a proprietary system. All self-contained, wireless and cellular. I have a dish of my own design on the roof behind the widow's walk, in addition to the basement server. This dish is undetectable from the street. The entire house is a cellular hotspot. No transmissions from within the house go to the outside. For someone to hack this, they would have to be inside the building."

"What about cell service or Internet?"

"No. That is all transmitted to and from the outside world. I'm talking about my security system, television, and appliances. We're still going to stay off our devices."

"Our friend said I should use mine like I normally would. It should look like you picked me up at the gym and I should let my father know where I am eventually."

She smiled. He didn't.

"Why don't you wait a while to text or anything until we talk through this more?"

"Sure." Annie sipped, and the drink tasted much better than she would have thought. "Wow. Pretty good."

"Yeah, fruit and spinach mostly. A little bit of honey for extra flavor."

Annie turned back to the glass window facing out to the water.

"How about entry from the bay?"

"It is a problem. They have very strict zoning laws, as you can imagine. The town won't allow any fencing, so I have an electronic fence. If anyone breaches the perimeter, I will be alerted with an alarm."

Annie nodded and finished the rest of her drink. Suarez took it from her and finished his as he walked back to the kitchen. He rinsed both glasses and immediately put them in the dishwasher. He started walking toward the staircase at the far end of the room.

He shouted, "I'm going to hop in the shower. I have some running pants and loose t-shirts. I'll bring something down for you when I'm done."

"No thanks. I have some clothes to change into in my gym bag. Its out in the Jeep. I'll grab them, then walk the grounds. Can I go out this door?"

Suarez stopped halfway up the staircase to answer.

"Yeah, just slide it to the right."

Annie looked up at him and said, "Remote?"

"Oh yeah."

Suarez tossed it, and Annie snagged it with her left hand, as she pulled her gun out of her bag with her right. "We're probably being watched. I'm sure Sheng hacked into a satellite a while back. He's got an eye in the sky. Keep your gun out of sight."

"Yeah. Got it. I'm just an innocent girl admiring the beautiful grounds."

Chapter 14

Sheng had not slept for the last two nights. He recognized that he was on one of his binges. He had worked himself up to a point where rest was impossible. It was his curse. His genius had given him access to the world's information. He felt as if there wasn't anything he couldn't know if he took the time to search for it. It was this knowledge that drove him to the edge of madness. Since he could know anything he wanted, he was compelled to search for it. All of it. He had to know everything. He could go on like this for days.

As he rubbed his face and stared at one of the nine screens in front of him, he knew his health was suffering. His mind left him for longer periods of time lately. He didn't know if it was from fatigue or if it was a major health issue. Sheng also knew these binges, as he called them, were his most productive times. When his mind left him was when he made most of his discoveries. He would type on the keyboard, absently writing code or searching in some sort of transcendental state, and the most miraculous things would appear on the screen.

This was how he'd discovered Hector Gomes.

Sheng had been looking for criminal activity in the Boston area. He knew that he would need participation from people outside the law for his plan to succeed. He needed a man who had some experience but not enough for the police to know about him. Last week he was on the laptop searching police files, and suddenly he had Gomes's picture in front of him. He didn't know how it got there. He must have left his mind for a time. As he looked at the picture, he knew. He knew all about Gomes and the kidnappings. He knew about the Murdocks and the priests. He knew how he would use them.

This was his gift. He was Sheng. He knew.

He picked up the cell phone and typed in the message. Gomes would see a text of random emojis. When Gomes inputted his code, the instructions would appear.

The Murdocks would break into Martinez's house tonight. They will die, and Gomes will go away. The capture of Martinez would happen afterward.

Sheng turned his attention back to the screen with the satellite image. This one was from a Google satellite. Hacking into a satellite was one of the first things he had taught his staff when he started his operation in China. It was relatively easy compared to some of the other security algorithms he had seen in the last few years. Sheng knew that he alone was the reason most companies and governments had spent millions to keep prying eyes away. It was no use, of course; he could see what he wanted. Sheng used the satellites on a rotating basis to maintain his surveillance of Martinez's house. He switched them to avoid detection, and it was this diligence that led to his mistake. The drone.

It had been an overreaction to use it. The frustration of the poor image from the Russian satellite had gotten to him. The damn Russians made shit. It was the only image that was grainy and unreliable. The rotation of the seven satellites was the ideal way to keep track of Martinez, but the two hours of bad reception was unacceptable to Sheng. He had reacted rather than thought it out. It was a foolish thing to do. An error that surely would have cost one of his old subordinates his life. Perhaps even Shizi, if he'd made such a mistake.

Sheng blindly looked at the image of the house from above. He may have dozed, because he saw something move on the screen and he jumped in his seat. He leaned in closely and massaged the touch pad to zoom in.

There was someone walking around the side of the house. It looked like a woman. He lost sight of her as she went under the carport. He glanced at his watch—it was nine thirty in the morning. When she emerged again, Sheng tried to zoom in more, losing resolution as he did.

It was a woman, and it looked like she had a gun in her hand. She held it close to her side, but it was there. Yes, it was a gun. Martinez had a bodyguard. They were moving him soon. Sheng watched her as she walked, her stride fluid, her steps synchronized. She had been trained, perhaps military or some sort of law enforcement.

As he watched her head to the back of the house, Sheng decided to change the plan. He sensed this woman could help him. If she could take out the Murdocks, it would make things less complicated for him.

Sheng knew how important it was that he never be connected with this. No one could know he was in the country. The bodyguard confirmed what Sheng already knew. The drone had tipped Martinez. The game was on.

He was glad now that his adversary was aware of the game. It would be an extra pleasure to outwit the American. The temptation was great to have Shizi climb the gate and kill the woman. Bring Martinez to him. But it wasn't worth the risk. Shizi was on the Americans' list of Chinese spies, and if Sheng himself was exposed, it would spark a national security concern for the Americans. If he was ever to be captured, Sheng had no doubt he would be traded for an American political prisoner in China and sent home, where he knew he would die one of two ways: in the airport upon his arrival, or in a prison camp after years of torture and degradation. It was clear that the best course was for the woman to kill the Murdocks and then get the policeman involved.

He dinged Shizi's phone, and he walked into the room after no more than thirty seconds.

"Pick up the policeman and bring him to me. You recall the words you will use?"

"Yes sir." Shizi spun and left the room.

Sheng pivoted in his chair to his lone desktop computer. He logged into the media software and started searching for his voice-changer program. There wasn't a New England accent in the dropdown menu so he typed "Massachusetts" into the search bar.

Chapter 15

Gomes went over the plan with the Murdocks once again. "There's going to be a bodyguard. Just one. You come in from the beach here."

He pointed to a spot on the Google map on his desktop.

Caleb asked most of the questions.

"This bodyguard, is he a pro? What kind of firepower will he have?"

"Nothing. Just a handgun, if that. This is your typical rich guy with some thick-necked retired boxer or football player or something. My man tells me it'll be a piece of cake. Take the bodyguard out, pick up the rich scumbag, and call me. This will be easier than breaking into one of the seminaries, believe me."

The moment the Murdocks left the office, Gomes turned off his phone as instructed then placed it flat on the table and picked up the hammer. A couple of well-placed shots, and it was broken into small pieces. He shoveled the pile with his forearm to the edge of the table and brushed the pieces into the zip-lock baggie he held at the edge. He would drop the pieces from his car on his way out of town.

The money was in the trunk. He thought he'd head to Florida. Gomes chose it because he didn't know anyone down there. He figured that he should lie low for a while. There was no way the Chinks were going to pay him the rest of the money. He'd probably be taken out if he tried to pick it up. No, it was best to head south by car, watch the speed limit, and live off the cash for a while until things settled.

He thought he might try to pick up a real job eventually. The cash would supplement his income so he could live decently. He was getting too old for this shit.

Chapter 16

S hizi waited in his car on Mayhew Lane. The feeling of summer was finally starting to take hold. He hoped they would finish this business soon. His years as a Red Army colonel taught him the value of a quick operation. The longer they stayed in one place, the more chances there were for things to go wrong. Sheng was getting flakier by the day. Once they were out of here and his bank account had another million or so, he would kill Sheng and get out of this miserable country.

He kept his eye on the back door of the Dock Street Coffee Shop, waiting for Officer Wells to emerge.

He knew how to approach the cop. Wells was like the police back home in China. Corrupt and not very smart. What other explanation could there be for a New England policeman not to notice a six-foot-four Chinese national who had been tailing him on and off for weeks? There was also the matter of the two hundred eighty-six thousand dollars owed to a Rhode Island bookie. A debt that Sheng had paid three hundred thousand for a few days ago.

Shizi knew the businesses that Wells had been shaking down. This very coffee shop was paying him a thousand a month to avoid a surprise inspection. Shizi knew all the signs of a corrupt policeman. Officer Wells had to be desperate to be running protection schemes in his own precinct—*shitting where he eats*, as the Americans would say, a clear indication that he was spiraling. Wells was easy prey.

Wells walked out of the door into the parking lot and headed toward his car, which was parked right in front of Shizi's. He was a large man. An inch or so taller than Shizi, but he was fat. Fat and soft. He would not be a physical challenge. As he walked to his car in his street clothes, Shizi stepped out of his car and walked forward to Wells's driver's-side door. He leaned against it and crossed his legs.

Wells noticed him as he approached. "Hey, shithead, that's my car you're leaning on."

Shizi smiled. A man like Wells made his job much more enjoyable. He slowly removed his sunglasses and slid them into his pocket.

"Mr. Corrigan sent me to speak to you."

He could see the wince on Wells's face.

"Who the fuck is Corrigan?"

Shizi stood upright and squared his legs.

"Please, Officer Wells, do not make this more difficult than it needs to be."

Wells made a feeble attempt to continue the charade.

"I don't know you or what you're talking about, man. Now get away from the car, or I'll run you in."

Wells reached into his back pocket. Shizi assumed it was for his badge, but he didn't want to be surprised by a gun. He knew about the ankle holster, and Wells didn't seem to be going for it, but the movement gave Shizi the opportunity to react to the "shithead" remark. He reached forward and grabbed Wells by the left wrist and twisted. Wells went down to a knee immediately. Shizi looked up and down the street. There were people strolling along South Water Street at the far end of Mayhew, but no one seemed to notice. He released the pressure on his wrist.

"You're going to take your hand out of your back pocket and stand up slowly, or I will snap your arm at the elbow."

Shizi turned his own wrist forward and pushed down. He knew Wells would feel the pressure at the elbow joint. It would be enough of a twinge of pain to make him cooperate. He released the pressure.

"All right, all right. Jesus Christ. I just spoke to Corrigan a week ago. What the fuck is this? He knows he's getting his money. Jesus. This is bullshit."

Shizi let go of his wrist and allowed Wells to stand.

"Mr. Corrigan no longer owns your paper. My employer has purchased the debt." He smiled. "This is a good day for you, Officer Wells. You have the opportunity to come to very agreeable terms with my employer to rid you of this obligation.'

Wells waved his hands. "No, no, no. We all agreed. I'm not going to use my position with the force to help with any illegal activity. I'd rather you break my arm."

Shizi smiled and squinted from the sun. He casually put his Ray-Bans back on.

"I would gladly accommodate you with your arm; in fact, I'm hoping to do so in the near future to teach you a little respect. As for your agreement, you have broken it yourself. We know you're collecting protection money from a number of businesses on the island. I could walk into this coffee shop and ask for the thousand for this month. Or perhaps the liquor store around the block with the expired liquor license. How would it look to your police department to have one of their men beaten on the street, only to discover that it was over late payment of gambling debts? After I disable you, we will release the names of the shops that you are extorting. I don't think it would work out well for you. It would be my preference, of course, but there is the matter of a debt to be collected. How would you pay if you were unemployed and in the hospital or in jail? Besides, I'm just a collector. I'm here to bring you to my employer. He wants to meet you and make an offer for payment in person."

"I got shit to do today. I'm not going to make it. I'm on duty later. Maybe tomorrow?"

Shizi didn't respond to the statement. It was all he could do not to smash this guy's nose into a thousand pieces. One upward thrust with the palm of his hand would do it. He took a deep breath then spoke slowly, methodically.

"Go around to the passenger-side door. Open the door. Sit down facing the street. Remove the pistol from your ankle holster and hand it to me slowly. When you finish, I want you to slide over the gear shaft and sit in the driver's seat. I will sit next to you, and you will drive to the location I give you. Do you understand?"

"What if I say fuck you and shoot you here in the street?"

"If you go for your gun, I will kill you where you stand."

They made a left on Katama Road and headed out of town. Wells behind the wheel and Shizi next to him, holding the gun on his lap. Wells spent most of the ride trying to figure a way out of this mess. He gave up the thought as they made a right on Navy Road. They drove in silence.

Shizi instructed Wells to pull into a driveway made of shells on Mattakesett Way. The house was halfway between the beach and a small airport. Across the hard-packed dirt road was a farm, isolated yet close to the airport and main roads. The location was ideal for Sheng's purposes. The house was used primarily for rentals, so their short stay would not raise eyebrows.

Shizi waved the gun to indicate for Wells to get out. They walked around the back to an outdoor staircase that led to the second level of the deck. The shells crunched beneath their feet. Wells turned to Shizi at the top of the deck. He could see the ocean in the distance and hear the crashing waves. He didn't know what awaited him behind the sliding glass doors that led inside the house, so he thought he'd make his pitch.

"You know that you're messing with a cop. I mean, I don't show up to work this afternoon and someone's coming for me. Already, I can have you for kidnapping a policeman. You don't want to add to that."

Shizi stared back at him blankly. He enjoyed watching Wells grovel behind a mask of bluster. He was surprised that this fat American had the courage to try. He felt a twinge of admiration for him. At least he was standing up for himself, making an effort.

Shizi had led many men to a door that stood between their pasts and futures. The door to a room where their mistakes and deceptions were about to be judged and their sentence to be determined. Some men fought, some cried. Shizi waited silently to see what Wells would do. He watched him stare out at the ocean, then he saw his chest drop. Wells wilted before his eyes, and it was glorious.

Shizi raised the gun for effect.

"Open the door."

The room was dark and dank compared to the glaring sunlight outside. Across the room was a large kitchen island covered with plywood. There was at least a half dozen laptops in a semi-circle atop the platform, and it smelled like the windows hadn't been open in days. The air was stale enough to almost be debilitating. Suddenly a head popped up from behind one of the screens like a meerkat on the lookout for predators. A small man came around the side of the island with his hand out. At first Wells thought it was a gesture of aggression, but then he saw the smile on the small man's face.

The man shook his hand and waved toward the couch.

"Please, Officer Wells, sit, sit."

Wells stood his ground.

The man continued with, "I'm hoping you were not treated poorly. My assistant was instructed to treat you with respect."

Wells relished the idea of bashing the collector. "Well, your boy here has a lot to learn about manners."

"Oh, that is not acceptable."

The man turned to Shizi. His voice raised. "What were you told? We will deal with this later. For now, don't just stand there like a fool. Go fetch us some tea."

Then he looked at Wells. "Would you like tea?"

"No thanks, I'm good."

"Water, anything?"

"Nah."

The man said to Shizi. "Ok then. Tea for me. Go. Get out of my sight."

This routine had been worked out with Shizi many years ago. Sheng had bribed hundreds of police officers over the years. It was always the same. Act deferential to them and their profession, then offer them money.

Wells sat on the couch, and Sheng sat in a leather chair across from him. He leaned in.

"Officer, I do deeply apologize for my assistant's behavior. I'm afraid he is not going to work out. My work demands a more delicate touch than this cretin is able to comprehend. Once again, I'm so sorry."

Wells sat taller. "That's all right. Just pissed me off a little is all." He raised an open hand. "It's okay."

"Thank goodness. I like to do business in a professional manner. Don't you agree?"

"Sure." Wells's bullshit meter was on high alert, thinking this was an amateur attempt at good cop/bad cop.

"I guess you're wondering why I invited you here."

"You know, grabbing a cop off the street isn't usually a good way to get off on the right foot. You bought my paper from Corrigan, your boy says. So why not meet me in a bar or somewhere and we can come to terms? You seem to know about my side income. You see I'm hustling. Let's work something out."

"You are right, of course. And I do know that you are making your best efforts to pay your debt. I have no doubt that if you were left to your own resources, you would pay in full, but I'm not in the position to wait. I was hoping we could come to an arrangement that would be suitable for the two of us."

"Well, I don't know what you have in mind, but I can't be pulling my badge or some shit. You know what I mean? I can't go outside the law. Hey, if I get busted, no one gets any money. Who the hell are you, anyway?"

Sheng laughed lightly. "Oh my. Forgive me. I have not properly introduced myself."

Sheng pulled out a gold card holder from his pocket and handed over a thick business card. The very card he'd printed an hour ago. It read, *Thomas Shin, Executive Vice President, MGM Casino,* in silver script. The white card was trimmed in gold. Sheng had researched "power fonts" to choose the cursive lettering.

Wells looked it over. "Casino?"

"Yes, Officer Wells. I amThomas Shin. I represent the owners of the MGM Casino in Macau, China. I am hoping you will be able to work with me. You see, I have a delicate situation that requires some discretion. In all honesty, we chose to ask for your help because you are in a delicate position yourself. I am hoping we can come to an agreement that will serve us both."

"Is this a shakedown? You gonna blackmail me or something? Let me tell you—people up here stick together, especially the men in blue. No one

is going to take the word of a casino guy from China over a local
policeman."

Wells put his hands on his knees as if he was about to get up.

"Please, Mr. Wells. Let me explain. Please."

Wells leaned back.

"There is a man on this island who is very deeply in debt to my
employer. Many millions, in fact. His name is Hank Suarez. You can look
him up when we finish here. Mr. Suarez lives in one of the large houses
along Edgartown Bay Road. He is a video game developer and his net
worth is in excess of nine hundred million dollars. Despite his wealth, he
does not seem to feel that he has an obligation to pay his debts. I have tried
to contact him many times. My assistant tried the house, but it is like a
fortress. Mr. Suarez owes the casino over eleven million dollars. I am here
to collect it."

"So what does this have to do with me?"

"I need your help to get Mr. Suarez out of his home and delivered to
me."

"How am I supposed to help you with that?"

"I do not think he would refuse an invitation from a police officer. Not
one in uniform. With a patrol car."

Wells shifted in his seat. *Maybe this isn't bullshit*, he thought. He
knew a little about how casinos operated, being a gambling man. This type
of thing wasn't unheard of. He also knew there might be a chunk of change
in it for him.

"You see, now we're getting into an area that I don't think I can help
you with."

Sheng ignored him, waved his hands, and continued.

"Your services may not be required at all. I want you as my backup
plan. Your debt will be paid whether you do anything or not. We will make
an attempt to persuade Mr. Suarez to come to us this evening. All I want
is for you to be in the area of Edgartown Bay Road between one and three
in the morning. I would like you to be the first officer to arrive at the scene
if the attempt fails and he calls the police. If the attempt is successful, then
no call will be made; you have your debt cleared and it will be as if we
never met. I am merely asking you to do your normal job. Take your

regular shift, just be in the area."

"What if he does call? I'll be first guy on the scene. What do you expect me to do then?"

'I was hoping that you would be so kind as to bring him to me."

"Be so kind? Bring him? In my patrol car? No, no. That's not going to happen."

"Officer Wells, I, of course, will compensate you for your troubles. Beyond the debt payment."

Again, Sheng reached into his pocket, and this time he pulled out a credit card. A platinum Amex card. He handed it to Wells. On the bottom left of the card was *MGM Corp.* with Wells's name.

"What's this?'

"It is a symbol of our gratitude. The card has a limit of one hundred thousand dollars. A corporate card. This is nothing out of the ordinary. We would like to pay you for your service to us. It is not a payoff or a bribe. The card will be activated when you deliver Suarez."

Wells turned the card over in his hand. It looked legit to him.

"Why don't you hire a lawyer or something? Grabbing a guy is a little Wild West, don't you think?"

"As a Chinese company, we have no jurisdiction in the United States. We do not see that we have much choice. I merely want an audience with Suarez. I have no plans to take him off the island."

"Yeah, you want your boy here to convince him, right? Have him do that wrist thing he did to me. He your leg-breaker?"

"My assistant is a military veteran. He's very convincing."

"A hundred grand, huh? And the debt to Corrigan?"

"That debt has already been paid as a thank you for listening to my proposal."

"A hundred grand," he repeated. "Can this come back to me? I mean, using the card?"

"No. It is a corporate card. We have over a thousand of them in use. It is a normal method to compensate independent contractors."

Wells turned the card over in his hand a few times then slipped it into his breast pocket.

"Independent contractor, huh? I'll see what I can do. If I can get him here. I'll tell you one thing. If he calls it in, I'll have to proceed according to normal police procedure. He would probably have to be brought in to at least make a statement, if I'm right about what you're trying to do. But if I'm the first officer on the scene, the protocol would be for me to transfer him back home." He shook his head in a nod of realization. "You know that, don't you? Yeah, instead of bringing him home, I drive him here. You do your thing, and nobody knows a fucking thing about it."

Sheng smiled.

"You are very wise, Officer Wells. That would be greatly appreciated. I was hoping you could bring him to me then. There is also a woman staying with him. I would prefer she be left behind, but if you must, you can bring her also."

"Whoa. You never mentioned that there's a broad involved. Who is she in all this?"

"I believe she is a prostitute. She just arrived this morning."

"I'll see what I can do with her. Some of those bitches can be real pains in the ass."

"I'm sure you will use good judgment. Remember, as soon as you bring him to me, I will activate the card. The casino would be very grateful to you."

Wells stood. "I'm going to take my car and get out of here. Your boy can walk back to his, for all I care. Looks like I'm going to have a busy shift tonight. Right?"

He chuckled, and Sheng laughed along with him. Sheng was thinking ahead now. He was sure that Wells would try his best to get that money. Sheng was thinking about the best way to kill him. Killing a policeman is always problematic. He called out to Shizi, who arrived in seconds.

"Officer Wells is leaving. I insist that you offer an apology for your rough treatment of our new friend."

Shizi turned to Wells and bowed.

"I'm sorry, sir."

Wells smiled broadly. "Not a problem. You listen to your boss here and be a good boy. Take it easy, fellas. See you tonight."

Wells walked across the room to the sliding door and left the way he came in.

Sheng walked back to his laptops, and Shizi waited for the word.

"Kill him as soon as he shows up with Martinez. We may want to use his patrol car to get to the airport. I have not decided yet ..." He paused, thinking. "Yes. Yes. Kill him right away. We will take his body with us. Take the patrol car and leave it at the airport, then dump his body in the ocean."

Shizi smiled. "Yes sir."

Chapter 17

T he day passed without incident. Annie walked the grounds two more times. Hank stayed inside and read. As she walked, Annie checked all the windows and doors from the outside. They were all locked up tight. She also locked the eight-foot-tall gates separating the front and back of the property on both sides of the house. She was unaware of the eyes on her.

Sheng had been watching her all day. The more he watched, the more he was convinced that she would kill the Murdocks. It was the way she walked that Sheng liked. The authority in her manner. This was not a woman to be trifled with. *Yes, she will kill them*, he thought. He had grown fond of her. It would be a shame to kill her, but it must be done. He had a greater purpose that she could not be a part of.

Sheng thought back to the days when he was in power, in demand. Women would be sent to him. Some he requested. Others were sent as gifts. He worked endlessly in those days and had little time for such matters. He did regret it now. Not having access to women. Perhaps when this matter was resolved, he could think about women again. Until then, he didn't want to clutter his mind, so he pushed the thoughts out of his head and watched Annie walk toward the beach at the back end of the property.

There was another set of eyes on Annie as she stood in the sand. Retired

Master Sergeant Charles Milan was also on a satellite feed. His view was much sharper than Sheng's. Milan could see the part in her hair and the Nike swoosh on her sweatshirt. Milan and his partner for this mission, whom he called "The Monk," had been on the island for two days. They came straight here after their meeting with Frank McGinley. They both understood the mission. Milan would be the front man and spotter. The Monk was the shooter. Like most snipers that Milan had known over the years, The Monk had many particular habits. The most notable of which was the fact that he hadn't said a word since they'd sat down with McGinley. Milan had seen this before. With what could be ahead of them, the choices that may have to be made, it was better to not become attached. Milan had spotted for half a dozen snipers in his time in Afghanistan, but he never came across a guy like The Monk. He didn't seem to mind the nickname either. He didn't seem to mind anything. The guy was a fucking block of ice.

They checked in to a small bed-and-breakfast in Edgartown. They shared a room, and Milan did not feel very welcome. He figured the owners thought they were a gay couple and they were not as accommodating as they should have been. Milan guessed that a sixty-three-year-old white man and a tall, athletic, black man who didn't speak wasn't their typical clientele. He wondered if they would be treated better if the owners knew they were heterosexual professional killers.

Milan studied the landscape and the terrain from his laptop. The satellite was tapped into with permission from the military after quite a few favors had been cashed in. Milan had full range of view. He could change perspective and viewing angles. Like Google Earth in real time. He was convinced that any attack would come from the beach. The back of the house faced Edgartown across a small inlet. The water was calm and not very deep. A small row boat or canoe could make an approach silently. He had driven by the house when they'd first arrived and the front entrance seemed pretty well-fortified.

The assault would likely come tonight. They were on a strict stand-down order. They were to wait to see if Suarez was taken. McGinley was convinced he would be taken alive. There wouldn't be a problem tracking him if he were nabbed with the satellite feed. Then they could move. The woman was on her own. From the way she carried herself, it looked like she would be fine. There was no way of knowing when things were going to happen, so they kept the gas tanks full and their weapons locked and loaded.

This was Milan's seventh mission as a Volunteer, and McGinley had been spot-on every time. Milan was confident that all would go as planned, but he was prepared if things got out of hand.

Chapter 18

Annie did what she could with the food in the fridge. Hank had eggs and a few vegetables that weren't quite soggy. She also found flour, baking soda, butter, and milk. Dinner was a cultural mash-up of frittatas and Irish soda bread.

It turned out okay, considering what she had to work with. When she had suggested they eat something, Hank had said, "I don't know. What can we eat?"

"What do you have in the kitchen?" she'd asked.

"I don't know."

She had rummaged through the cabinets then. One of Annie's great loves was cooking. It always brought her peace. Concentrating on the task in front of her and following a recipe brought order to her chaotic life. She loved hearing a guest gushing over her meal. She was a good cook, so it happened often. Tonight there was no gushing. They ate in silence.

Hank cleaned up as Annie did one more loop around the property. She sensed that he enjoyed the cleanup as much as she enjoyed making the mess.

It was a nice night. The sun was setting off to the west, the spire of the church steeple in town splitting the yellow ball in half. Annie allowed herself a moment to relax. For the first time, she noticed how tired she was. She was usually a ball of energy by this time of night, but after sleeping in the back seat of a car and that hardcore workout this morning, her legs and body in general were starting to wear down. She knew she had to stay alert, probably through the night. It would be a long one.

She walked out to the edge of the water, her shoes sinking slightly into the sand. She looked as far as she could in each direction. There was nothing. She closed her eyes to hear the lapping of the waves, a bell methodically chiming from a boat rocking up and down. She heard the clinking of glasses and laughter far off in the distance. Annie thought it would be nice to come back here in better circumstances. When she could look out at the setting sun without a gun in her hand.

When she got back inside, Hank had jazz playing from invisible speakers. The house was lit up, and he was pouring himself a drink. Annie walked over to the bar.

"No drinks, no music, no lights. Not down here. You can go upstairs if you like, but I have to have quiet."

Hank was clearly taken aback. He was not used to being ordered around. He put down his drink.

"Oh, okay. I didn't think it would be a big deal. I mean, one drink."

"No, not tonight. Cut the music please."

He walked over to a cabinet and pushed the white door. It clicked open, and he reached in without looking and pressed something. The music stopped.

"Now the lights please." All the while Annie had the gun in her hand.

Hank walked over to the outlet and shut the lights.

"What now?" he asked.

"Now I sit. You can go upstairs if you like." She took a seat on a white lounge chair facing the sliding glass doors looking out to the backyard and the setting sun. She laid her gun on the armrest.

"Can I make some coffee? I can manage that without making too much noise, I think."

Annie smiled. "Yeah, that would be great. Is the alarm set?"

"Shit. I forgot. Can you imagine? I was waiting for you to come back in."

He took the remote out of his pocket and clicked one of the buttons. Annie heard the automated sound of a big bolt sliding into place. She looked at Hank, and he sheepishly grinned.

He loaded the filter and poured the water into the coffee machine in the fading light, then stood in silence, leaning on the counter behind her. He had changed earlier to white pants, a cotton button-down shirt, untucked, and loafers without socks. She was happy he didn't wear flip-flops. Annie hated to see a man's feet. It was a thing with her. It was the hair on the toes that got to her.

As the machine started to pop and gurgle, he asked her how she liked it.

"Just a little milk, please."

"It will only be a little. We're running out."

"That's okay; I can have it black also."

"You're good for now."

He walked over with two mugs in hand. There was a lobster on hers and a jumping marlin on his. The coffee smelled great and tasted better.

"What kind of coffee is this?"

"This is Italian roast. I grind it.'

"I can tell. I'm used to the canned stuff."

"You've been missing out. I'm gonna sit for the sunset, then I'll go up."

"Cool."

He lowered himself into the adjacent white chair, balancing the coffee mug in his hand. They sat in silence for the next hour. Annie listened closely to everything. He stood after a while, took her lobster mug, and came back with a refill in silence. She thanked him by raising her cup. He raised his in return. After the sun finished its descent, the room was completely dark, but Annie's eyes adjusted to it.

Hank didn't go upstairs; he stayed. After a half hour in the dark, he whispered, "Watch this."

The tip of the moon jutted up from the horizon. It rose at a pace that Annie had never seen before. It was a little unsettling to her. It was as if she were watching an unearthly phenomenon. During the moon rise, there was a moment when the reflection on the water was like a silver carpet heading directly through the glass doors. As it continued to rise, the moon's glow walked its way across the carpet to Annie's chair. The glow continued up her legs and body until it rested on her face. Hank had anticipated this, she realized. It was his chair after all. That was why he hadn't gone up to his room earlier. He wanted to see this, and Annie didn't blame him.

Annie felt the light on her face, and knew he was looking at her. *What is he thinking?*

"It's beautiful," she whispered.

"Yes, this happens a couple nights a month, depending on the weather, of course. We got lucky," he whispered back, not taking his eyes off her. "It *is* beautiful."

The moon continued its rise and the silver carpet rolled out to sea.

Hank turned back to the inlet. It was quiet. Just a few lobster boats bobbing on the water. They sat in silence a while longer.

"How did you like the bread?" Annie asked in a soft voice.

"It was great. I was going to compliment the chef, but you got up from the table to check out the grounds."

"Hey, I'm on the job."

"Yeah, it was pretty awesome. How did you make that out of the little I have in the house?"

"Irish soda bread was always a go-to for my mom. If we had milk, eggs, and flour, she could make just about anything. She had the touch. I could never make it like she could. I couldn't make *anything* like she could."

"She must have been a hell of a cook."

"That she was. She got the Irish bread recipe from a friend. It used to piss her off, the friend. She would ask how an Italian could make Irish bread like a Dubliner. My mom used to say that you had to cut a cross on the top of the batter and bless it before it went into the oven. I didn't bless this one."

"Well, it was as good as any bread I've eaten in a while."

"Thanks. She died this past February."

Annie was shocked that she had said it out loud. She momentarily wished she could take it back, but it was out there. Hank didn't respond, and without thinking, Annie continued.

"Two months we had. The doctors saw how bad it was and sent her home to die."

"Cancer?"

"Yeah, pancreatic. Fucking brutal to watch her fade so fast. The thing is, she must have known something was wrong for a long time, because it was so far along. I was pissed off that she let it get to that point without doing anything about it. Tell someone. Tell me, I guess."

Annie felt the need to unload. To finally talk this through. She couldn't talk to her father, fearing that the topic would be too much for him.

Hank asked, "You still angry?"

Annie took a deep breath. "No, now I'm just sad. The thing that is so devastating about it is the finality of it all. The realization that I will never see her again. Ever. It's hard to wrap my head around it. I mean this was, or we were, different than most mothers and daughters. She was my best friend. You know, I don't want you to get the wrong idea; she wasn't a typical Italian mother. It wasn't like I needed my mommy in the traditional sense. She was a smart, professional woman. Worked in the insurance business in downtown Manhattan on Pine Street. Amalgamated was the firm. Started as an assistant—she would say secretary—and worked her way up to senior vice president. She'd travel, give major presentations, all over the world. I couldn't imagine standing up in front of people like that, but she was a star. One time she was in Paris and was supposed to meet with someone who was her equal, you know, another vice president. Let's face it; there are hundreds of them in these big companies. So she goes in, and the guy asked if she could present to the board. They sent the proposal ahead, a proposal she wrote up, and they must have loved it. So she goes upstairs with this guy. To the top-floor boardroom. Walks through the door, and there's a long table with about a dozen men sitting around it. Can you imagine? She walks in and the entire room stops and watches her enter. Shit, I get goosebumps just thinking about if that had been me. So, she looks across the room and out the window is the Eiffel Tower. You know what? She blew the room away. Got this big account. There was a big bonus that year, because that summer we went to Paris for vacation."

"Wow, she must have been a hell of a woman."

For the first time, Annie's voice cracked. "My father told me that story. She would have never.'

They sat in silence for a while, looking out at the bobbing lobster boats. Annie stood up to stretch her legs and went over to the glass doors. She looked at her watch and was surprised to see that it was one in the morning. She turned to Hank.

"You should head upstairs and get some sleep. I'll be up all night."

"No. I don't think I'm going to sleep much knowing there may be a kidnapping attempt tonight. I'll hang out here."

"Sorry for unloading on you. You don't need to hear my problems."

"No, no. It's fine. Hey, I haven't had a real conversation for a long time. In case you've forgotten, I haven't been living a very social life for the last two years. I haven't said more than ten words to anyone in a very long time."

Annie went back to her chair and plopped down with an old man's grunt.

"It was the bread that got to me," she said.

"The bread?"

"Yeah, baking. The smell in the house. That was our thing. Every Sunday, my mom and I would bake together. That's how we reconnected. Not that we ever had a problem. I mean, I never spent more than a week without speaking to her, but as an adult, as an equal, I guess. The thing is, I was a pretty shitty teenager, you know? I was always rebelling against something. I wasn't even sure what. I remember an old line from a movie I watched with my parents, can't remember which; it was a young Marlon Brando who said it. Someone asked him what he was rebelling against, and he answered, "What do ya got?" That was me. I didn't come around until I was twenty-four or -five. Some guy who I soon learned was not worth the tears broke my heart. I went home for a few days. My mom got me in that kitchen, and before too long, we were talking like girlfriends. Baking, that was the connection. She taught me everything. Giving instructions and advice along the way. God, she was amazing. I started going home every Sunday. We'd have something new to bake each time. One of us would have an idea and off we went. For hours. The smell of a cake in the oven. A glass of wine and time with someone you love. That's heaven. The thing is, I knew it then. I knew the whole time how lucky I was."

Annie's voice cracked through the last sentence.

Hank waited for a moment before speaking, maybe to give her some space. Then he said, "Yeah, I know the feeling. I was pretty tight with my old man."

"Did he pass?"

"No, but he thinks I did."

Annie's open-hearted admissions made Hank feel like doing the same. He had carried the weight of the pain that he'd inflicted upon his father for two years now. Of all the sacrifices he had to endure, brought on by his own ego—his need to be the best, the smartest, the richest, all the things that mean nothing to him now—being without his father was the worst. Knowing that he had caused him so much pain. The one person on earth who had always been there for him. Who gave up everything for him. And Hank had let him down. He returned his love and support with lies and deception. Hank knew when his father believed he had died, it had caused an unbearable tear in the old man's heart. It was a shame that Hank could hardly live with. This life that he chose was wearing on him.

It had been over ten years now since Hank had led anything close to a normal life. It started when he was approached by the military to work on drone technology. That led to more pro-bono work on behalf of causes that he felt strongly about. Most were innocent enough. Streamlining water delivery in Africa; setting up a database for immigration patterns; tracking extreme weather events ... but it was inevitable that there would be conflicts. He had allowed people to push him in directions he shouldn't have gone. It was his ego, he knew. The button that could be pushed to manipulate him. Before too long, he was hacking into terrorist cells and the Chinese and Russian governments. It was during a job to trace the communications of a domestic terrorist that Frank McGinley came to him. Recruited him into the Volunteers. Not as a soldier but as a member of the executive committee. McGinley the puppet master, pushing the ego button. This brought risk to his friends and family.

That was when his visits to his father had become less frequent. Soon enough, Hank was spending much of his time underground, in hiding. It was an ordeal to visit his father. Inevitably he saw him less and less. Now he may have lost him forever. It was a broken feeling inside of him. This knowledge. Hank would feel physically weak when he allowed himself to dwell on what he had done to his father.

Annie spoke, and Hank jumped in his chair, startled. He had drifted off.

"You were close, you and your father, I mean?"

Hank gathered himself. He wanted to let it out, but he knew there was still a need to remain guarded. There was no way to tell how this night or the next day or so would play out. She couldn't know any details. Nothing that someone like Sheng could use to find him or his father. Hank knew it wouldn't take much information. Sheng could track anyone.

"Yeah, we were pretty tight. We didn't bake much, though."

Annie chuckled.

"We had a little ritual. I would go over his house with a six-pack of beer. He liked Modello. I would try to bring different brands, you know something a little more expensive, but he would have none of it. He had this little Coleman cooler, just big enough for a six-pack and ice. We'd load it up and go sit in the backyard and talk. That was it. Many times I had to come over unannounced or late at night, and he would just get out of bed and come downstairs with the cooler in his hand. We'd sit out back and just bullshit, you know? Sports, news, whatever. He raised me himself. Very smart man. An engineer with IBM. Yeah, very smart."

"He thinks you're dead?"

"Yes, he does, and I know it fucking killed him."

They sat a while in silence. The rhythm of the conversation had been established. One side opened up, and the other waited to see if there was more. Giving room. Complicit in sorrow. Hank leaned forward in his chair.

"I used to fight with him a lot. Well, mostly about one thing. You see, he was a brilliant engineer, but he never got the credit or pay or recognition that he deserved. It used to make me crazy. I would ask him how he could let others take the credit for his work, why he didn't ask for a promotion or a raise. I couldn't understand. I would insist that it was because he was Puerto Rican. How could he let them treat him like that?

"He would tell me it wasn't important to him. That he had all he needed. I was so fucking stupid and blind in my own ambition that I didn't see it. His wisdom. He knew that a promotion would take time away from us. He wanted to be there when I stopped over. Those nights in the backyard on folding chairs was his raise and promotion. All the recognition he would ever need. And there I was, fighting him over it. Well, I was real smart, wasn't I? I have more money than I could ever spend, but this is the longest I've spoken to a human being in over two years. No friends, no family."

Hank put both his hands on the armrests and groaned as he stood. He rubbed his hands across his face and walked toward the glass door. He said aloud to himself, "Ah fuck. I shouldn't be telling you any of this. I don't know what the hell is wrong with me." Then he turned around and walked back toward Annie.

"I'm getting some water. Want anything?"

"Yeah, I'll take a water."

Hank reached out his hand to her, and at first, she didn't understand. "Your cup."

"Oh yeah." She handed it over.

Annie faced forward, out the glass doors. Hank Suarez was not the arrogant prick she thought he would be. He was something more. He was nice. She thought that *nice* might be good for her. Hank came back with her water and handed her a glass.

He remained standing. Next to her but facing out to the inlet.

"Can I ask your name? Just your first name I think would be best."

"Annie."

He repeated, "Annie." Then sat.

"You should head upstairs. Its two thirty. Close your eyes for a while."

"I think I'll close my eyes down here, if you don't mind."

"No, go right ahead."

"Thanks, Annie." He sat back in his chair.

Chapter 19

Metallica started blasting from the speakers. Annie jumped up from her chair.

"What the hell?"

Hank leaned up in his seat and fumbled through his pocket. He pulled his remote out and pressed. The music stopped.

"That's the alarm."

"Yeah, I figured." Annie looked out the glass doors, then reached her hand down to him. "Gimme that thing."

Hank handed it over. She looked at it. The remote was like a key fob with four recessed buttons. Annie spoke rapidly, almost frantic.

"How do you work this thing?

Hank pointed at the various buttons as he said, "This one is for the car, this for the alarm. This opens the door you point it at, and this locks it. Got it?"

"Yeah, got it." She put it in her sweatshirt pouch.

Hank stood, and Annie stepped over to him and put her hand on his back.

"Get up to your room and lock it down." She said it with such authority that Hank started moving as soon as her hand rested on his back. He started toward the staircase, then stopped.

"I can help. I can do something."

"No, you can't, and that's not how McGinley wants it. You know this. Get up those stairs. Close your door and lock it. Stay put until I say. I'm here to keep you safe."

Hank stood still for a moment. No one ever spoke to Pap Martinez like that, but then he hadn't been Pap Martinez for a long time. Annie chambered a round into the gun and waved at him with her other hand.

"C'mon, get going."

Hank smiled at her, turned, and headed up the stairs. Annie waited to move until she heard the door close and the lock click. She walked along the perimeter of the room to the side of the glass doors and looked out. She saw two shadows along the hedges lining the perimeter of the property. The moon was bright enough for her to make out the men after a few seconds. Both had guns raised above their heads. They didn't seem to be making much of an effort to stay out of sight. Annie was relieved somewhat to see that they didn't look like military or seemed trained at all. She had seen this type before. They were thugs. It struck her as odd.

They did have guns, though, and they were on Hank's property, which gave her all she needed to execute the plan she'd put together this afternoon. She headed to the front door, pointed the remote at it, and clicked. The door unlocked, and she slipped out, clicking it locked the second the door closed.

Sheng watched the Murdock brothers approach the house from one of his laptops. He quickly typed in the password into three others, and soon had an eye in the sky on all four.

The Monk had the midnight-to-four shift. He saw the men as they walked along the beach from a half mile to the north. He was going through the protocol of expanding the perimeter when he noticed their car parking in a small harbor lot. He watched them walk along the beach, and as soon as they took their guns out, The Monk walked over to Milan's bed and shook him awake. They were in the car when the men set foot on Suarez's property. Milan watched on the laptop as The Monk drove.

Annie walked out the front door and around the side of the house toward the large gate on the carport side. She manipulated the gate handle.

The Murdocks had split up, each taking opposite routes around the house. They tried to jimmy windows and turn doorknobs.

As they drove along Katama Road, Milan knew that something was wrong.

He spoke to The Monk as if he were speaking to himself.

"This is bullshit. These two. They're a couple of fucking mutts. This is a charade. She's gonna pop the two of them easy enough. When you get within a block, I want you to pull over. We can watch from the car. I don't think we have to reveal ourselves yet."

The Monk grunted.

On the carport side, Caleb Murdock came to a high wooden gate. It was as high and thick as a stable door. He rested his head against the hard wood and listened. Not hearing anything, he lifted the handle, and it opened with ease. He walked through and saw the side door to the house in front of him. The porch light was on. As he approached the porch, he heard the gate close behind him. Then he heard a woman's voice.

"Stop there. Drop the gun on the driveway and kick it away from you."

Caleb didn't drop the gun. He turned on the woman with his gun at eye level. She fired. He went down.

From their respective points of view, Milan and Sheng saw the flash. One shot and he was down.

Sheng quickly plugged a cell phone into the USB port on the laptop with the voice simulation software. He hit the speed dial on the phone. Two rings, three, now four. A weary-sounding woman picked up.

"Edgartown Police."

Sheng inputted his broken English that came out like a Maine fisherman.

"I heard a gunshot. By Edgartown Bay Road. Oh God. I see a man with a gun."

"A gunshot, sir?"

"Yes. Come quick."

"Where on Edgartown Bay Road?"

"I just passed number forty-seven. Near there."

"Is it number forty-seven, sir?"

"I don't know. I'm driving.'

"What is your name, sir?"

Sheng hung up and went back to the screen.

———————

Annie stood over the man for a couple of seconds then went over to the gate, and from the respective satellite feeds, it appeared that she locked it again. She walked to the front of the house, around the front porch, and eventually got over to the other gate. While she was walking, Billy Murdock hustled in the direction of the gunshot. It was a clever setup on her part. She would circle around the house, locking and unlocking the gates, until she had him cornered.

———————

She opened the other gate and picked up the stone she'd set aside this afternoon and put it in the doorway to prevent it from closing behind her. Annie slowly walked around the side of the house to the back. All the while, she had her gun up, staying close to the footprint of the house.

———————

At the other gate, a pathetic scene played out. Billy Murdock had seen his brother's body through the slots of the gate and was trying to climb the gate to get to him.

———————

Annie heard the gate rattling and a man cursing around the corner of the house. She peeked around the corner and couldn't believe what she was witnessing. She's seen some stupid smash-and-grab jobs before, but this clown was a fucking idiot. He was at the top of the gate, but his pant leg was stuck on the handle. He was trying to pull himself over but didn't seem to understand that his pants were holding him back. She did take note that he still had a gun in his hand.

She leaned halfway around the corner and yelled over to him.

"Drop the gun. Drop it."

He is definitely not a bright bulb, she thought. He turned his body, and she heard a loud tear of clothing. He swung his arm wildly and took a shot at her. It came nowhere near her, but the very idea incensed her. She pulled her trigger and put one in his ass cheek. He screamed, "Caleb!" and fired again. This time he came closer, so Annie put the next one in the center of his back. He fell off the gate and landed on the ground with his left leg still attached to the handle. He hung head down, dangling from his one leg.

In their separate locales, on their separate missions, Sheng and Milan watched it play out from the satellites. Sheng was almost aroused by her ruthlessness. Milan admired her efficiency of movement and the planning. Taking what her environment provided and using it as a tactical advantage. *She will do well as a Volunteer,* Milan thought.

Wells was sleeping in his patrol car behind the bike rental shop in the parking lot at North Beach when the call came in.

"Possible shots fired. Edgartown Bay Road. On or about house number forty-seven."

Wells hoisted his seat to an upright position and fumbled for the mic.

"Officer Wells, North Beach Patrol. Do you hear me?"

Wells tried to remain calm, in character.

"Yeah, I got you, Rose. Firecrackers, you think?"

"Not sure. Folks are always partying along there."

"Yeah, fucking rich New Yorkers on that block."

"Don't get me started on that. Did you see that slide into second last night in the Sox game? Fucking Yankees."

"Yeah, I saw. I'll head over."

Sheng expanded his screen and watched Wells's patrol car turn on the lights and pull out of the lot, heading south on Edgartown Bay Road.

Milan looked down the road over his laptop and saw a patrol car heading toward them. It drove by with its lights on at a very relaxed speed. There was one cop, and he looked like he was going out to pick up the drycleaning. If his lights were on, he should have been more intense, and if he were relaxed, his lights shouldn't be on. *This is bullshit*, he thought. Something was being set up. It was too easy for the girl. There was another step waiting to take place, one he had no clue what it could be.

He turned to The Monk.

"Get your gear ready. We stay with them from here on."

The Monk grunted again. This time with more feeling.

Chapter 20

Annie raced to the glass sliding doors, clicked the remote, and heard the lock open. She slid the door open and ran into the house, turned to the stairs, and went up them two at a time. She banged on the door at the top of the stairs.

"Hank, Hank, come out."

The door swung open, and Hank stood for a moment and looked at her. She looked rattled.

"What happened?"

"I think I killed them both."

"Both?"

"Yeah, there were two of them. I'm pretty sure they're dead."

"Okay, okay, let's get you downstairs, and we'll put this together."

Hank put a hand on Annie's shoulder and turned her around. They walked down the wide stairs side by side. Hank got her to the chair where the moon's glow had hit her earlier and went to get her a glass of water. When he returned with it, she took the glass with a slight tremble of her hands.

"That was the first time I've ever pulled my weapon. Jesus."

He didn't respond, as if giving her time to soak in the events.

"I didn't think, you know. I just reacted."

He cleared his throat and said, "Well, you did great. You had no choice. I heard the gunshots. You had no choice."

"Yeah I know, but still. Shit. Two of them."

Annie sat silently for a moment, and Hank reached down and put his hand on her back just beneath her neckline.

Hank knew he had to take charge. After all, she'd just saved his life. It was his time to step up.

"You stay here. I'm going to go outside and clean things up. I'm sure whatever backup McGinley sent will be here any minute."

"Where the hell were they ten minutes ago? What the hell?"

"I don't know. I don't know. I'm sure there is a reason. There's a reason for everything when Frank is in charge. I'm going outside. Stay here."

He walked toward the door and glanced back at her. She was staring blankly out the glass doors. He couldn't see her face from where he was standing. If he could, he'd have seen a tight smile come across her lips. The look of pride from a job well.

This, Annie thought, *is something I'm good at.*

The moment he stepped outside, Hank saw the body. He was lying on the driveway face down. Blood streamed slowly from the man's side and formed a small puddle by the front tire of the Jeep. Hank walked around the body and came to the half-open gate door. As he pushed, Hank was surprised by the weight of it. Once he stepped through the gateway, he saw the other body hanging from the door. He almost stepped on the guy's head. He did a quick sidestep to avoid it. Hank saw a gun still in the upside-down man's hand, and he looked over to make sure the other guy had a gun near him. He did. The night was dark and silent. Hank thought it would be best to leave the bodies untouched. As an executive committee member of the Volunteers, he had run high-tech operations. Hacking and uncovering hackers, covert messages, research, and the like. Hank had never been a part of anything like this. He did know from speaking to other committee members that there was a protocol for this type of thing. Cleaners, they were called.

Hank thought it best to wait for the cleaners to show up. He headed back to the door to check on Annie when he saw the lights. Police lights reflecting off the leaves above Edgartown Bay Road. There was no siren, just the lights. He quickly rushed inside.

"The police are here. Give me the gun."

Annie blindly lifted the gun in her hand, and Hank took it.

"Listen. I did the shooting. You're just a girl I picked up. Do you remember who you're supposed to be?"

Annie sat up straight in the chair and suddenly seemed as alert as ever.

"Yeah, I'm a receptionist at a chiropractor's office in Middle Village, Queens. My name's Rochelle, and I picked you up."

Hank laughed and responded in his best Queens accent, the borough where he was raised.

"Should I call you Ro?"

Annie responded in kind. "Get the fuck outta here."

They both laughed. Like that, Annie was back.

Their laughter was broken up by the burst of a police siren. The lights now bouncing off the interior walls of the house.

"Where's the remote?"

Annie looked confused for a second, then, "Oh yeah." She reached into her pocket and pulled it out. "Here it is."

Hank put his hands on her shoulders and stared deeply into her eyes.

"You did your thing. You saved me. Now it's my turn to be in charge. You have to follow what I'm saying now. Don't speak. I mean, not a word. I did the shooting. You're in shock. You've never seen anything like this. You got it? Not one word."

"Yes, I got it." Annie smiled. "I'm taking the rest of the night off."

"Good. Wait here."

Hank unlocked the front door and walked out with his hands above his head.

Chapter 21

The entire house was a crime scene. Annie sat in her chair, kept her mouth shut, and observed. It was an opportunity to see her life's work through the eyes of a civilian. It was an education. Police were crawling all over the house. A few knew what they were doing, the rest ... well, the best she could say was they were not up to New York Police Department standards. A couple of fools were walking all over the house. Opening doors, stepping all over the carpet. One even went into the fridge and drank what was left of the milk from the carton.

The big cop, the one who first came to the house, was a creep. Her instincts were on high alert around him. He didn't say much as he waited for the others to arrive. Annie figured either he didn't know what to ask or he was waiting for one of his superiors to get there to back him up. She'd seen plenty of cops like him on the force. Either incompetent or crooked. Most were a combination of both. It didn't help that he kept staring at her chest. Fucking creep.

The room fell silent as soon as the chief walked in. It was like a game of freeze. They waited for him to get fully into the center of the kitchen until they started moving again. Annie could tell they didn't like him much, but it was clear they respected him. He was one to be careful around.

A tech called over. "Chief Riggins, could you come back outside please?"

Annie could sense the chief had been about to come over to her and

Hank, just before the tech called for him. He glanced their way then walked out the side door. The area where the bodies were.

Annie thought about them—the bodies. She was more convinced now than ever that something was off about this whole thing. She wondered now if any of what she had been told was the truth. Popping those two seemed to sharpen her thinking. *Nothing like the clarity of death to open my eyes*, she thought. She was charged, energized by action. One thing was very clear to her now. McGinley had sold her a line of bullshit. There was no way two amateur mugs were going to be the ones to come for Hank Suarez.

Annie didn't doubt that Hank was for real. He was too smart to be anything other than who he claimed to be. She had been around enough dirtbags in her life to learn who was full of shit and who wasn't. Hank didn't have the lying gene. It wasn't in him. This was a cause for concern. He was supposed to take things from here. Talk the cops into thinking he'd pulled the trigger. Still, they would be brought to the station. No doubt. Maybe that was the plan? She didn't know. She wasn't sure of anything at this point, and she didn't like it.

The chief came back in with a smile on his face. He walked directly over to Hank.

"You a cop?'

Hank was startled by the question. "What?"

The chief smiled and turned to Annie. "You. You a cop?'

Annie was pissed off but not surprised that he would assume Hank had done the shooting. She'd been up against that attitude for all of her twelve years on the force. She took up her role as the wiseass Queens receptionist and answered, "No, are you?"

The chief smiled and went back to Hank. "Who did the shooting?"

Hank squirmed in his chair then looked down at the floor before looking up sternly, a dead tip-off that a lie was on its way.

"I did."

"Why?"

"What do you mean, why?'

"Tell me what happened. Did they shoot at you, break any windows? Did they say anything?"

"They were on my property with guns."

The chief leaned over to get in Hank's face. 'So why didn't you call a cop, huh? Who goes outside after they see two guys with guns and gets into a gun battle? You see my dilemma?"

"I just thought. ..."

"Yeah, you thought. You thought what? Two guys coming on my property, so I'm going to go outside and get into a gun battle like it's the fucking movies. Is that what you thought?" He turned back to Annie. "What's your name?"

"Rochelle Denardo."

Back to Hank now. "What type of gun did you use?"

"A Glock police special."

"Bingo, you're right." Chief Riggins opened his big fist to show a shell casing. "What do you use? A twenty-five or a thirty aught six?"

Annie knew that was total gibberish. An old trick.

"Twenty-five." Hank said it with confidence; she had to give him that. It was over now. He was blown. Annie hoped he had the good sense to keep his mouth shut from that point on.

"Yeah. I use a twenty-five myself. That's why I asked if you were a cop."

Annie looked over at Hank and smiled when she saw the look of resolute thinking on his face. Riggins was blown to Hank now. He had overplayed his hand by trying to appeal to Hank's ego.

Hank looked up at him and said the word that made every crime-scene cop cringe.

"Lawyer."

Riggins smiled and mildly chuckled; it sounded more like a rhythmic grunt than a laugh. He turned back to Annie.

"You did the shooting. This guy? He's not the type. The groomed nails. Expensive clothes, nice house. No, not him. I don't think he's got the balls. We'll run tests. I'll find out. Why, Rochelle? Why would you run outside and face two gunmen ... a nice girl like you?"

He was trying to get a rise out of her. It wasn't working. He squatted down to come face to face with her. "You're not from around here. I know that. You come up here from New York with that thick accent, which by the way I think is a little too thick, and all of a sudden I got two dead shitheads on my hands." He smiled. "I've been on the job close to thirty years now. I know what I know. So before I cuff the two of you and put you in a can with a couple of meth-smoking hookers, I'll do you the professional courtesy and ask you again, and keep in mind I know the answer. Are you a fucking cop?"

"Lawyer."

Riggins stared into Annie's eyes for a moment then suddenly stood. He walked away and whispered into the big, creepy cop's ear. The cop came over to the two of them. He flicked his fingers upward, gesturing for them to stand. They did, and Annie looked over to Hank, who looked downright peaceful. If it was meant to reassure her, it worked. He smiled at her, and she smiled back.

The cop turned her around and put on cuffs. Annie didn't resist, didn't say a word.

The cop went over to Hank and performed the same routine. Hank did speak.

"Aren't you supposed to read us our rights or something?'

Before he answered, Annie knew what the cop's response would be.

"You got the right to keep your fucking mouth shut."

He laid a hand on Annie's back and roughly shoved her toward the door. Hank followed on his own.

Chapter 22

Charles Milan watched on his laptop as Annie Falcone and Hank Suarez were put into the squad car that had rolled past him an hour ago. He quickly punched in the code to change the coordinates so he could lock onto the car. He tried to convince himself there was no way to lose track of them. After all, they're on an island.

This was the part of any job that made him nervous. Leaving someone under his watch in the hands of the bad guys. There was the very real possibility that this cop was so corrupt that he might shoot the two of them right now. Pull off the road, pop 'em both, and get back in the car. Milan knew he had to rely on the knowledge of Frank McGinley. When they had their meeting, Frank said there was no chance Suarez would be killed. They had to take him alive. He didn't say anything about the girl. Milan learned from his dealings with Frank and his predecessor that what wasn't said in a meeting sometimes became the most important detail.

Milan took comfort in the fact that he hadn't lost anyone yet. He only came close once. It was about fifteen years ago, and the one he almost lost was Frank McGinley himself.

His eyes were on the screen, but Milan's mind was fifteen years in the past. He looked over at The Monk. He had his eyes closed, sitting upright in his seat, like one of those mannequins that people use to get through the diamond lane. Milan knew he had to pay close attention, but he couldn't keep his mind from wandering.

The McGinley job had been on 16th or 17th Street in Manhattan. The

East Side. McGinley had his place there. Milan was on the job as a Volunteer for William Brogan.

Brogan. *Jesus.* He hadn't thought about that guy in years. Goddamn, he was a hard case. He remembered his stare. Brogan could look right through you. The first time Brogan leaned in to him, he nearly shit himself, and he was a Navy SEAL on loan for the Volunteers. It was Brogan who'd recruited him. They had been on a number of jobs together before the one with Frank. Milan tried to remember what branch of government Brogan came from. NSA? CIA? Justice? It didn't matter. No one had more juice than Brogan back then.

The job had been to stake out Frank's house. There was a female serial killer hunting him. Like most jobs, Milan didn't know many details. He did know that this chick was a piece of work. She had killed two highly trained operatives in the mountains of Colorado. Left them to the animals. All the men were motivated to capture this bitch. Brogan had told him all about her after the job was done. She was a hitter for the mob. She'd put down seven that they knew of, not including the two in the mountains. Milan and his men were in a Con Ed truck in front of Frank's place. They knew she was in the city.

The intel said that she would go for Frank. It was as solid as the intel Milan was working with for this case. Except it wasn't as solid as they'd thought. The killer outsmarted them. She went to Frank's girlfriend's house, killed her, and waited for Frank to arrive. Wouldn't you know? Frank left his briefcase at the girlfriend's, so he'd stopped by to pick it up before heading home. It was as simple as that. A forgotten bag. These were the things that haunted Milan. The little mundane things, a forgotten bag, lost keys—it could be anything. He knew that no matter how well-prepared he was, he could never have full control.

Milan had seen a lot of bad things in his life. Some of the violence he'd seen in Afghanistan was hard to believe. The things that humans would do to one another was hard to fathom at times, but the scene at Frank's girlfriend's home that day was somehow worse than anything else. It was shocking to see so much blood in a civilized setting. That was what had stood out then ... and what had sent a chill through Milan tonight sitting in the car. The way the girlfriend was slashed, cut, tortured. The cop who

Brogan had watching the place was cut from her left cheek down to her chest. She was near death when they got there. Almost gutted with a buck knife. When they arrived, the killer was lying in the kitchen with her head smashed practically flat.

And Frank. Jesus Christ, the beating he took. His face wasn't there. It was a shattered plate. There was nothing, no definition, no eyes, no nose, just blood. How he'd survived and killed that woman was a mystery. Milan took great pride in his own fortitude, his ability to overcome any obstacle, but he wondered if he could have survived what Frank had gone through. As they wheeled Frank out on the stretcher, Milan had thought, *If this guy gets through this, if he ever leaves the hospital, he would be the strongest man I've ever known.*

Now, fifteen years later, he was taking orders from McGinley, who had taken over from Brogan. He was different from the old man, but just as much of a hard case when he had to be.

He looked down at the laptop to see the squad car turn off Edgartown Bay Road and make a right onto Katama Road. As soon as it cleared a small dirt road on the right, a car pulled out. Milan zoomed in to see the car follow at a discreet distance. He punched The Monk to rouse him and used the touch pad to expand the screen. He couldn't make out a face, but it was one man. The guy followed the squad car until it drove around the back of the police station. Milan watched as the sedan pulled to a stop at the far end of the parking lot and turned off its lights.

He said to The Monk, "I was right. The house was bullshit. Someone is tailing our cop."

The Monk responded by reaching behind him to the back seat and coming back with his sniper rifle. He laid it across his lap and stared forward out the window, silently telling Milan to drive. Milan handed him the laptop and turned the ignition. He knew the area well enough by now to find a spot to keep both the sedan and the front door of the police station in view. He pulled out and headed into town.

Once he got to the spot, Milan opened a window, cut the lights and engine.

It was a beautiful night. The next phase of the operation was made a bit more complicated by the man who had followed Annie and Suarez, but

Milan had his orders. No reason to change anything at the moment. The turn of events just heightened his alertness level. He looked toward the parking lot past The Monk's profile, which was almost invisible in the car. Milan remembered the stillness these snipers had about them. The ability to fade into the background like a cheetah in tall grass. He was ready; The Monk was ready. They just had to wait an hour or so for the next step.

Sheng's satellite feed failed him as the squad car pulled onto the main road. He quickly recalibrated to lock onto another satellite. The frustration was enough to make him scream, which he did in the empty house. Once he had a new one online, he went directly to the police station parking lot just in time to see the squad car go around to the back of the building. Shizi soon pulled in and cut his lights. After a moment, Sheng's cell phone rang.

"I'm here. He has both of them in the patrol car and walked them into the building."

Sheng answered in a New England accent through the voice-changer, forgetting that he'd used the phone to call in to the police earlier. "Okay. Stay with them and let me know when you are headed my way." Sheng realized his error with the voice-changer as the words came out. He didn't acknowledge it, of course, and Shizi knew better than to comment. "You know what to do if they come out with anyone other than Officer Wells."

"Yes sir. I'm prepared. Pull up and kill them all."

"Yes. Shizi. You are an honorable soldier. I regret not having an army of men like you, but we are refugees, are we not? Men without a country. I am stealing a satellite feed to run an operation as important as this when I used to have the best technology at my fingertips. I could scramble the Red Army with a phone call. Now I am as feeble as one of my first-year students. You will kill them if you have to. It will blow up our plan, but we can fight on, can we not? Come back another day. We can do it."

Shizi had only heard Sheng speak with emotion after he had been on one of his marathon sessions in front of a screen. Shizi knew Sheng had gone many days without sleep. He thought that it might make it easier to kill him. Sheng would be unstable and vulnerable. One day, maybe two, and Sheng would be dead.

"Go to sleep, sir. I'm here and will call as soon as there is any movement."

"Yes. You will."

Chapter 23

April 8, 1900
Bethesda Fountain
Central Park
New York City

W oodbury Kane sat on the wall and watched the children splash about in the fountain. It was unusually warm for early April, and he loosened his cravat.

He was a bit early for his appointment. Jacob Riis would be on time as usual. He was a very punctual man. Kane wanted to have a few moments to review the events of the last couple of weeks before giving the information he had received to Jacob.

The Ice Trust Scandal was in full swing. The papers had been covering every twist and turn of the sordid business. Riis had been feeding information to the *Times* and the *New York Journal*. Randolph Hearst himself had taken an interest and was pushing the *Journal* to dig deep. Of course, they weren't as much digging as accepting information that had been uncovered through Kane's network of Volunteers. From dockworkers and ice delivery men to city attorneys and judges, Kane had an ear on the street that no journalist could match. His men, his Volunteers, were supplying information to Kane, which he passed on to Riis, who sent it to the papers. Kane knew this was the key to bringing down Tammany. It may not happen overnight, but doubling the price of ice, a vital commodity to the common working man, cut into the support of the ward bosses. Taking advantage of the working man, the people whom Tammany had long depended on for support and votes, would prove to be their ruin. Kane was sure of it.

Kane had confirmed information that could change the course of New York City politics for years to come. He knew of direct involvement by Mayor Robert Anderson Van Wyck in the scandal along with a number of Tammany ward bosses and their families. The mayor, a Tammany crony, along with a select group of political players were given stock in the American Ice Company before the price hikes. He had proof through his dockworker Volunteers that ice deliveries had been blocked for any company other than American Ice. They were creating an artificial shortage to spike the value of ice, and therefore, skyrocketing the value of American Ice Company shares. The very stock they were given in advance had more than doubled in price since the artificial shortage, and the working man was stuck paying the very expensive bill.

Kane was lost in thought about how to acquire the final bit of proof when Jacob tapped him on the shoulder.

"This is something new. Meeting with me in public. Here I was this past year thinking you didn't want to be seen with me." Riis smiled down at Kane, temporarily blocking the sunlight. Kane looked up at the dark image of his friend.

"Why don't we walk a bit? The sun is quite warm today."

"Sure, sure. Lead the way."

Riis stepped aside, and Kane rose. Both men were dressed much too formally for a stroll in the park. It couldn't be helped. They were formal men. They headed northwest toward the Bow Bridge.

"Why meet me here? I've become accustomed to our meals at this point."

Kane smiled. 'I thought it would be good for us to get some air, don't you think?"

"Yes, I've been hunched over my papers for days on end now."

"How goes the autobiography?"

"I have to say, Woody, I regret the entire undertaking. I still have no reason to believe that a solitary soul would want to read my life story. I sound like a self-righteous fool, and a colossal bore to boot."

"Come now, Jacob. You're hardly self-righteous."

Riis chuckled. "Yes, hardly."

They came to the bridge and found it too crowded to even rest an arm on the railing. Kane pointed north.

"Come, Jacob. Let's walk until we find a proper bench to sit on. Perhaps in the shade."

They walked and exchanged pleasantries while inquiring about each other's personal affairs. Kane came to enjoy Riis's company. He often thought back to the dinner with Teddy at Delmonico's and the comradery he felt that night. Until then, Kane never would have imagined that a man like himself could become friends with Jacob Riis, who, for all his success, was still a working man. True, he was no longer working the coal mines of Pennsylvania or tramping through the Lower East Side tenements, but he could still fit in those worlds in a way that Kane never could. Even now, as a distinguished writer, Riis referred to himself as an ink-stained wretch. Kane would always be an elite. It was in his blood.

The fourth bench they came to after the bridge was open, so they sat.

Kane, anxious to share information, began. "I have information that will bring down Tammany. Yes, there I've said it."

Riis chuckled again. From the beginning of their relationship, Kane had been the blusterous one. The man who would bring down Tammany! He had stated this so often that it had become an inside joke between them.

"What information do you have, my friend?'

"Well, as you know, I have been taking your advice to personally go down to the docks or to the stables to speak to the workers there. 'That's where all the news is,' you told me. So I have been going downtown to the waterfront every day for the last couple of weeks. I've also spent some time around the courthouses."

Riis smiled. "I'm happy to hear this unexpected turn of events."

"Don't get your blue collar in an uproar. Where do you think I'm getting all the news I'm passing on to you?"

"Believe me, I appreciate the news. It kills me every time since I can't write a word of it under my byline. I'm aware we can't arouse suspicion that we are working toward the downfall of Tammany, but oh, how I long to be back behind a news desk. It is great that you're doing this. I mean it. Now, what do you have that will make me jealous today? Please don't make it something so juicy that it will make me cry."

Kane took out his handkerchief and handed it to Riis.

"Prepare to weep tears of joy. A dockworker who took the oath of the Volunteers confirmed that Mayor Van Wyck and John Carroll, the personal representative of 'Boss' Croker, who is the leader of the Tammany party, took a steamship up to Maine to the headquarters of the American Ice Company. They met with the president of American Ice, Charles W. Morse himself." Kane smiled and slapped his thighs for emphasis.

Riis, as was his way, showed very little reaction, always thinking things through before responding.

"Let's go back," Riis said. "A dockworker took the oath of the Volunteers? You received information from a dockworker without any payment? I find it hard to believe."

"He's a dock commissioner."

"A dock commissioner is a lot different than a dockworker, Woody."

"Well, he works on the docks. He runs the place."

"Yes, but—" Riis stopped. He knew he could never explain the different levels of the working class to someone like Woodbury Kane. A dock commissioner was a very powerful man along the East River. Riis guessed that Kane happened to catch him on a day that he was on-site. Most commissioners spend their days in an office, coordinating shipping transit. Riis smiled when Kane responded.

"I got the sense that he was a man of high character and would be useful in the future. He offered me tea. A very nice man."

"The word of a dock commissioner who took the oath as a Volunteer is as good as yours or mine, I would suspect. It is very valuable information, Woody, but hardly enough for me to use your handkerchief over. Very good for the next issue of the *Journal* or the *Times*, but I'm afraid not enough to bring me to tears."

"I wasn't finished. I mentioned the courthouse, yes?"

Riis leaned in, obviously intrigued. "Yes, you did."

"A family friend is an attorney downtown and, more importantly, a notary. I asked him if anything relating to American Ice came across his desk, to let me know. Don't be concerned about his discretion; his family owes quite a sum of money to mine, which I am holding in escrow. It's substantially less now because he shared some very interesting information. Mayor Van Wyck was given 2,600 preferred shares and 3,325 common shares of American Ice at a fifty-percent discount to par. According to my notary friend's calculations, it is worth over three hundred eighty thousand dollars."

Riis didn't put the handkerchief to his eyes; he balled it up in his fist.

"He knows this for sure?"

"Yes, and his notary stamp is on the stock certificates."

"This is incredible, Woody. You are truly going to bring down Tammany with this news. Where are the stock certificates being held? When can we get to them?"

"Don't get too excited now, Jacob. There is a bit of a problem obtaining the certificates."

"Don't tell me. You can't have told me this only to let me down."

"No. No. I think there is a way to get the certificates. It won't be easy, but there is a way."

"Explain please." Riis was getting agitated.

"He carries the certificates with him at all times. In his breast pocket. He obviously doesn't trust a bank or the attorney's office."

"That, my friend, is a problem."

"I remember you telling me about a famous pickpocket from the Five Points. What was his name? Drip, Dipper?"

Riis sat up straight. "The Dip. That was his nickname. They called it dipping. Dipping into someone's pocket." He pantomimed the act with his right hand. "That was a few years ago. I don't think I can find him now. I don't even know his real name."

"Well, that is the only thing I can think of. We can't strong-arm Van Wyck and steal the papers. It would make him look like the victim. We certainly can't have our names attached to any of this."

"Let's walk."

Riis stood and headed north on the path. Kane stood and followed. They strolled side by side. Kane, being a head taller, leaned over to his left as Riis spoke.

"Monk Eastman would know where The Dip is."

"The gangster?"

"Yeah, I recall The Dip being part of his band of brothers. A real crude bunch they are. Thieves, burglars, racketeers. Mostly Jewish and Irish. It's to be expected, I guess."

"Do you still have any connections with these people? Could you arrange a meeting for us? Try to get Eastman to sit down with us."

"I think I can get him in a room, but not with you. You're too recognizable. And believe me, these types are as loose with secrets as any neighborhood gossip. I'll meet him alone. I can say I'm meeting him for research for a new book, if word gets out that we met. I suspect Eastman wouldn't like you much, anyway."

"Not many do," Kane joked.

"Yes, I think Eastman will meet with me. He has been up against the Five Points gang for years. You know that Tammany has been backing the Five Points? They use them for some of their more underhanded deeds."

"Jacob, of course I know about the Five Points gang."

"I know. I was just walking through this in my head. Eastman would be open to any idea that hurts the Five Points in any way. Yes. I'll get a meeting."

He turned to face Kane and put out his hand, which Kane shook.

"I guess we are partners in crime now."

"I knew you would lead me to the dark side eventually."

Riis smiled. "Welcome, my friend. I will try to meet with Eastman as soon as possible. You have to stay out of this from this point on. We've discussed separation of duties for the good of the larger enterprise. This, I believe, is one of those cases. You can't have a hand in this. Tammany has been trying to denigrate your good name since the Ward Boss Costello affair. If your name comes up, it will sour the effect of revealing the stock certificates."

"Yes. I agree. You will keep me informed of your progress?"

"Absolutely. If I manage to arrange a meeting, I will let you know. If he is not keen to the idea, I will tell you. If Eastman is game, I'll come to you with the certificates in hand."

"Good luck, Jacob. Be careful."

"I'll be fine. Monk Eastman isn't going to harm me. My hunch is that he may know more about us then we think. I think he'll come around."

"Good. Thank you, my friend."

"Thank me? You gave us the opportunity to make this city a safer and more prosperous place to live. You should be thanked, and not by myself alone."

"I don't think we should apprise our esteemed governor of this. Not at all."

Riis nodded. "I agree. Teddy cannot be anywhere near this. We take this one to the grave."

"That won't be for many, many years."

"Of course. Don't worry for me. I have been in far more precarious situations than sharing a drink with Monk Eastman."

"I know you have."

Riis stepped back and tipped his hat. 'I'm off to meet with a gangster. Et Omnia Recta."

Chapter 24

April 10, 1900
The White Horse Tavern

J acob Riis nursed his ale. It was a few minutes before midnight, and he was usually asleep two hours by this time of evening. Monk Eastman returned his request by courier this afternoon. The note merely stated the time and place.

Riis was a bit uneasy about the meeting. He never confided in his friend Woodbury just how acquainted with Monk Eastman he was. He had met him during his research for his first book, *How the Other Half Lives*. Eastman was a street thug at the time. Only fifteen years old, but many years older in life experience. Riis first encountered Eastman after watching him and his gang stalk and then rob a gentleman who was foolish enough to wander through the Five Points after dark. Riis had been fascinated by the action. A boy would signal ahead as the gentleman passed. The young thugs would walk alongside the gentleman. They would move closer slowly. Before the gentleman realized it, he was shoulder to shoulder with a gang of pickpockets, hoodlums, and scoundrels. Riis had read about the hunting method of hyenas in Africa. What he'd seen wasn't much different. Jacob had scrawled the details of the hunt onto his pad.

Eastman had then approached him—it was clear even then that he was a leader of men—and asked him if Riis liked what he saw. At the time, Riis himself was a bit naive about the ways of the Points and thought that he might be better served if he made haste and left the area. Eastman shouted him down and his fellow thugs started to circle around him. Eastman walked over slowly, his eyes threatening.

"Are you here for a show, mister?"

Riis tried his best to stand resolute. "No. I'm here to write a book."

Immediately, Eastman's eyes lit up. He waved his arms to tell his crew to back off. "A book? You a writer?'

"Yes, I like to think so."

"What do you write about?"

"I'm venturing to write about the lives of the people living here."

"A writer, here? Why would you want to write about this place?"

Riis relaxed as Eastman's gang backed away.

"I find this," he waved his arms, "very interesting. Did you know that no one knows how you live? How the people down here live?"

"Oh, I know that. I just don't think anyone would care. I hope you're planning on paying the cops a cut of your writing money."

Riis pulled out his pad. "Tell me about the cops."

"Tell you about the cops? Are you stupid or just crazy?"

That had been how their relationship started. Over a pad. Eastman turned out to be a great source for Riis. He knew the area, of course, but it was more than that. Eastman knew the back stories and the back alleys. When Jacob showed up one night with his photography equipment, Eastman had backed off. He didn't want to be photographed. Bad for business, he'd said.

Riis stayed in touch for a few years. When the book came out, it garnered quite a bit of notoriety, and Riis suddenly became the toast of the literary set. Since he had spent years laboring in obscurity, he didn't put much stock in his sudden fame, and after the initial flurry of excitement, he went back to his writing.

He had heard that Eastman had spent some time behind bars in the years since Riis first roamed those streets with him, but he was out now. It had been a while since Riis had seen him. Riis learned that Eastman was still in the Points. In fact, he had moved up a bit in that world. Gone were the days of rolling drunks or stealing from prostitutes. Riis also knew that Eastman was in a heated rivalry with the Five Points gang. The Five Points were mostly Italian now, and with Eastman's gang of Jews and Irishmen, there was a natural friction. There was open warfare on the streets. Riis didn't think that Monk Eastman was very long for this world, so he was glad that he had accepted his invitation to meet.

Riis looked up to see Monk Eastman walking toward him with a wide grin. Riis immediately assumed he was mad as a hatter. He couldn't have looked more unstable if he tried. He was wearing a pork pie hat that was two sizes too small and had a number of gold teeth. His hair looked like it hadn't been washed, ever, and his shirt was untucked beneath an undersized jacket. Riis assumed this look was for effect. The Monk Eastman he had always known had a reputation as a "thinking man's gangster" and now ran one of the most notorious and organized gangs in the city. This getup had to be a joke, or perhaps he had gone mad since Jacob had last seen him. Before Riis could slide out of the booth, Eastman was upon him, practically racing to the head of the table to greet him. Riis tried to slide out of the booth to shake his hand, but Eastman was too fast for him, already reaching out his hand. Riis half stood in the booth to shake it. Eastman smelled of whiskey. This wasn't his first saloon of the evening.

It had been over ten years since their first meeting, and Eastman was a little wider on his short frame—maybe five foot six, tops. His nose looked like it was smashed flat with a cast-iron pan. There was an angry smirk on his face when he spoke.

"Well, now ... my old friend, Jacob Riis. You're quite the toast of New York now, aren't you?"

"Oh, I don't know about that. Please sit."

Eastman slid into the booth bench across from Jacob. A waiter appeared without beckoning. Riis had waited ten minutes for someone to take his order when he first arrived. Apparently, Eastman was more the "toast" of this part of town.

"What you havin'?" Eastman bellowed.

"This is an ale."

"One ale for my friend here, and I'll have my bottle."

The waiter scurried away.

"Jacob Riis. I thought I'd never lay eyes on the likes of you again. You dress a lot better. No old jacket for you no more, huh? Those books of yours must be sellin'."

There was something in the way he spoke that was different than Jacob remembered. Although his words were friendly, they sounded aggressive and threatening. It seemed Eastman had become the type of man who would call someone "pal" as a precursor for a fight. He spoke like a gangster. Jacob felt he should tread lightly. If Eastman's dress and demeanor were meant to intimidate him, they did ... in a way. Jacob still felt he was a man that could be reasoned with.

"I believe we have a mutual interest."

"You think so? Could it have something to do with you feeding stories about the ice scandal to the dailies? Could it have something to do with some rich guy roaming around the docks and asking a lot of stupid questions?"

"I'm sure I don't know."

Monk leaned in, and Riis felt the heat of his breath, smelled the whiskey.

"Don't talk to me like I'm that kid you met a few years back. You're here to do business, right? You're not going to get anywhere by talking like a fool. I know this town. I know more about you than you think, and I know the people you spend your time with. I make it my business to know. This isn't one of your books. We're not in a story. I came here outta respect for you, but you won't walk out of here if you try to snow me. I got three more appointments tonight. You tell me what you want, and I tell you how much it's gonna cost ya. Got it?"

Jacob was initially set back but gained his footing quickly.

"I don't think discussing the people I spend my time with has any benefit to you. It would be wise to keep my friends out of this."

"Why? You think they're better than me?"

"Of course they are."

Eastman threw his head back and laughed with a roar that rattled the entire booth.

The waiter came over, cautiously, with their drinks. Another pint for Riis and a brown bottle without a label and a glass for Eastman.

Eastman waited for the waiter to leave. Riis had the sense that no one would be paying for the drinks tonight.

"You have salt, Jacob Riis. I give you that. I saw it the first time I met you. And what you did, coming down to the Points … well, it was a good thing you did. Too many people living like animals down there."

"Well, Monk, it gave me a chance to meet you. I do have a proposition for you. It's rather risky, although I'm sure you won't be too concerned with that part of it. The task could be rather complicated, though."

"What's the complication? Risk I can take. Complications I don't like."

Riis figured he didn't have much time and it was best to be direct with a direct man.

"I want you to rob the mayor of New York."

Eastman didn't pause or flinch.

"Of what?"

"Stock certificates."

He took a minute to fill his glass with the brown liquid from the brown bottle. He lifted the glass and emptied it. A little dribbled down his chin, which he didn't bother to wipe. Riis watched as the liquid dripped onto the front of Eastman's shirt.

"That's interesting. This have anything to do with all the ice scandal stuff? The papers want another headline? How much you getting paid to feed them the stories? See, I'm trying to set a fee here."

"The reason I want the certificates is none of your business, and I want you to volunteer to steal them for me."

Eastman didn't laugh at this rebuke. He sat back and stared into Riis's eyes. Riis knew he had to stand his ground if he had any chance at getting those certificates.

"I don't volunteer for nothing. I work, I get paid. That's the American way. How you gonna pay me?"

"Bringing me those certificates would go a long way toward taking down Tammany. If Tammany goes down, what do you think happens to the Five Points gang?" Eastman settled back in his seat and Riis continued. "You know Tammany has been propping those Italians up for years. How many times has one of their men walked away from an arrest? Do you get the same treatment? Tammany is using them for muscle. You know this. Anything that hurts Tammany helps you. That is your payment."

Eastman smiled, and Riis counted four gold teeth.

"This stock thing. Is it gonna have an immediate effect, or is this one of those long-term things?"

"I think somewhere in between."

Eastman poured, drank, and dribbled again. Riis ignored his ale.

Eastman put both of his hands flat on the table.

"Where does he keep these certificates?"

"That is the complication. He keeps them on him at all times. I was hoping that you could put The Dip on the job."

"He keeps them on him? That's better than a safe or something?"

"I don't think he trusts anyone. These are documents that he wants to be kept private. I don't think leaving them with a bank or attorney would suit this situation."

"Smart man. And here I am thinking that all politicians are stupid."

"Not all. Most."

"Yeah." He looked at the bottom of his glass and thought. Riis waited. After about ten seconds, which really seemed like an hour, Riis broke the silence by taking a sip from his ale. Eastman poured a glass but didn't drink.

"You can forget about The Dip. A working girl stabbed him in the shoulder a couple months ago. He don't got the feel no more. His arm's all outa shape." He smiled broadly. "I'm gonna do it myself."

"You? Really? Listen, Monk. We don't want any smash and grab job. This has to be discreet—or Mayor Van Wyck, and by proxy, Tammany, will look to be the sympathetic party. This has to be subtle."

"I don't look subtle to you?" Eastman laughed again in his very unsubtle way. "Don't worry yourself. I have a plan. I always have a plan."

"Are you going to share it with me?"

"Oh, now. Look who's sharing. You gonna share with me?"

"You know I can't. If you really know the people I'm working with, as you claim, you would know that I can't say any more to you."

"Yeah, yeah. I want something else, though. I want a promise before I tell you my idea."

"What promise?"

"Write about me in one of your books."

Riis saw it then. The same expression Eastman had worn the first day they'd met. He was still a kid looking for attention.

"Why is that important to you?"

"I want to be remembered, you know?"

"Yeah, I think I do. I can't promise, but I'll do my best. No. I *can* promise this. If I can't write about you, I'll write a character based on you."

"And you'll tell me who it is?"

"Yes. That I promise."

"Okay. I wouldn't need The Dip for this, anyway. This will be easy. I got three whorehouses over on Allen Street. Van Wyck is over there a couple times a week. I'll get word when he's there. I walk into the room and take them. Easy."

"I thought you didn't like complications?"

"No, this is a good plan. Who's gonna talk after getting robbed in a whorehouse? He's married, I figure. I know he's running for reelection. Nah, this is good."

"You're not worried about reprisals?"

"I don't know what that word means. What? You mean that someone's gonna get back at me? I don't care. This would be a stick in the eye to the Five Points. Show them that no one is safe. Not even their boy. Plus, I would love to see the look on his face when I introduce myself."

Riis was convinced now that Eastman had gone crazy. At least it was crazy on their side. For the moment. Eastman was smiling ear to ear.

"Sure thing. I take the certificates, and I'll let get word to you when I have them."

It seemed too easy to Riis, so he said what he wished he didn't have to. Thinking that he may be pushing too hard.

"This is a private matter, Monk. It stays between us, and I need those certificates. I can make sure they're worthless if you try to negotiate after the fact. It will be bad for you if you don't follow through."

Surprisingly, Eastman wasn't insulted in the slightest. He hardly considered the words. Instead of striking or roaring in laughter, he put out his hand to shake. Riis realized this last part, the threat, was likely part of every deal Monk had made in his life.

"You're gonna write about me. Remember."

"Monk, I assure you, if you pull this off ... even if I can't write about it, someone will."

Chapter 25

April 14, 1900
P.J. Clarkes Saloon
New York City

J acob Riis entered the pub through the side door on 55th Street as instructed. The dining room entrance was on his left, and he could hear the chatter of the lunch patrons through the closed door. He looked up and climbed the narrow staircase to the private dining room. There was a landing at the top of the stairs with a window looking out to 55th. There was a stack of upside-down chairs linked together five-high. It was a bright day, and the sunlight through the window temporarily blinded him. He turned away from the sun and heard two voices. The plan was to meet with Woody. He couldn't imagine that anyone else would be invited to this meeting. Jacob thought perhaps he had made a mistake as to the time or location. He meekly went around the corner, convinced he was in the wrong place at the wrong time.

As he entered, he saw two men sitting at a table in the center of the room. Woody was there, and he stood to greet him. Jacob was surprised to see the other person in the room was John Morgan. The son of the great J.P. Morgan himself. Riis was temporarily frozen in place. Kane walked over to him and put his arm on his shoulder to walk him out of earshot of Morgan. Morgan remained seated, no doubt waiting to be formally introduced.

Kane whispered in Jacob's ear, "I know this wasn't planned, but he has been asking to meet with you for some time."

Riis, always worried about Kane's flair for the dramatic, leaned in to reprimand him.

"We are not supposed to inform our benefactors of the details of our operations. You know this."

Kane held Riis's hand a little more firmly and looked into his eyes.

"You work your side of the fence and I'll work mine. The man has been on our team from the beginning. He has supported us financially and, more importantly, politically. This, this thing that we're doing is bigger than the two of us. You want to bring down Tammany, make things right? Well, you're going to have to work with others. We'll need him for the next step in our plan. You're going to have to give up some control from time to time. So smile and play nice."

It was the first time Woody had taken such a forceful tone with Jacob. Rather than being offended or put off, Jacob considered it a further entrenching of their friendship and Woody's dedication to the cause. He smiled up at him.

"Okay. Why don't you let go of my hand and introduce me to your friend?"

Kane smiled back and turned to Morgan, who rose from his seat. He reached out with his arm toward the table and stood with a stiff back to make the formal introduction.

"Jacob Riis, I would like to introduce you to John Morgan."

Riis walked over to the table and extended his hand. They shook.

"It's a pleasure to meet you, Mr. Morgan."

"Please call me Jack."

"Okay, Jack it is."

Morgan seemed quite pleased. His smile was broad, and he put his other hand on Riis's to shake with both.

"Et Omnia Recta."

Riis smiled back. "Yes, Et Omnia Recta."

Kane interjected. "Let's sit, shall we?'

They took their seats; Morgan poured a glass of wine for Riis, topped off Kane's and then his own. The gesture was not lost on Riis. He doubted that Morgan had ever poured his own glass, let alone the glass of a guest. Morgan spoke.

"First, I want to say that I am a big fan of your work. Your book was seminal. It changed the way I view things, the city we live in. It truly did. I'm thrilled to be of any help I can be in this noble cause you and Woody have taken up."

"That's very nice, sir."

"Jack."

"Yes, Jack. That's very nice. I thank you."

"I would like to invite you to my home to discuss some of your work and your viewpoints on the future of our great city. Many of my contemporaries would be well-served to learn from your experiences."

Kane interrupted. "Jack, I think it would be best for our relationship to remain discreet. At least until we get this business behind us."

"Yes. I think you're correct." Morgan turned back to Riis. "Perhaps a private meeting? I'll have my man send you some dates."

Riis said, "Yes. That would be nice."

The feeling came over Jacob that he would be more comfortable with another meeting with Monk Eastman than a private meeting with Jack Morgan, but he knew it would be for the good of the organization to establish comradery with the controlling member of the Morgan family empire.

Woodbury Kane raised his glass. "To the Volunteers. Et Omnia Recta."

Riis responded by saying, "Cheers." Morgan, the more formal, "Et Omnia Recta."

They sat a moment in silence. Kane had the impression Jacob was acquiescing to Morgan. It made sense, since a man like Jack Morgan was more familiar with a man of Kane's background than Jacob's, and Woody was, of course, far more comfortable with the gilded set than Jacob. Kane started by filling Morgan in on their progress.

"Jacob has acquired the stock certificates that I mentioned to you earlier, Jack. He was wise enough to bring them directly to the *New York Times* and the *New York Journal*'s editorial boards."

Morgan was obviously intrigued and didn't wait for Kane to finish.

"How did you get your hands on them, Jacob?"

"I think it is better if you didn't know that, Jack," Riis replied.

Kane quickly interjected. He didn't want there to be too much interaction between Riis and Morgan. He could already hear the slow drip of condensation from Jacob's words. Knowing Jacob as he did, he knew that if Morgan asked many more obvious questions, the drip would turn into a flood.

"Jacob is right, Jack. We have to keep most of our work to ourselves to protect you and, more importantly, to protect the integrity of the operation. An infinite amount of conflicts could arise if each of us knew all of the others' affairs. It's best practice to keep a distance."

Morgan sipped his wine and nodded. Happily wrapping himself in the cloak of secrecy.

Kane continued. "The shares have been returned to Van Wyck, is that correct, Jacob?"

"Yes. This morning, I'm told."

"Good, good. The headlines come out tomorrow. The papers are going to run with this story for quite a while. Excellent work, Jacob."

"Thank you. It was your idea, let's not forget."

"Ideas and results are separate matters. You did a fine job."

Riis nodded.

Kane turned to Morgan. "Jack, could you share with Jacob what we discussed last evening?"

"Yes, yes." He smiled and leaned both elbows on the table. Riis and Kane instinctively aped him.

"On behalf of my dear friend, John D. Rockefeller, I want to thank the two of you for your efforts. John D. and I feel we are on our way to a better, more equitable New York City. Our dream is to raise all boats. It is good for the people of this great city, and let's be clear, it is good for business. John D. and I were up late into the night. Long after you left us, Woody." He patted Kane on the top of his right hand. "We believe we have the ideal candidate to run against Van Wyck in the upcoming mayoral election."

He paused for dramatic effect, and Kane took the cue.

"Whom do you have in mind?"

"Seth Low."

Kane and Riis shared a brief look. Seth Low was their choice. Kane's job last night was to subtly direct Morgan and Rockefeller to come to the same conclusion. The trick, of course, was to make them believe they'd thought of it. Kane was a master at getting men to do what he wanted. Whether it was the charge up San Juan Hill or a real estate transaction. Woodbury Kane had that gift.

Morgan continued. "He's uniquely qualified. As you know, he is the former mayor of Brooklyn and now the president of Columbia College."

Both Riis and Kane nodded their approval and let him continue.

"I've known Seth for quite a while. He is a very serious and driven man. He has been thinking about a run for quite some time, and has a vision for this city. He calls himself a fusion candidate. He's emphatically anti-Tammany. A Republican, in fact. He wants to run as a candidate of the Citizens Union Party and the Republican Party. He'll need the backing of both parties to ward off the rigged voting that Tammany is sure to implement. He has just completed the final stages of moving the Columbia College to Morningside Heights, and knowing him as I do, I believe he is ready for a new challenge."

Kane and Riis were feigning rapt attention. Kane had also known Low for many years, but he knew better than to take the spotlight away from Jack Morgan. After all, he was the bank. He let him continue.

Morgan leaned back, and Kane and Riis again shadowed his movement. "John D. and I feel that the main issue Low should run on is police corruption. The ice scandal will be a great part of this. You, my friends, have done excellent work. This news, tomorrow's headlines, will further erode the support of the working man from Tammany. The very voter they count on. We just feel that a scandal is a scandal. There may be a half dozen more before election day in this city."

He chuckled slightly. His tablemates echoed him.

"We want to stress the corruption," he added. "It is such a large problem that to not address it would be political suicide to a candidate who plans to run as a reformer."

Riis asked, "Does Low have the will to reform in office? Do you know any of his ideas?"

"Yes. Yes, I do. I think that you, in particular, Jacob, would appreciate some of his ideas. One of his initiatives will be to make the municipal unions a merit-based program. The nepotism and payoffs for good-paying union jobs have kept them out of reach for the common man. Seth plans to do away with all that. I will make sure he has the support in the city council to pass such legislation."

Kane and Riis were wise enough not to mention the irony of Morgan's message. They knew the way Seth would do away with nepotism and payoffs was to use those exact same methods. Since they had just recruited a gangster to rob the mayor of New York in a brothel, this seemed like a minor infraction of their ethical standards. It was something they'd discussed at length during the formation of the Volunteers. They knew there would be times when the law had to be broken, when justice served would be in their hands alone. It was something that bothered Jacob far more than Woody since he still had a working man's sensibility.

They agreed eventually that both of them had to be on board with it. If either objected, the other must respect that and find another way to get the task completed. It had worked so far, and on this issue, there was complete agreement. Van Wyck could not serve another term. Reform was desperately needed.

Kane regained control of the meeting. He put both hands flat on the table and announced, "I think it is agreed. Seth Low is our choice for the next mayor of New York City."

The three men raised their glasses, silently toasting, and sipped.

Kane continued. "Now for next steps. Jack, what are your ideas?'

Morgan puffed out his chest a bit and said, "I will take on the task of raising money and awareness for Seth. I'll have my top man arrange the social calendar. I'll also rally the banking community. I do have to tell you, gentlemen—this will be no easy task. Bankers do not like upheaval, and the word 'reform' is not one that will be greeted with open arms."

"We know we can count on you, Jack," Kane said, his eyes boring into the other man's. "Jacob and I will continue to try and find out whatever we can to help the cause."

Riis jumped in. "I haven't thought of this until now, but since the ice scandal story will be out in the press, I can start writing about Van Wyck. I can submit an opinion piece to the *Times* or the *Journal*. I will go after Van Wyck now that the news is out. Woody, why don't you work your new legal connections, see if you can find out some information about police corruption or payoffs. Any little story will have an impact. The key will be to keep them coming so the story stays in the minds of the voters."

"That sounds like fun, Jacob," Kane said, raising his glass.

They sat silent for a moment until Morgan asked the question they all had on their minds.

"And what of Mr. Roosevelt, our fine governor?"

Kane and Riis squirmed in their seats. They didn't know how to respond. They had discussed this situation at length and had not come up with a good answer. J.P. Morgan, Jack's father, made his hatred of Roosevelt well-known. Jacob and Woody could not gauge exactly how Jack Morgan felt about Teddy. Kane had been reasonably sure that it wouldn't become an issue, but now here it was.

Morgan let them off the hook and continued speaking. "Does the governor know of my involvement in this organization?"

Kane answered, "Yes."

"He approves?"

"Wholeheartedly. The results are what matter to Teddy. We all feel confident in your dedication, and we all feel that you and John D. will be invaluable to the cause."

"Will you inform him of the outcome of this meeting? If you do, and he does not approve, I think it may be a problem. John D. and I will not be overruled by a party not intimately involved in the discussions. We all know Mr. Roosevelt has a strong will. I will not continue to provide assistance and counsel if I feel my decisions may be summarily dismissed by our governor."

Riis responded this time. "Teddy has agreed with Woody and myself that he should only be informed on issues of great importance. I think all would agree that the mayor of New York is an important issue so we feel that we must apprise him of this. Be assured that we have complete authority and discretion to complete our tasks without Teddy's approval. We are the executive committee of the Volunteers. You, Jack, are on that committee. Right now, until Mr. Rockefeller makes an appearance, it is a committee of four men. If we all agree, then our task is to inform Teddy of our decision. He is one man, one voice, one vote. Nothing more."

Morgan rose from his seat and put out his hand. Riis shook it.

"Well said, Mr. Riis. Well said indeed. Let's set to our tasks now then, shall we? I will arrange a cocktail reception at my home. Woody, I hope you can make it."

"I think I can do that."

"Jacob, can I convince you to change your mind?"

"I don't think so, Jack. Some of the things I'm thinking about writing may not sit well with the banking crowd. No, I think it is best for you and me to keep our friendship discreet. At least until after the election."

Morgan slapped Jacob on the shoulder. "I will get you to my home eventually, Mr. Riis. Mr. Roosevelt is not the only one who doesn't take no for an answer."

"It will be an honor, Jack."

Kane clapped his hands together. "Will you join us for lunch, Jack?"

Morgan started walking toward the staircase. "My friends, nothing would make me happier than dining with such noble men, but I will not eat in a saloon. Good afternoon, men. I will be in touch."

He turned down the steps and Kane and Riis practically hopped up and down with delight. Things could not have gone better. They will get their man as mayor. Tammany was on the run. It was a great day in New York.

Chapter 26

C hief Joe Riggins looked up at the clock. Four thirty. He was thinking about how he was going to get his daughter to her softball tournament this morning. She had to be at the ferry at six thirty to get over to Nantucket. It was to be an all-day event. She had three games today and, if they were successful, a final tomorrow night under the lights. It was a big deal, and she would be very pissed off if her dad wasn't there. He could call Lucy, the sitter, to take her to the ferry; that wasn't the problem. As a single father and a cop, it was difficult to find the time to be around for these things. He somehow had thought if he was in a smaller town, he would be able to do it all. He was wrong. If anything, there was more bullshit to deal with on this job. It wasn't bullshit on the same scale as Boston, but it was time-consuming bullshit nonetheless. He resigned himself to the fact that he wasn't going to make it. He figured he'd wait a while longer before waking Lucy and asking her to take his daughter to the ferry.

Riggins turned his attention to the stack of paperwork on his desk.

He opened the file on the drone one more time to see if there was anything he had missed. After the incident with the tourist and his brief interview with Hank Suarez, he had it hand-delivered by one of his officers to a buddy on the Boston force who specializes in surveillance technology. He received the report through a scanned email this afternoon. He read through it immediately and had many of his suspicions confirmed. After a brief glimpse five minutes ago, the words on the page haven't changed. The report said it was a highly sophisticated device. What stood out to Riggins was that the tape on the drone had been erased remotely after it was disabled. Someone had been taping something then wiped the tape clean after it went down—and could get into unfriendly hands. Something wasn't right. He'd had Suarez and the New York cop in separate holding rooms for the last hour or so. He held his head in his hands and tried to piece together the connection. Why would a New York cop——it was obvious to him that she was——be protecting a software developer who was being spied on with a high-tech surveillance drone? It wasn't witness protection; those guys wouldn't spring for a decent hotel, let alone a mansion.

The mansion? Suarez had paid cash for it. That was undeniable. He had copies of the bank transactions. A twelve-million-dollar home to hide a witness? No. Not a chance. Could be heavy government shit or organized crime. Neither of those fit because of the two shitheads the woman popped. They both had sheets a mile long. Low-level shit. There were a few notes about suspected kidnappings, but Riggins knew the type. Irish punks. Boosting liquor stores or stealing social security checks from mailboxes. That was the level of criminal expertise the Murdock brothers had. If it were a big government thing or the mob, experienced shooters would have been on this. Riggins wondered briefly if he should call the state or federal authorities to see if he could get some clarification. He shelved the idea for now. Maybe he'd make a call after nine when he was more likely to get someone who was on the ball to pick up a phone. For now, he would brace the rich guy. There was no way the woman cop was going to cooperate.

He thought about the look on his daughter's face when he got home, whenever that might be. How he hated to disappoint her. This has been planned for months. She understood his job, of course, but she was a teenage girl, and he would catch hell from her. He got up to go into the holding room to question Suarez. Chief Riggins knew it would take all of his will not to rip this guy's head off.

Annie Falcone had fallen asleep in her chair, her head cradled in her arms as she leaned over onto the table. Before dozing off, she had considered the circumstances. They were in a police station. Her job should be done. No one was going to grab Hank out of the station. She didn't know what was next for him, but she was out. She felt a pang in her chest when she considered the fact that she may never see Hank again. They may have taken him out a back door already. She wasn't concerned about herself. If anything, her father would bail her out, literally and figuratively. Annie thought that maybe her dad could track Hank down when the time was right. It wouldn't be bad to meet with him in a more normal situation. Maybe over a drink or a meal. It was that thought that had prompted Annie to lay her head down, wondering what they would talk about and where she would like to meet as she closed her eyes.

Hank was in a fantastic mood. For the first time in years, he could envision a way out of this life in hiding. The last couple of hours should cement his identity as Hank Suarez. With his house now the center of a major crime scene, the police must have done an extensive background check on him, the deed to the house, his past jobs or relationships, and anything else they could think of. The longer he sat alone in this room, the closer he was to winning his freedom. There was no doubt that the FBI or CIA or someone would be in the station house before long. He knew from past missions with the Volunteers that once discretion was blown, it was time to go big. They would pull out all the stops to nail Sheng now. He remembered the type of drone that was used from that first night's questioning from Chief Riggins. Hank knew the approximate flight capacity. He was certain that Sheng was on the island. Of course, he might have fled by now, but Hank knew him well enough to know he wouldn't give up easily. He was still around; Hank could feel it. They'd shut the place down to get to Sheng. Stop all boats, planes, helicopters, or any other route to the mainland. Sheng was boxed in, and Hank's identity was rock solid. Even if Sheng managed to slip away, Hank knew from experience that his foe would have to dig himself a deep hole to climb into. Sheng was smart, no doubt; but not even he could evade the Americans and the Chinese for too long. If he survived this, it would be years before he could emerge. Things were working out. Finally.

He was dog-tired, but there was no way he could fall asleep. There was too much to think about. He allowed himself to daydream about his future. It had been a long time since he'd allowed himself this luxury. He would ask Annie out for a drink or lunch or something. He would like to get to know her better. He would move back to New York. God how he missed the city and all the restaurants and bars and theaters. There were too many for him to count. The idea of walking around the West Village after a nice meal and music with a woman, with Annie, on his arm was more than he could have imagined only hours ago. He'd sell the house here. It didn't matter if he took a loss—he'd had enough of this place. Hank was a city kid. He could use the proceeds to buy something nice. A high-rise near the park. Doorman, elevator. Yes. Something nice.

Hank knew that he was distracting himself from the one thought that was dearest to him. The idea of a reunion with his father. He didn't want to go there in his mind. To let himself get excited by the prospect of seeing his dad again and have it ripped away would be too much to bear. So he pushed it away. Like he'd been doing for two years, he blocked any reunion out of his mind and concentrated on the work he had left behind, and the projects he wanted to get started on again.

Hank learned over the last couple of years the value of distance and time. He had walked away from a lot of his projects—unwillingly, of course—but this allowed the projects to grow on their own. To breathe. His more complicated projects benefitted from the time away. He thought of the code that needed to be changed, of course, but there was more. Most of the work he'd left behind involved human interaction. Hank knew now that he never could have completed those projects to his own satisfaction. He woud have been mired in frustration ... because he wasn't qualified to finish any program that involved human emotion. And that was his ultimate dream. To use technology to better the world. To do that, he would have to find a way to appeal to a user's better nature.

The last two years in relative isolation had taught him something he never could have learned in any university. It taught him humility. It took a long time, but it finally sank in. He was too ambitious, too wrapped up in accomplishment and money to see what a miserable shit he had become. He had become that know-it-all tech asshole he had always hated. In essence, he was the polar opposite of his father. The opposite of all the things he admired in a man. Hank had learned that he must be a man of high principles if he could ever influence others to act in a profound way. He had to become a better man to complete his life's work, to achieve its goal.

It hit him then. In that room. He had received exactly what he deserved. The two years. The money lost. The time apart from his father. He deserved all of it. To have so much knowledge and talent, with unlimited resources at his fingertips, and to not put it to good use was unthinkable to him now. He did good work with the Volunteers, for sure; but he knew in his heart he was capable of much more. He knew what kind of a man he used to be. He'd write code for video games with barely any effort. Make big bucks and date models. Hank knew now that he was one of the few men in the world who could truly change civilization for the better and he had barely lifted a finger. It was a crime. He had deserved this sentence.

Chapter 27

Riggins took a deep breath as he held his hand on the doorknob of Suarez's holding room. In his other hand was the case file he had assembled. He knew Suarez was too smart for a bum rush. Riggins had to control his emotions, even though he couldn't stop thinking about how this asshole was keeping him away from his daughter's softball tournament. Unable to make it to ten, he stopped at the count of three and opened the door.

Suarez had his head in his arms on the tabletop. He looked up immediately. Riggins guessed he had either been sleeping or crying because his eyes were puffy and red. No matter. He had things to discuss.

He put the file on the table in front of the empty chair across from Suarez and slid into the seat. He leaned back and opened the file to an earmarked page, but he didn't look at it. He wanted to speak to this guy first. See what he had.

"You call that lawyer yet?"

Hank rubbed his eyes and tried to focus. The lack of sleep seemed to be hitting him all of a sudden. "No. Not yet. Am I under arrest?"

Riggins smiled. "You're what we call a person of interest."

"Really. What's so interesting about me?'

"Well, for one thing, you say that you just shot two men, but you don't even know what kind of ammo you used. For another thing, I think you're full of shit."

"You hold people in here for being full of shit? If that's the case, you should be about full up."

"Maybe I should be more specific. You're full of shit *and* you're from New York. That's enough for me until a lawyer springs you. Until then, I want to ask you a few things."

"You think I'll answer?"

"Maybe not. But it would be in your best interest to do so. You see, I got two dead guys on my island. I don't like that. It's a pain in the ass for me. You understand. So unless you have a reasonable explanation for it, this is all going to fall on you."

Hank didn't respond. Riggins forged ahead.

"I know this isn't the Big Apple, but we do have ballistic tests here. I'm waiting for the results now. My guess is that you didn't shoot the gun. If that is true, you lied to a police officer during a preliminary investigation. They call that 'obstruction.' Serious shit."

Hank crossed his arms and leaned back in his chair. Riggins continued.

"I'm going to talk to the girl next. If she bails on you, you're fucked. I hope you know that. Tell me what the hell happened out there, and I'm sure we can rack this up as self-defense. I don't give a shit about the two men she shot. Two less mooks in the world is not going to keep me up tonight."

Nothing from Hank.

"All right. You want to be a hero. Okay. I'm sure your girl will think differently."

With that, Riggins snatched the file, stood, and walked out the door. He didn't go in to see Annie. He went to the men's room and then to the breakroom for a fresh cup of coffee. He waited ten minutes, then went back into Hank's holding room. He didn't wait to sit.

"She shot 'em. She was there to protect you. Says she doesn't know anything about you or whatever shit you're into, but she pulled the trigger. Now you're in deep shit, Mr. Suarez. Two dead bodies, lying to a cop. You better call that lawyer."

Hank was getting tired of this routine. Tired of this room, tired of the predicament he had gotten himself into. He smiled at Riggins and spoke. He made sure to be very selective about what he said.

"She didn't say anything to you. I won't either. Riggins, is it?"

Riggins sat down with a grunt. "Chief Riggins."

"Chief Riggins, I respect your job. I really do. I have the utmost respect for the police and any first responder. With that in mind, I want to be honest with you. This is not going to go anywhere. You will not arrest me or her. It would be best for you if you would just go back to your office and wait until you get your ballistics back. You can pursue this any way you want, but I assure you, this is going nowhere. I'm just trying to save you some aggravation."

***

That was the worst possible thing that Hank could have said. Far from appeasing Chief Riggins; it pissed him off.

"Who the fuck do you think you're talking to? I'm twenty-four years in. You think I haven't heard every line of bullshit there is? You fucking condescending prick. I'll bust your fucking face and throw you down the stairs. Make it look like you resisted arrest. You think I haven't done it before? Try me, you fucking asshole. Some fucking rich asshole gets up in my face. Are fucking kidding me? This is going nowhere? I'll say where it's going to go. I'll come up with something to keep you here for a good long while, believe me. We could lose a file. Maybe the judge can't come in this morning to hear your plea. Respect my job? Respect my boot up your ass. That's what you'll respect."

Suarez responded by smiling again. He seemed to be enjoying himself.

Riggins had to stand again to calm himself down. He walked around the table twice and then out of the room. He stood in the hall and thought it through. His problem was that the prick was right. If Suarez and the girl kept their mouths shut, he had nothing. Sure, he could delay things and the ballistics will prove him right, but it was a small offense. If this guy had a half-decent lawyer, which Riggins was sure he did, the two of them would be playing house again in a couple of hours. He had to know, though. The drone, the half-assed robbery attempt. The house for cash.

He had to know. He took a deep breath and stared up at the ceiling. There was a time in every investigation when a detective had to come to grips with the fact that he wasn't going to get all the answers. Or much satisfaction. It was the same for a chief or a patrolman. He was about to resign himself to the fact that he would never get the answers he wanted, but he did have one last card to play, and he thought it just might work. He didn't have to bullshit the guy. He had his theory, and he figured he'd lay it out for Suarez. See if he got a nibble. He walked back into the room and sat down, opened the file again, and spun it around to face Hank.

"Okay, I get it. You got nothing for me. He pointed at the scanned photo of the drone. "This is what I don't understand. The drone. See, at first I thought you were part of a money-laundering operation, but the house sale was legit. No angle unless you planned on flipping the house. No, that would be too complicated. Too clunky. I know you're full of shit. Your bio is perfect, but I've been on the job too long not to have a gut about this. There is something off about you. So I figure you're one of two things: you're a witness against the mob, or there is some big government thing going on. Now, I rule out you're a mob rat since the Feds would never spring for that house. I have a copy of the deed and the record of the transaction. It is your house. See right here?"

He turned to another dog-eared page, the file still facing Hank. "So I'm going with the government cover-up. Plenty of that going on these days. What stuck in my gut was the drone. Why would someone be surveilling you? If the Feds have you wrapped up, who the hell is watching you? I had a buddy check it out. There was a recording device on this thing. Someone erased the recording after it crashed. That's a pretty sophisticated device. I reached out to some agency guys I know in Boston. Their FBI division doesn't have this technology. This is high-level stuff. Now, you compare that to the low-level mugs who were sent out to kill you. Yeah, sent to kill you, not rob you.Well, you can see why it don't add up."

Hank leaned back in his chair and smiled. He was starting to like this guy.

Riggins continued. "That's why it doesn't make sense. Those two things. The drone and those two guys. So I've been thinking about this for the last couple of hours and this is what I came up with. Whoever you think is protecting you is not your friend. There is no way any responsible agent of any branch of law enforcement would have allowed that shit show to go on at your house tonight. I don't care if that chick is a fucking ninja. I know the protocols. Backup would have been there long before my lazy-ass cop showed up. I hate to tell you, Mr. Suarez, but someone is hanging you out to dry."

Riggins pulled back the file, closed it, and went on some more.

"All of this puts me in a bad situation. My guess is that if you get sprung, someone is going to come after you again. I don't know if your girl is very good or very lucky, but I don't like the odds of you coming away unscathed twice in a day. The numbers are against you. My concern is that if you do get killed, I'm the stupid cop who let you walk." He tapped the file with his big hand. "There's a paper trail now. I have cops and Feds all over this file. They're all gonna shit on me if this goes bad. So we're married on this. At least holding hands. So here's what's going to happen. Your lawyer springs you; I'm following you home. You get on a ferry; I'm sitting next to you. Holding hands, you see?"

Hank chuckled.

"So what's it going be? You want me up your ass for the rest of your life, or are you going to talk to me?"

There it is, Hank thought. Riggins should have walked away to let him think about it. He pushed too hard. Like back at the house. This guy was pretty good, but Hank wouldn't back him in a poker game. He was a bad bluffer. It was clear to Hank that he had been playing him from the start. Nice theory. Pretty close, in fact. There were a dozen things Hank wanted to say at that moment, but all he said was, "I'll wait till nine and call my lawyer. Thanks for your concern."

Riggins stood and pointed a thick finger in Hank's face. "Fuck this, and fuck you." And then he walked out of the room.

Chapter 28

Charles Milan spoke to The Monk without expecting an answer. "It's been long enough. I'm going in. Stay down. I want it to look like I'm alone. I'll park around back."

Milan had spent the last hour or so surveilling the parking lot and surrounding area of the police station through the satellite feed on his laptop. The Monk kept an eye on the man in the car that had followed the patrol car transporting the girl and Suarez. All was clear on both fronts. The lot was quiet. So was the watcher.

Milan was a stickler for preparation. He never understood the concept of playing it by ear or winging it. He had his approach, his demeanor, and the words he would say memorized like a script. Before turning the ignition, he did a mental checklist like he'd done a hundred times before. FBI badge, government plates on their drab sedan, business card, name and cell number of the executive assistant director. McGinley assured Milan that the National Security Branch director would be prepped, so his cover was clean. Milan knew his lines. Showtime.

He started the car and slow-rolled it into the parking lot entrance and around to the back. He took the long way around so the watcher couldn't tag his plates. The Monk had the back of his seat lowered and was lying flat by his side. They pulled into a spot near the back entrance that Milan had seen from the satellite. It was under a tree and shrouded from the parking lot lights. They were in complete darkness. The Monk sat up. The spot was reserved for police, but his federal license plate entitled him to the spot. He shut the engine and spoke to The Monk again.

"Cover my back. If that guy from the lot comes anywhere near this back entrance, I want you to take him out. Got it?"

The Monk nodded. Milan got out and walked across the lot to the back door.

Shizi watched the car as it went around back. He was unable to gather any identifying characteristics, so he called Sheng who was watching from his satellite feed. He picked up in one ring.

"Yes."

"A car just went around the back."

Shizi could hear the sound of Sheng's barstool scraping along the floor. He was moving closer to his laptop.

"Yes, I saw. Give me the license number."

"It was out of range. I didn't see anything."

Shizi heard Sheng typing.

"I do not see anything either. Looks like an unmarked police car. I wonder why it is coming in at such an hour."

"Maybe they called in off-duty officers. They're probably stretched because of the crime scene at the house."

Sheng didn't respond for a second. A sign that he was deep in thought.

"That is probably it, but keep an eye on that car. If it leaves, I would like the license plate numbers."

"Yes sir."

Chapter 29

The back door was locked, and no one answered the buzzer he'd held down for over thirty seconds, so Milan walked around to the front. He realized the watcher would have eyes on him once he turned the corner. He tried to keep his head down, facing away from the lot. He had no idea what kind of surveillance would be in use.

He was uncomfortable with this part of the operation. Since he couldn't communicate with McGinley, it was on him to figure out the best way to go forward. The watcher was a wrinkle he hadn't anticipated, but many operations have unexpected bumps in the road. All he could do now was to adjust and trust his years of experience. He determined the plan should move forward as originally designed. They had to draw Sheng into the open. Milan was confident that McGinley was right to think Suarez would not be killed, but the girl ... that was another matter. He thought about her dilemma as he went up the stairs to the main entrance. If he were running this for Sheng, the girl would not make it off this island alive. He could walk in right now and tell the cops that the guy is out there. That alone would save the girl and free Suarez. It would also guarantee that Sheng would flee. If he went through with his plans, he was signing her death warrant. Milan knew what he had to do.

The front door was unlocked, and Milan walked straight into the lobby of the small precinct house. Straight ahead was the desk sergeant sleeping on his folded arms on the raised desk. On one of the chairs that lined the wall to Milan's left was the cop who had been first on the scene. He was asleep also. Milan looked at him. Tall, fat, out of shape. He concluded that the cop would not be a threat. As he approached the desk, Milan made a fist. He banged it down on the desk, and the sergeant jumped, almost falling backward off his chair. He flung his legs out to balance himself and let out a grunt. Before the cop could speak, Milan pulled out his badge.

"Walter Hernandez, FBI. I'm here to see Chief Riggins."

The sergeant scrambled to straighten the disheveled state of his desk. He was stalling to clear his head. Milan waited as he shuffled papers and picked up a pen and moved it to the other side of the desk. The sergeant looked up.

"What now?"

Milan pushed the badge closer to the sergeant's face. "Walter Hernandez, FBI. I'm here to see Chief Riggins."

The sergeant smirked like every cop Milan had ever met when introducing himself as a federal agent. He could read his clichéd mind. *This is our turf.* Same thought, same face, same hint of defeat. All cops knew that if the FBI came around, they would end up out of the loop or running for coffee. The sergeant straightened.

"I'll see if he's in."

"Yeah, you do that. Who's Sleeping Beauty here?" He thumbed over his shoulder to the sleeping officer.

"That's Wells, the officer of record. He's waiting around to get the credit for any collar that may come from this. You know, the gunfight. Shit. You know, right? Or why would you be here? Yeah, you know."

"I know. Call the chief please."

"Yeah, sure. No problem."

Milan was tempted to ask him to go for coffee but thought better of it. The desk sergeant hit a button on his phone and was answered with a groan.

"What the hell?" Came across the line.

"There's a FBI agent here to speak to you, and, Chief, we're on speaker."

"Thanks. Send the son of a bitch in."

The sergeant smiled and extended his arm to the right. "First door. Past the water fountain."

"Thanks."

Since he didn't like being called a son of a bitch, Milan didn't bother to knock when he got to the door. Chief Riggins didn't rise to meet him. Instead, he looked up briefly and went back to his file. Milan went directly to the front of the chief's desk and held out his badge. Riggins didn't bother to look up. He kept his head down when he spoke.

"Didn't take long, did it? Maybe you can tell me what the fuck is going on in my precinct?"

Milan didn't answer the question. He formally introduced himself, as was the protocol.

"Walter Hernandez, special agent, National Security branch."

Riggins looked up. "National Security? You out of New York?"

He reached out his hand to indicate he wanted a closer look at Milan's badge. Milan handed it over. Riggins looked at it closely. Even running his fingertips across the business card that was affixed to the fold-out badge case to feel the raised stamp. He handed it back.

"Have a seat."

Milan sat in one of the leather chairs facing the desk, folded the badge case, and slipped it into the inside pocket of his windbreaker.

"Chief, as you can imagine, I'm here about the incident over on Edgartown Bay Road this evening."

"Incident? That's what it was? I thought it was a shootout on my island. I have two dead guys in the morgue. You have any background on this *incident*?"

"Nothing that I'm at liberty to share. This is an ongoing operation."

"Well, if you don't share, how are we going to get along, you and me?"

Milan wanted to set the rules of engagement early. "I have no interest in getting along with you, Chief Riggins. I need some information and cooperation."

Riggins was having none of it.

"You here alone? I don't know you from a hole in the wall. You want cooperation? I'll wait till nine and call my local field agent."

Milan leaned in and pulled a different business card from his jacket pocket. It was the card of Executive Assistant Director Adam Koontz. Koontz, the number one man in New York and the head of the National

Security Branch, had been prepped by McGinley. Koontz was asked for the favor in return for a bust that was handed to the Bureau by McGinley a couple of years ago. The arrest of the terrorist with the sarin gas in Queens. Koontz was ready for the call.

Riggins eyed the card. "What am I supposed to do with this?'

"I would like you to call Director Koontz please."

"Now? It's quarter past five in the morning."

"Yes. He's expecting the call."

"What the hell." Riggins picked up the desk phone, but Milan held out both of his hands and shook them to stop him.

"No, no. Use this please." He pulled out the burner phone from his side pocket.

"A burner? What the hell is going on here?"

"We think our communication may have been breached."

"My phones too?"

Milan sat back. "It's best to be careful."

Riggins shook his head. He had never experienced anything like this. A lone Fed coming in, handing him a burner. He knew who Koontz was, of course, but this was way out of line with anything he'd dealt with in the past. He didn't know which way to go on this. He wanted to make it clear he wasn't on board with this type of nondisclosure. The lack of openness between their respective departments made him uneasy, so he decided to let Hernandez know how he felt. To have it on record.

"I don't like this. You understand. I don't know what's going on, but I want you to know this is not the way I like to run things. It's my precinct and my jurisdiction. My bust. It's always the same. You guys come in after the shots are fired and the dust has settled. Only to stir it all up again." He shook his head. "God. I hate this fucking bullshit."

Milan sympathized. He had dealt with all kinds of police officers over the years. He had not once had a cop who was happy to hear from a federal agent. He understood. Most locals wanted the problem solved and put away with no complications. That was their job.

He smiled. "Chief Riggins, I appreciate your frustration. Please press the number one on the phone. Director Koontz's number is in memory."

Riggins shook his head and pressed.

The phone was on the night table of Director Koontz's bedroom. It was plugged in but had never been used. A burner phone. McGinley had told him there was a breach of all communications on the particular operation he was working on, and the burner phone was necessary. Koontz knew better than to ask. The guy had handed him the biggest bust of his career, which led to the bump to director last year. He owed him one.

The phone rang.

There was no way to trace a phone that had never been used, Koontz knew. Although with the level of hacking and security breaches they'd seen in the last couple of years, he was reluctant to pick it up. He looked over at the clock. It was five fifteen. His wife stirred slightly; she was used to late-night or early-morning calls at this point. She rolled over and put a pillow over her head. He unplugged the phone from the charging jack and picked it up.

"Koontz here. Wait a minute." He walked out of the bedroom and down the hall. He put the phone back to his ear.

"Director Koontz. Who is this?'

Even though Riggins knew he was calling Koontz, he found himself caught off-guard when he heard the man's voice. He stumbled with his words.

"Ah, Director Koontz? Is this Director Koontz?"

"Yes. You called me. Who is this?"

"Sorry, sorry. This is Chief Joe Riggins, Edgartown Police."

"Okay, Chief Riggins. Who gave you this number?"

Riggins held his hand over the phone and whispered to Milan.

"What's your name again?"

"Walter Hernandez."

Riggins went back to the call. "Agent Hernandez, sir."

"Okay, Chief. Listen carefully. This is a high-level security call. I want you to cooperate with Agent Hernandez completely. This is a national security investigation. Do not impede this investigation in any way or it will reflect very poorly on you and your department. Hernandez will explain all or nothing. It's his case from this point on. Do you understand?"

"Yeah, I got it."

"Hand the phone to Agent Hernandez please."

Riggins handed it over. Milan put it to his ear.

"I'm destroying the phone now," Koontz said to Milan. "Are we done here?"

"Yes sir. Thank you."

Koontz hung up. Milan turned the phone around, took out the battery, and put both the phone and the battery back in his pocket.

Riggins leaned back in his chair, crossed his arms behind his head, and asked, "What can I do for you, Agent Hernandez?"

Milan straightened up in his chair. "Who knows about the drone?"

Riggins smiled. "Ah, the fucking drone. I knew there was something funky about that. It's a real military-grade piece of machinery."

Milan didn't have time for idle chatter. Sheng was out there, likely with his bags packed. There also was a man, who was no doubt a killer, waiting in the parking lot. He tried to sound urgent yet polite.

"Yes, Chief, I understand, but this is a fluid situation. I'm going to have to urge you along. There are pieces that have yet to fall into place. If you could please just stick to brief answers, I would greatly appreciate it."

"Okay. I sent it to a friend in the Boston Police Department. He sent me a report," Riggins said with an edge to his voice. "Since you're so rushed for time, I'll tell you this also. I had a forensic accountant, a civilian who lives on the island, go over the sale of the house. Let's see ... what else? Oh yeah. I made a few calls to detectives that I have known over the years. Two in Boston, one in New York. I also haven't been shy about asking opinions around the station. It's called 'working a case.' That's what a cop does before a fed walks in and takes it away from him." He pushed a file across the desk toward Milan. "It's all yours."

Milan opened it and glanced at a few pages.

"This looks like you put in some time on it."

"Only days, nights, and weekends."

Milan let out a deep breath and took a moment to think. He made sure to take a polite approach.

"Thanks for this. It will help build a case when the time comes. I only need your cooperation for a few hours, then hopefully I can bring you back in for the arrest. Sound good?"

———

"Sure." Riggins knew the case was not likely to be taken away from him at this point. That's why he had done all that legwork. Why he had put so many eyes and prints on this file. The Feds couldn't make this go away now that they knew so many officers were aware of the investigation. He imagined that once the morning paper came out, the shooting story would go wide. As far as Boston, for sure. Maybe New York. He'd used the filing system he taught himself many years ago. He called it "filling the bucket." Document everything. Fill that bucket with data so high no one could lift it alone. They had to let him stay involved now, and if the shit hit the fan, his ass was covered.

———

Milan closed the file and placed it on his lap. He knew they would have to go big on this case, since so many people knew about it. McGinley would have to put on a show when this was done. It made for more pressure to get Sheng as soon as possible. Now he had a couple of police forces, the FBI (since he'd used the badge), and McGinley counting on him to bring this to a successful conclusion. Only McGinley and Suarez knew how important this operation was, but now a lot of people knew that something strange was happening on this island. He was going to have to tap dance at the end of all this. He didn't like dancing. He asked Riggins another question.

"Who was the first officer on the scene?"

"At the house? That was Officer Wells. Why?"

"I'm going to ask you to trust me on something. I want you to release Suarez and the woman. I want Wells to take them back to the house. Tonight. Now."

Riggins leaned in to speak softly to Milan.

"Listen. Wells is not the guy for this."

"Why not? Wouldn't it be protocol to have the first officer on the scene bring them back?"

"Yes, but I don't think Wells is your guy."

"Why not?"

"He's under investigation by our Internal Affairs office. He's been extorting from a few local merchants. We think it's gambling. We have him dead to rights, but we're just waiting for the lawyers to give us the go-ahead. You know, unions and shit."

"Yes, I know."

Milan stood and paced a few steps, thinking. The cop must be part of this. He was being bribed or paid off in some way. That was why he had driven up to the crime scene in such a casual way. He had already known it would happen. Could Sheng have gotten to him? Milan all but slapped himself in the head as if he were in a V8 commercial. Of course. Sheng must have researched every cop on the island. He had to find an unwitting accomplice. He had no power anymore. Except for the mug in the parking lot, there couldn't be anyone that Sheng could trust. He was as deep in hiding as Suarez. Maybe deeper. What better way to get Suarez to come peacefully? In the back of a patrol car. The scene at the house was a setup. It all made sense now. The amateur hoodlums, the lazy cop. If the gunmen killed the girl and took Suarez, that would have been fine. If the girl killed the gunmen, then Sheng would have the cop arrive on the scene and hand-deliver them both to Sheng. Or maybe even just Suarez; the girl was expendable. It made sense. Milan turned back to the desk but didn't sit.

"I want Wells. Have him bring them back. This is very important. You have to keep this between us. I want you to wait by the phone. Don't leave this office. Your highest priority now is to keep this quiet. Keep a tight lid on it. When Director Koontz said it was a national security situation, he wasn't bullshitting, but even he doesn't know the exact nature of this operation. It's just you and me, Chief. No phone calls. Nothing. I will call you when this is done. I think it will be soon. You can't be involved until this is resolved. Believe me, it's in your best interest."

Riggins leaned both arms on his desk and stared into Milan's eyes. "Who the hell are you?"

Milan didn't answer. "Wells is asleep outside. I'd rather he didn't see me. Wait a couple of minutes and call him in."

"You didn't answer me. Who are you?"

"I'm a friend." Milan walked out of the office.

Riggins waited two minutes and stood. He walked to the door, opened it, and stuck his head out. "Wells, wake the fuck up and get in here."

Chapter 30

Wells stood in front of Chief Riggins's desk, rubbing his eyes. "What you want, Chief?"

Riggins looked at this jerk. He couldn't believe that he was going to hand over Suarez and the New York cop to this guy. He had forgotten her name already since whatever name she used was clearly bullshit, so it didn't register with him. Although she did do a nice piece of work at the house, he thought he should give her respect, but she didn't show him any, and it was very late, so he decided that he didn't give a shit.

"Go and take those two shitheads back to their house."

"No charges, nothing?"

"No. We don't have anything on them, and the guy's lawyer is some big shot, so we're going to let them go. I want you to take them directly to the house. Don't say a word to either of them. His lawyer is pissing vinegar that we held them this long. And, Wells, don't mess with the scene when you get there. I don't think we have everything we need from the house or them yet."

"Got it."

Wells walked out of the room, and Riggins picked up the phone to call the babysitter. He wasn't going to make the softball tournament. He figured that he may be here for a while. He quickly slammed the phone down, having almost forgotten about the security breach. The last thing he wanted was anyone knowing anything about his family or their whereabouts. He didn't want to risk calling anyone. This was going to leave his daughter stranded. He was already dreading going home. Damn, she's going to give it to him.

———————

Wells walked into the female cop's room first. He wanted to check her out again. He'd been thinking about her rack for the last couple of hours. He walked in without knocking only to wake her up. Her hair was in her face and her eyes were racooned from running mascara, but she still looked pretty good to him.

"C'mon, sweetheart. Time to go."

Annie looked around the room and then back at him. She seemed disoriented for a moment. Suddenly she stood up straight and stretched. There was the rack he'd been thinking about.

"Are we free to go?"

'Yes, you are, little lady. Come on with me. I'm going to take you home."

He put his hand under her armpit to move her along, and she almost took a swing at him as she stood.

"Keep your hands off me."

"Now, now. You don't want to get yourself in trouble with me, do you?"

"Just keep your distance. I don't want no cop mauling me."

"Oh, we have a princess." He reached around his back, took out his handcuffs, and held them in her face. "You want to be a bitch about it, I can put these on. Although, a girl like you may like it." He swung the cuffs like a hypnotist. "You like it rough like that? You want to take another swing at me?"

Annie took a deep breath but remained silent.

"All right. That's a good girl. Why don't we make it easy for the two of us? I'll follow you out, and you wait at the front desk. I'll go fetch your boyfriend."

———————

Annie walked around the table slowly, keeping an eye on Wells. She headed out the door and went straight to the front desk. The sergeant pulled out the large envelope that she'd emptied the contents of her pockets into when she'd arrived. He turned it over, and her lip gloss and iPhone tumbled out. She looked at the phone and turned it on, then uncapped the gloss and put a swirl on her lips.

The same cop who'd dragged them to the station walked into the room. "You're next, Suarez. Stand up."

Hank did what the cop said. He had stayed wide awake since Riggins had left, anticipating the arrival of a federal agent or a lawyer or anyone but this big cop. This was a concerning development. McGinley would not trust him in the hands of a local policeman. Something was wrong.

"I'm still waiting to call my lawyer."

"Well, I got word from the chief. Your lawyer called. You're going home."

The chief, he thought. It wasn't like McGinley to get local police involved like this. He couldn't shake a feeling that he'd had since the shootout at the house. *Where the hell was the backup?* This was nothing like any operation he remembered. Usually, things were buttoned up. Gunplay in a domestic neighborhood, local cops on the scene ... none of it made sense.

There was nothing he could do about it now. This operation was still active, and if the plan had gone wrong, he had no way of knowing. The only choice he had was to continue relying on McGinley to do the right thing. He walked around the table and out the door.

Annie saw Hank come out of the room and it was all she could do not to run over to him. Not to embrace him, but to scream, "What the hell is going on?" She didn't do either. Instead, she looked at him and screamed with her eyes. He saw it and gave no other response than an *I don't know* look.

She stepped away from the desk to let him get his belongings. A watch, wallet, and his universal remote. Without a word, Wells started walking toward the front door. Annie looked over at Hank again and got the same silent response. They both followed the big cop out.

Shizi sat up in the car when he saw the three exit the building. He called Sheng.

"They're coming with our cop."

Sheng was right on it. "I have them. Yes. Here they come."

"How close should I follow?"

"Wait for them to leave the parking lot. I have a good view. You can stay a safe distance away. Leave your phone line open and on speaker. If Officer Wells strays from his assigned task, I will let you know. I want you to follow him in and then block his patrol car in the driveway. Do you understand?"

"You're not going to let the policeman go, are you? I still get to kill him?"

"Of course, you are going to kill him. You have done a fine job, and you deserve your reward."

"Thank you, sir."

Wells walked to his patrol car with Hank and Annie following close behind. They both scanned the lot instinctively but saw nothing. The sun was starting to come up. Even though it was very early, it felt like it would be a hot day. Wells went to the driver's door without saying a word. Annie and Hank split up and went to either side and got in. They pulled out without a siren or lights.

Milan was watching them leave from his laptop. He knew he would have to give them plenty of room. The watcher was still in the lot, hadn't even turned his lights on yet. The patrol car was moving out of sight range, yet the watcher sat there. It hit Milan that there must be some other form of surveillance. The watcher wouldn't let them get so far away without making a move. Sheng must have an eye in the sky. He quickly made an inventory of all their movements in the last half a day. They'd stayed out of range during the shoot-out. His gut had been right to stay back on that. He also had kept a wide berth of the watcher's car when he'd driven into the lot. Both decisions played out in their favor. *The little things,* he thought. Even the little things had to be done with precision. It sometimes surprised him how making what seemed like a minor tactical decision could come back to haunt or help an operation. In this case, his decisions had helped. Staying away had been the only thing that prevented this whole thing from going to hell a while back. He was reasonably sure that Sheng did not know about him, or The Monk. The eye in the sky did raise a major problem. He would have to wait with The Monk in this car until the cop took them wherever he was going. It wouldn't be back to the house. That much was sure. The cop was taking them to Sheng. It was happening now.

He heard the watcher's engine turn over. The Monk leaned forward like a German shepherd anticipating the car moving. Milan put his hand on his chest.

"We have to wait. Stay alert. We will see action soon."

Chapter 31

They turned right out of the lot and proceeded along Katama Way. Hank and Annie stayed silent in the back seat of the car. They glanced at each other once, then looked forward. The sun was starting to come up to his right. It was as dark red as a beet.

They were both hungry, tired, and lost in thought. Assuming they were on their way to Hank's house, Annie thought about a shower and a change of clothes. Something to eat and a cup of coffee would be nice too. They hadn't eaten in almost twelve hours. She wondered if there was anything she could put together in the kitchen for a hearty breakfast. It was her way to cope with stress. A type of meditation method she had learned from her mom. When she needed to calm down, she would imagine a meal preparation in her mind. Going step by step, she would think of a meal, then lay the ingredients on the countertop. She would add each item to the bowl. Once they were added, she would mix slowly, deliberately. When everything was blended properly, she would put it in the oven, and then emerge from her imagination refreshed and focused.

Annie was still whisking the eggs when Hank spoke.

"Why are you turning onto Herring Creek Road?" He was leaning forward and talking to the cop, who did not respond to the question.

"Why go this way? You're going out of the way. You'll have to circle back when you get to the airport."

The cop responded by locking the doors. The snap of the locks was like a shot to Annie's head. She shifted from *cook* to *cop* instantaneously.

Hank started rattling the cage divider in front of them.

"Hey, man. What the hell? Answer me." He sounded panicked.

The cop's answer was to speed up. Annie looked around her for landmarks, in case she would need to tell someone where they were. She looked behind them and saw a lone car about a half mile back. It had its foglights on—a sign to her that they were being followed by a professional. A citizen would be using full lights most likely—most people didn't even think about foglights. She turned to Hank and put her hand on his arm and gently pulled it away from the cage in front of him.

She whispered to him, "We have to be calm now." She held his arm tightly and nodded with her head to the back window.

Hank turned around. He turned back to her and mouthed, "Following us?" Annie shrugged and gestured with her palms down to stay calm. Hank sat back. Annie continued to look around for information. She was hoping to see a mile marker, but did not.

They came to a three-way intersection. In front of them was some sort of café or diner. Behind the diner was a small airfield. They took the second left onto Mattakesett Way. Annie had the direction from the police station firmly planted in her head. She could get back blindfolded if she had to. The road turned from asphalt to hard-packed dirt about a half mile in. To the left was what looked like a farm, and on the other side was a string of long, pebbled driveways. None of the houses were visible from the road. Annie turned back again and saw the car behind her. It still had its foglights on, and it gave Annie a chill. A trained agent following them would know to turn off their lights before entering a straight path. This wasn't their backup; it was an escort.

She and Hank were on their own. Again. A quick thought of punching Frank McGinley's ugly face crossed her mind, but only briefly. She knew that a clear head was of paramount importance. She had no access to a weapon and was likely to be boxed in at any moment. All she could do now was to keep her wits about her and make sure that Hank remained calm. She reached over and held his hand. She could feel the panic radiating from him as they pulled into the gravel driveway. They proceeded around a bend after going about twenty yards. Annie looked behind her to see that the street was no longer visible.

Chapter 32

Milan watched the patrol car and the trail car from his laptop. As soon as he saw the following car turn into the desolate dirt road, he handed the computer to The Monk and turned the ignition. He lit out of the parking lot at high speed. There was no doubt in his mind they were going to kill the woman. There was no scenario where they wouldn't. He had to admit to himself that it was the logical move. The streets were deserted as he hit the main road at over eighty miles per hour. Eyes focused straight ahead, he addressed The Monk. He had no time for his game of solitude.

"I need recon. What's happening now?"

The Monk didn't answer. He tried to lean the laptop into a position where Milan could see it from the driver's seat.

"Goddamn it. I don't have time for this shit. They're going to kill that girl. Give me a fucking answer."

The patrol car came to a stop facing an aluminum garage door. The yellow light of a motion detector came on, shining through the windshield and up to Hank's and Annie's thighs in the back seat. The rest of their bodies were still in relative darkness. The two of them sat in silent recognition that this was an abduction. The cop had brought them to Sheng. Annie and Hank realized things would move fast now. Unable to speak freely, they independently thought of ways out of this mess. Hank squeezed

Annie's hand a little tighter. The sound of crunching gravel broke the silence. A car pulled up behind them. No doubt it was the car that had been trailing them since they left the police station. Annie turned around in the back seat to see who it was. The lights were out, but she could make out a lone man in the driver's seat. He cut the engine and got out of the car. The cop opened his door and walked around the back of the patrol car to greet him.

<hr />

Visions of that bloody apartment twelve years ago were flashing through Milan's head. The sight of McGinley's girlfriend cut open from neck to waist was as clear to him as the dashboard in front of him. The Monk finally spoke. He sounded exactly how Milan thought he would. He spoke like a Marine.

"They pulled into a driveway. Big house, garage in front. They're waiting. Okay, now the trail car pulled in, boxing them in." Milan pushed the pedal to ninety. "The cop just got out of the car, one man in the trail car. He's out. They're meeting at the side of the cop car."

<hr />

Wells didn't attempt a handshake. He looked at Shizi with a smirk.

"All right. I did your fucking job for you. I got them here."

Shizi didn't respond. He looked past Wells to the driveway to estimate where the splatter of his head would land. It would be his responsibility to clean up. It would be a problem if any blood or other residue were found after they left the island. He took a step to his left to induce Wells to slide over a few feet as well; the backsplash would clear the patrol car. Wells obediently took the few steps. He spoke again.

"You're not talking to me? Okay. That's fine. Here's the way it's going to happen. You take him up to your boss. I'll bring the broad back to the house. What you do with him, I could give shit."

Shizi reached behind his back for the gun tucked in the back of his pants. Wells continued.

"After you bring him up, come back down with my card." Again, Shizi didn't respond, but he did smile. "Why you fucking standing there? Move your ass."

Shizi pulled out the gun and shot Wells in the face.

Annie jumped in her seat at the sight of the shot, which she clearly witnessed but barely heard because of the silencer on the gun. It almost seemed like a movie. Hank was looking forward but turned when Wells's body fell next to his passenger window. He turned to Annie in panic.

"Holy shit. Holy shit. What the hell?"

Annie didn't have time to panic. She held her hand up to him. "Shut up. I'm thinking."

She looked through the cage in the patrol car. There was a shotgun mounted on the driver's side in front of her. She looked to the side of the cage, but there was no way to wrap her arms around it and reach the shotgun. Annie quickly realized it was futile. Every cop car she had ever been in had the same setup. She cursed herself for not thinking clearly. She turned to Hank and put both hands on his arms.

"Listen. They're going to kill me. I just saw him kill a cop, and they don't need me for anything. You have to keep your head and save yourself. They want you. Forget about me. All of your thoughts now should be about how to stay alive."

Hank stared at her in disbelief. He tried to lift his arms but she held fast.

"Annie, no. I still believe we're going to get out of this. I believe in the Volunteers."

Annie shook her head. "Face it, Hank. Your guy blew it. There's no way out of this for me."

The man opened Hank's door.

"C'mon, get out." He waved the gun at Hank.

Hank turned and stared into her eyes. "I'm not going without you."

Annie pushed him on the shoulder. "Go."

Hank turned away from Annie and looked into the cage in front of him.

"Move it," the man said.

Hank hesitated a beat then looked up at the man who stood over him. The man pressed the gun flat against Hank's forehead. Hank sat firm.

"Fuck you and fuck Sheng. I'm not getting out of this car without her."

The man cocked the pistol and shot. He put a hole in the floorboard of the car. The back seat smelled of burnt metal. Hank closed his eyes.

"Kill me, you fuck. Fucking kill me."

The man spoke in a calm voice. "She can come with us. Get out of the car."

Hank took a moment to consider the words, then stepped out of the car. Annie slid across the back seat and got out behind him. The man put the gun to the back of Annie's head. She felt the heat from the barrel. The man looked over at Hank.

"If you do anything stupid, like try to run, I shoot her in the head."

Hank started toward the back of the house. "Yes. I understand. Now let's go speak to Sheng."

———

The Monk fell silent.

Milan turned to him. "What? What the hell?"

"He shot the cop. Head shot."

"What about the two of them?"

"It looks like there may have been another shot inside the car. They're stepping out of the car now."

"The girl. She shot?"

"No, not yet. He's got the gun to her head and he's walking them around the garage to the back of the house. I lost them." The Monk tried to massage the touchpad without success, then looked forward. "I don't know how to work this software. You're going to have to take it. I'll drive."

Milan was already planning the assault. "No time. Look for a place to set up. Keep in mind there is likely an eye in the sky."

"Okay, okay. Let's see." He leaned into the screen. "There's a resort of some type across the road from the house. I could set up there. I'm not sure of a sight line, but if I get on the roof, I'm pretty sure I can get an angle to the driveway." He looked around some more. "The only access to the back of the house would be from the dunes between the house and the beach road."

Milan pulled off the road——throwing gravel and dirt six feet in the air. "Gimme." The Monk handed the laptop over. The protocol for the operation went into effect at that moment. Milan's job was to spot and identify the best way to get The Monk to deploy his skill. Milan on tactics, The Monk on the trigger.

The Monk could feel his pulse rate slowing. He was instinctively going into shooter's mode.

Milan stared at the screen and waited a few seconds to speak. He turned it sideways to show The Monk and pointed with his finger.

"Okay. I'm going to pull into the resort parking lot. No rooftop. Remember that he has a satellite view. Here, at the end of the parking lot, I think I can get us within ten yards of the tree line. We'll need cover from the satellite. Hopefully, we'll make the ten yards without notice. We can work our way through the brush from here to across the street from Sheng's place."

Milan plotted the route with his finger on the touchpad as the curser tracked the route.

"Can you get a straight shot from here?" Milan stopped the little arrow at a spot in the brush across from the curved driveway.

The Monk leaned in and looked closely.

"Plenty of trees. I'll find something. No, no problem. I'll get my shot."

Milan looked over at him. The Monk was as intense as a prize fighter heading into the ring.

"Okay, good. You follow me once we get to the lot. I'll get to the base of the driveway and signal with my flashlight when I'm in position. Don't signal back. You'll be facing the house. I'll assume you are good."

"Got it."

"Pack your rifle away; we're heading over to the parking lot." Before pulling out, Milan turned to The Monk. "Listen, this turns to shit, you know what to do."

The Monk nodded, and Milan pulled out onto the road.

Chapter 33

Hank could feel the moisture in the air as he reached the top step. The gray deck was so weather-beaten that it looked like it may collapse under the weight of the three of them. He looked out to the ocean to see the sun, half up now, shrouded in a morning haze. Yes, it would be a hot one. He moved to the center of the deck to allow Annie and the man to get up the stairs. There was only one way he could think of to find a way out of this. He would try to negotiate with his life for Annie's survival. It was clear that Sheng would go to great lengths to keep him alive. Otherwise, they both would have been dead long ago. The fact that the man agreed to take Annie along was telling. To take an unnecessary risk was the antithesis of everything Hank knew about Sheng.

Hank knew that he had to stall for time. There had to be someone out there backing them up. He had been a part of many Volunteer operations and never once had things gotten this far without some form of intervention. There was a very good chance that Annie could have been killed not two minutes ago in the car. The man could have killed her and wounded him. He could easily be in the trunk of that car now. None of this made sense. What bothered him most was that he had no control over his own life at this point. It was like walking through traffic blindfolded, not knowing what was going to run him down or when.

A frightening thought suddenly came to him. What if there was no backup? What if it was better for the Volunteers, for the country, if he was sent to China? Or killed? He knew an awful lot of things that could make men in powerful positions very uncomfortable. With a new president, a new administration, he couldn't know the new power players. Since the FBI chief had been fired, there could very well have been a purge in the Bureau. The CIA, NSA, those fucking spooks——there was no way of knowing their priorities. They could all be cleaning house, and he could be just another piece of trash.

Annie stepped up onto the deck with the man still pressing the gun against her head. She managed a weak smile, and Hank smiled back. *Stall for time*, he thought. *Keep believing and push the doubts away.* There was nothing else to do.

The man looked at Hank.

"Open the door."

Hank walked over to the sliding glass door and pulled it open. A stale smell hit him like a handful of dust. He wondered when this door was last opened. Hank knew that smell. He'd spent half his life engulfed in it. He'd thrown out clothes when even a washing couldn't remove the smell. It was the odor of the room of a binge coder. A cave. An airless, soundless, showerless environment. The rank odor had a common moniker. BO. Body odor. Hank had seen coders go weeks not leaving their room. Top-level programmers could fall into a fugue state. A type of self-hypnosis. Sheng was the acknowledged master of this discipline. It was his method. Hank had heard that Sheng had taught his team in China this form of self-induced mania. Since he had accomplished so much with his Chinese hacking team, it seemed like the stories were true. Sheng had them all coding like mad men. The smell told Hank that Sheng would be in an erratic state. He would be functioning on very little sleep and food. Dealing with someone in such a state could be very volatile. Hank had to stay alert to find an angle to save Annie's life.

He walked into the dark room. The only light came from a bank of laptops spread across the kitchen island. Half of the room was shrouded in a faint glow. The half where Hank stood was starting to brighten from the hazy sunlight from outside. He waited for Annie and the man to enter behind him. Once all were in the room, the man pushed Hank in the back to move him forward and closed the door behind him. He pointed with the gun to a leather couch. Hank headed toward it, but the man stopped him.

"No. Not you. Her. She can sit. You stand here."

Annie walked over to the couch and sat. She looked over at Hank with her big, brown eyes. He felt like shit. He got her into this dilemma. He knew that she had no idea of the level of danger that could come her way from all of this. He was sure that McGinley bullshitted her to get her on board, because the man had done the same to him when he'd been recruited. Using people for the greater good. Hank never once thought of the moral repercussions of it until someone he cared about was in danger because of it. *Et Omnia Recta* seemed like a reckless vigilante motto now that he was looking at those brown eyes. He did care for her. He knew that now. A little late for sentiment, but there it was. He hadn't given a shit about much lately. Now, though ... now that he had found something, someone, to care about, he would fight for it.

Sheng's head popped up from behind the bank of laptops. He was Hank's age, but looked at least ten years older. Hank wondered when he had last been outdoors.

Sheng stared at Hank and rose from his chair.

"The great Pap Martinez has come to pay a visit."

Hank didn't move. Sheng walked from around the kitchen island. He was older and frailer than Hank would have imagined. It had been over fifteen years since he had last seen Sheng. It was at a conference of some sort in San Jose, California. Sheng was a visiting Chinese scientist; Hank was on his way to his first hundred million. They went back further than that even. To MIT, where they were top students. Sheng was a little shit even then. Hank remembered his temper, the tantrums he would throw. Before the start of their junior year, Sheng was gone. Went back to China. Their only interaction since the conference was when Sheng had Hank kidnapped, drugged, and held ransom on behalf of another criminal. Sheng's payoff for that job was his escape from China. Hank's was the setting for his false death. They both had received something from it. Hank had paid a high price of course. Sheng ... well, Hank didn't give a shit about any price he may have paid.

Sheng walked across the room with a broad smile.

"It has been a long time. Yes, a long time." He circled around Hank with his arms behind his back. A man evaluating livestock.

"You look good, Pap. Yes. You have taken good care of yourself since I last had you taken against your will. You really must find better help. This keeps happening. No. This is not very good for you, Pap. A great man like yourself getting kidnapped not once but twice, by the same man no less. How smart can you truly be?" Sheng paused, as if waiting for Hank to respond. Hank refused to say a word at this point. Sheng continued. "Such a great man. A hero to his country. A spy against mine, but that is the way it goes. No? A hero or a spy, it all depends on what side you're on."

He then turned to Annie. His man was standing silently by the side of the couch, the gun still pointed at her head. Sheng walked over to her and leaned down. "Did you know that you were in the company of such a great man? The greatest spy in the world, after me of course."

She did not look him in the eye as he spoke. Sheng leaned in closer.

"Did you know when you shot those men that you were protecting a mass murderer? I knew. I know Pap Martinez better than anyone. He created your drone technology." He straightened and pointed back at Hank. "This man here. He is responsible for thousands of deaths. Innocents. Sure, your government claims they were only targeting terrorists. You can ask him. Ask him about the schools, the playgrounds bombed. Ask him about the thousands of soldiers executed in my country because he jammed our government communications. He knew, you see. He ran the program to trace back to the military. He knew there would be retributions. He's an assassin. A hired killer for the capitalists of the world. It's the money. Ask him. Ask him how much money he has. A billion? Who knows? He tried to fake his death. Tried to fool Sheng. No one can fool Sheng. I know. I know all of it. I know you are here alone. I have a satellite system set up. The police asked him about the drone, and he hired you to protect him. You are police, I would assume?" He raised a hand to Annie, as if to stop her from commenting. She was looking at him now, and her expression was turning from blankness to one of concern. "Now don't lie to me. I saw. I watched you dispatch those men. Did you think that would be my lone attempt on Mr. Martinez here? Did you think those men would be my soldiers? It was a game. A game, you see. How can you be so foolish to think I would send such men to capture the great Pap Martinez?"

He stared at Annie's puzzled face and smiled broadly. He threw his head back and clapped his hands, then looked at Shizi.

"She doesn't know. She doesn't know! This is wonderful." He turned back to Pap. "You put her in such danger based on deception. Oh, Pap. I see it now. You lied to her. Lied to get what you wanted. The greatest liar of all. Pap Martinez. Did you lie to get in her pants?" He swiveled back to Annie. "Did he?"

Annie didn't answer. She glared at Sheng and thought about how she would like to punch his punk face in.

Chapter 34

Annie turned her glare to Hank. It was true. Hank was Pap Martinez. She could see it now. The hair. Maybe his chin and ears were different, the teeth also, but it was him. She had seen the YouTube video of what she had assumed, along with the rest of the world, to be his death. She thought back to everything he had said over the last day and wondered how much of it was lies. She had been lied to from the start. McGinley, that lying sack of shit, put her in grave danger. Annie wondered if her father knew what was going on. He would have never approved this. McGinley had to be lying to him also.

Pap Martinez. *Jesus*, she thought. She had spent the last day with one of the most influential Americans of the last twenty years. Every New York cop knew what Martinez had done for the city. He was a hero to many New York cops and firemen. The money he gave for 9/11 families was well known. His thesis on anti-terrorist security was the template for the department. The things he had said last night were starting to gain perspective and weight. Annie realized that Pap's idle musings could very well have had or could soon have a global impact.

She understood now why she couldn't know who he was. What she couldn't understand was why none of the big agencies, the FBI or NSA, were involved. There was no way she should be here. No way that she was even remotely qualified for such an assignment. Annie was completely puzzled. She hoped that the kindness, the soft words, and the comfort he had provided her as she spoke about her mother wasn't also a lie.

As if on cue, Sheng provided some clarity as he spoke to Martinez. "You didn't tell her? Oh, such a liar you are." He then spun to face Annie again, his demeanor becoming more frenzied. "Tell me now, young lady. Did he tell you how much danger you were in? How did he hire you? I see everything. I saw you get in the car outside of the gym. I watched you walk the grounds at the house. I watched you dispatch those men. Done with such efficiency. Yes, I do appreciate a direct woman. In a different time, perhaps I could have offered you a job. Maybe work with Shizi here." He smiled, but Shizi remained stoic. "Yes, that would be better. You are much more pleasant to look at than Shizi." He turned to Shizi. "What do you think, my friend? Do you think I would enjoy her company to yours? Come now, do not be such a bear. We could all work together, no?"

Shizi shifted in his stance and answered, "Whatever you think, sir."

Sheng let out a laugh and reached up to clap Shizi on the shoulder.

"Yes, yes. Oh, she is pretty all right. Still, I prefer you." He laughed again. He walked back to the kitchen island and briefly slipped behind the fortress of laptops. After scanning the screens, he spoke from behind them.

"No one out there. No one follows. Like you, young lady, at first I was confused. I can see the doubt on your face. You must be asking: why? Why would you be all alone here with this man? Where are the soldiers? If this is the great Pap Martinez, why would the entire United States Army not be out there? I do not know how you were hired. That is something I must know. How did he find you? Who sent you? We will find that out later. Shizi can be very persistent with his questions. It is clear that you have been sent to die for him. He will try to negotiate with me, of course. As Americans, you all feel that there is always a deal to be made. Perhaps he will offer you up as a mistress to me. Yes, that would be an American tactic. Offer the woman to save the man."

He walked out from behind the screens with a gun in his hand. He walked slowly around Pap. Not addressing anyone in particular. He walked and waved the gun.

Annie was starting to get really confused. Sheng was jumping from thought to thought. He walked over to the glass door and looked outside. The room was silent for thirty seconds. A lifetime.

He turned and walked back to the couch and addressed Annie directly. "You see, we are both fugitives from our own country. I fell out of favor with my superiors, and I imagine that Pap has done the same. We know so many things." Pap was still standing by the side of the couch so Sheng spoke to the back of his head. "We know so much, don't we? It can be a threat to leaders who are not as knowledgeable as we are. They think about what we know. What we can use to unseat them. This makes men in power very uncomfortable. Yes. It is a great burden to be us. Is it not, Mr. Martinez?"

Pap didn't respond, but looked at Annie instead. She could see something like regret in his eyes. She stared at him, wanting to believe that he was for real, that he was the type of man she hoped he was.

Pap stood taller then and spoke for the first time. "I hired her for the day. I thought you would have a satellite feed. After all, you were the one to first master that hack. I sent a letter. An old-fashioned paper letter, in the mail. Didn't think of that, did you? I planned for this in case you caught up with me. She knows nothing. She's former NYPD. Disgraced, thrown off the force for insubordination. She was supposed to provide security until I could make plans for my departure. I have no argument with you, Sheng. I can make a deal, yes. I can offer you a way out from this life on the run. They'll take you. My government. They do it all the time; you know this. They'll take you. You'll have your own lab. Whatever you want. You'll live better under my government than you could ever live in China."

Sheng smiled. "But what will become of you?"

"I'll continue to run. You're correct. I'm not just running from you. My own country wants me silenced. I turned off too many people over the years. It's my greed, my arrogance. You were right about me all along. I believe you are in a similar position."

Sheng slapped Pap hard across the face, and Annie jumped slightly at the sound. "Don't toy with me. You have no idea about my situation. Manipulate and lie."

Pap held strong, insistent. "It can work. I have a number of places I can go. This is no lie. Like you, I do know too much for my country to be comfortable with me. There was an election. They want me out, but it would be a great political victory to have you. Let me take out my phone.

I can arrange it in a minute, but you can't kill another cop. Not NYPD. You must know this. They'll chase you down. There won't be a deal if you kill a New York cop."

"And what of a Massachusetts policeman?" Sheng turned back to Shizi. "You see now how the Americans work? Making an arrangement for me to turn on you for my freedom. Sure, give them a cop killer. That would enhance my bargaining position; maybe they'll give me a prison cell with a view. Police, police. Always a problem to eliminate. This country has too much respect for law enforcement. In China there is no such reverence. We see the police for who they are. Racketeers, extortionists. Always with a hand out. No, no Pap. My loyalty goes to my men, not a badge. I'm not an American huckster. I believe in rewarding my trusted soldiers. I don't turn them in. I think I will allow Shizi the pleasure of torturing this little bitch. Yes. You can watch and see how your lies hurt people. That would be fun. She will tell us how she got here."

He turned to Annie, and she thought about how he was so much like a spinning top, whirling around on the floor.

He said to her, "You will tell us, yes?" He then threw his hands in the air. "Enough talk now. You are both coming with us. I have a plane ready. When we get out far enough, we will throw the fat cop out the door. If the lovely, young lady wants to tell us more, she can make the journey with you, Mr. Martinez. It is true that we cannot leave a dead policewoman behind us. It will make things far too complicated. If she is a cop at all." He jabbed a finger at Pap. "You are such a smooth liar. It is impossible to know what is true. You will come with us. Shizi will work the girl for information. If she cooperates, you will have a companion on your journey. If not, she flies like the fat man. We will be far gone by the time they find the bodies. You will be in China, and I will be enjoying my freedom." He turned and pointed the gun at Annie.

She knew there was no way she was going to live through this. They were going to throw her out of the plane along with the fat cop no matter what she said or did. They wouldn't find her body. And if they ever did, Sheng would be far away somewhere, impossible to find.

Sheng approached her and said, "I think you may be a problem. This is going to hurt."

He shot her in the foot. Annie screamed, and Shizi reached down and covered her mouth with his big hand. Pap started toward her, but Sheng put the gun in his face. "You want her to live, you come easy. Perhaps I will change my mind. Maybe she can come with us. She is quite pretty." He turned to Annie. "Stay quiet, and I will have Shizi tend to the wound. Another sound and I kill you here."

Annie stopped screaming but the pain brought tears to her eyes. She rolled onto her side and pulled her leg up to her body. Sheng shooed Pap over to the couch next to her, and she felt Pap's arms around her.

Sheng yelled at Shizi, "Go now. Get a tourniquet and some bandages from the kit. We do not want her to lose her foot, do we? Go. I will watch them."

Annie rocked in Pap's arms as she writhed in pain. Shizi came back with a first-aid kit and applied a tourniquet and bandages with surprising skill. After he finished dressing the wound, he rolled Annie to her side and bound her hands behind her back with a zip-tie handcuff. He did the same to Pap.

Sheng was typing frantically on each of his laptops. He said to Shizi, "Let's get them down to the car. I wiped out all of my data. Put them in the trunk, then come back up here for the laptops. Is everything else packed away?"

"Yes sir. We are ready to leave."

"Okay. Let's go then."

Chapter 35

Milan and The Monk got out of the car and walked the few steps to the brush surrounding the parking lot of the resort. It was thick with exposed roots in the sand to step over. Both men had seen far worse and made their way through swiftly and quietly. Milan already had the route committed to memory from his laptop surveillance. He led The Monk around the bend near the end of the property that ran alongside the road where the target house sat. Once they turned and began to walk parallel to the road, The Monk started looking up to the treetops. He would have to climb. There were only a few trees high enough for him to have a view of the house over the remaining tree line. He thought about the slope of the driveway bend. He would have to go past the house and set up beyond the entrance. That would mean passing in view of the garage. The Monk tapped Milan on the shoulder. He pointed toward his chest and signaled that he was going to go deeper into the brush to pass by the house. He then pointed up to a tree that he saw about a hundred yards away. It was certainly tall enough for a perch, and looked sturdy. Milan nodded.

The Monk had the proper rifle for the job. The M110 semi-automatic with AN/PVS-10 night sight. He thought that he may not need the night sight, depending on the angle of the rising sun. He had chambered the rifle and balanced the scope as they pulled into the parking lot. He had been dismantling and reassembling the weapon since they'd arrived on the island.

Only once in his career did he have a misfire. It was in Iraq, and sand had jammed the trigger mechanism. He was able to recover from that without any adverse repercussions, but he'd learned a valuable lesson. One that he would never forget. Clean your weapon.

The rifle was ready and would fire smoothly. It would require minimal adjustments once he got to the top of the tree. He was glad that he'd kept the strap. Since his balance could be compromised in the tree, it would be good to use the strap to wrap around his arm for leverage. He came to the tree and looked up. The lowest branch was about eight feet above him. He stabilized the weapon behind his back and jumped. He grabbed the thick branch with both hands and walked his legs up the trunk. The moment he was able to swing one of his legs around the branch, he swiveled up to his belly, flat on the limb, without the rifle touching anything. He reached up to the next branch, which was not quite four feet up, and started his climb. Within a minute, he was near the top of the tree. He swayed a little, but as he held his breath and steadied his movements, the tree stabilized.

The Monk looked out across the road and could see the garage clearly. It was about fifty yards away, he estimated. The scope would confirm it, of course. But he had complete confidence in his feel for the shot. From this distance, he could hit heads on a spinning dime.

Milan was in position in the brush across the street from the house. The Monk saw the brief flash from Milan's mini flashlight.

The Monk then leaned his back against the trunk of the tree. He had one leg wrapped around the branch for balance and the other knee bent so he could rest the rifle on it. Wrapping the strap tightly around his left forearm, he pulled the rifle onto his kneecap. He was stable and in shooting position. He could stay like this for hours.

He scoped the garage door and made his adjustments to widen the perspective. He honed in on the police officer to make his adjustments. Only the cop's lower body was visible from this angle. There was no movement. It was rare to have such a close shot. He thought for a moment that he should make the shot without the scope, but that would require disassembling it from the mount. There may not be time. They could come out any second. It worried him that he may not be able to get everyone in the frame of his scope at once if they came out separately. There was the chance that he would have to take up to five shots.

He calmed himself and allowed his heartbeat to slow. The Monk found that place in his mind that slowed everything down. Years of training went into the next ten seconds. He was trance-like in his concentration. The shot would happen. It would find Sheng.

Chapter 36

Annie tried as hard as she could to contain her moaning, though the pain was great. She wanted to speak to Pap, to tell him to stop standing up for her. They were going to kill her. It made sense that they didn't want to leave a police officer's body lying around. They'll throw her and the other cop out of the plane without a second thought. She hoped she would be as dead as that fat bastard before they tossed her. The idea of dropping from that height was the focus of many of her nightmares. She would force them to shoot her if she had to.

The man walked over to the door and slid it open. Sheng stood over Pap and Annie on the couch.

"I'm very sorry for putting you in such pain, but you strike me as the kind of woman who would put up a fuss. So now we go. You go quietly, and I don't shoot the other foot. Let's go."

Annie looked up at him like he was fucking crazy, because he was.

Pap stood and helped her up. Annie grimaced through the pain as she rose. The man walked over and took her by the zip tie cuffs. They dug into her wrists, and he used them like a tiller to steer her forward. Sheng did the same with Pap.

Annie went out the back door first and squinted in the sun. It had fully risen while they were inside. The man steered her left to the deck stairs. No one spoke. They went down the steps slowly and carefully. They were so narrow and steep that each person had to take one step at a time. Annie down one, then the man. Pap down one, then Sheng. To the bottom. They got to the gravel walkway at the base of the steps and headed toward the garage in front of the house.

Milan heard the crunching of the gravel. Lifting his flashlight, he sent one flash in the direction of The Monk's tree. He didn't turn; his focus was directly on the side of the house where the sounds of steps were coming from. The girl came around the corner first. The big man was behind her. Next came Hank Suarez with a little man almost completely hidden behind him.

The Monk spotted the girl, limping, possibly shot in right foot. The man was taller, a clear shot. Hank Suarez came next with a man behind him, smaller. From this angle, he could barely identify him. The man looked up, and The Monk had him. It was Sheng. The Monk shot the big man first. One shot. Forehead. Clean. As the man fell dead, The Monk turned the rifle toward Suarez. He couldn't get a clean shot at Sheng. He waited. One, two, three. He took aim at Suarez's right shoulder. The shot should go through and disable Sheng, which would allow for a kill shot. Suarez would have to be compromised for this to work. The shot would clearly peirce his lung. He prepared to seal the deal.

The Monk heard a shot then a second. Sheng slumped down to his left, and Suarez bent over in pain. As Sheng fell clear of Suarez, The Monk made a head shot before he hit the ground. He turned back to the girl. He smiled and took his finger off the trigger.

He'd kept the time in his head. The firefight had taken eight seconds.

The big man went down in a heap on top of her. He was dead. It happened too fast for Annie to remember; she just knew. Knew that the mission was to kill Sheng. The shooting would continue until he was dead. With Pap in the way, he would be killed as well. She reacted. She saw the big man's gun not two inches from her. She rolled over in the gravel and grabbed for it behind her back. Annie didn't fumble with it. She grabbed it and gripped. She estimated where Sheng and Pap were standing and fired low in that direction, figuring that it wouldn't be a kill shot but might provide clearance for the guy—she assumed a sniper—who had shot the man.

After that, she heard two shots.

Chapter 37

Milan walked up the driveway, pistol cocked. He saw Annie lying on her side. Blood was oozing out of her foot. She tried to take aim at him from behind her back, but he spoke.

"Et Omnia Recta."

She dropped the gun.

"Motherfucker. About fucking time. How is he?"

"Who you asking about?"

"Hank."

"Looks like a shoulder. He's down, but he'll make it. How about you?"

Annie had to know. "Sheng. Did you get him?"

"Not me, but yeah, he's dead."

"Good. Fuck 'im."

"How are you?"

"My foot hurts."

Milan crouched down and took a closer look. He picked her foot up, and she winced.

"It looks like it went clean through. It will hurt like a bitch, but you'll be okay. So you know, lots of bones down there. Recovery will take a while."

"Did I hit anyone?"

"Nah. Your shot hit the garage. What did you expect, shooting from behind your back? You hit the garage door, and it spooked Sheng. He panicked and let off a round. It grazed Suarez but cleared a space for the shooter. Ballsy move, though."

Annie smiled. "Yeah, I guess."

"What's your name?"

"Annie."

The Monk walked up the driveway with the rifle at shooting position. He lowered it when he got within ten feet of Milan and Annie.

Milan chuckled and turned to The Monk. "Look. It's fucking Annie Oakley."

Chapter 38

The Monk scooped Annie up like he was ladling water. He brought her around to the back of the house and laid her down in the dewy grass without a word. He returned with the big man and tossed him in a heap near the side under the deck. He went back to the front of the house and came back with Sheng under his right arm. He carried him as easily as a sack of laundry and tossed him on top of the other man. Annie managed to get up on one elbow.

"What about Hank? Is he going to be okay?"

He didn't answer as he returned to the front of the house. Annie lay back and closed her eyes. The foot was throbbing, and she hoped help was coming soon. The other man said it was his shoulder. His shoulder. *Can't be that bad, can it?* She closed her eyes.

Once the bodies were secured, Milan pulled his cell phone out of his pocket. While he waited for it to boot up, he looked at his watch: 6:20 a.m. It had been a long night. He closed his eyes and tilted his head back to face the sky. He gave a silent thanks that the girl was okay. He then glanced at his phone; it was ready for him to make the call to McGinley.

McGinley picked up on the first ring. "Charles, how are we?"

"All secure, Frank."

"Sheng?"

"Dead."

"The others?"

"He had a bodyguard; he's dead. There's also a local cop dead. Not our shot. The bodyguard took him out. The girl and your man are wounded but should be fine."

"Shit. A dead officer."

"The cop was working for Sheng. Likely, he was blackmailed to cooperate. He was dirty."

"No matter. A cop's a cop."

"Yeah."

"How bad are the wounds?"

"The girl's worse than our man. Her foot. His shoulder. I gave a quick look; the foot was shot straight through and the shoulder was a graze. We were lucky on this one, Frank. We cut it too close."

"I knew this one would be bad. We had no support. Just your instincts. You're a solid man, Charles."

"Want to tell me who this motherfucker is that we went through this trouble for?"

"Can't do it, Charles. Sorry. Besides, the mission was Sheng."

"Yeah, I know. You made that clear."

There was a pause, and Milan silently cursed McGinley for unnecessarily putting innocent lives at risk.

"Who knows?" Frank asked. "How big is the net here?"

'It's big. Half of New England knows about the drone. The local chief was all over this. Did a hell of a job with what he had to work with. I think we go big on this. The cop was part of it, but I think we can use him to feed the media. Local hero bullshit."

"Yeah. That's good. Get the chief on the line. Have him go very big with this, I agree. I'm talking helicopters and sirens. I'll contact Director Koontz and get a shitload of agents over there. I want this in all the papers. I can feed some info to the *Times* and the *Wall Street Journal*." He paused then came back. "Yeah, I like it. Local cops take down Chinese spy. Okay. Get our man to the designated drop point at the airport. I want them wheels up before the police arrive. "

"On it." Milan didn't hesitate. He disconnected and turned to The Monk.

"Get our man out. You know the drop point. Take this car. Do you have the keys?"

The Monk looked inside the vehicle. "The keys are here."

The Monk walked over to Pap and put his hand under his good arm. He picked him up and started walking him toward the car.

Pap was dazed but asked, "Where's Annie?"

The Monk didn't speak, so Milan did. "She's fine. We have an ambulance on the way. She'll be fine."

The Monk put him in the back seat and got behind the wheel. Milan walked toward him to say "good job," but The Monk had already turned around to back out, then sped out of the driveway. Milan walked to the back of the house to make some calls and tend to Annie. He had a show to put on.

Chapter 39

February 4, 1904
The Metropolitan Club
10 East 60ᵗʰ Street
New York City

W oodbury Kane was a little unsteady on his feet as he walked out the front gate of the club. He pulled his watch from his pocket to check the time: 3:10 a.m.

It had been a long evening of cards and brandy. He thought it best to walk back to his residence at the Algonquin Hotel to clear his head in the brisk winter air. The street was empty at this hour so he was alerted immediately to the sound of footfalls behind him. He picked up his pace, and the steps behind him increased to keep up. Kane had experienced many late nights in the city and was not the type to let any ruffian from the shadows distract from his evening plans. He turned to confront the men, who were now just ten yards away. They stopped in their tracks.

Kane knew them from the newspapers and the precinct-house posters. The men were Razor Riley and Biff Ellison. Riley and Ellison were gunmen for Paul Kelly, the head of the Five Points gang. Kane smiled as he looked at the handguns pointed at him. The men must have thought it odd—him smiling—but they held Browning M1900s, the very handgun Teddy carried at all times. Theirs didn't have pearl handles like Teddy's, but Kane was sure they were just as deadly. He attempted to take control of the confrontation while they were confused.

"Gentleman, have you come to have me escort you to the police station? I believe there's a precinct house not far from here. Would you kindly follow me?"

Riley and Ellison were hardened men and not the type for witty repartee. Ellison practically grunted his response.

"Shut up and keep walking. Turn right on Fifth."

Kane turned around and started walking. A sense of calm came over him. He had always had the ability to stay calm in tense situations. In fact, the more dangerous the moment, the clearer his thinking would be. As he walked, he thought about this particular dilemma he found himself in. It was clear this was not a robbery, or they would have shot him in the back immediately. There was something else at play. He was being taken somewhere.

They walked up the east side of Fifth Avenue for a few blocks. Kane was alert now that the brandy cobwebs had been waved away at the sight of the Brownings. Ellison spoke again.

"Cross over here."

The streets were empty, the city still asleep for a few more hours. As Kane crossed, he saw a man sitting on a bench along the rock wall that separated the Fifth Avenue walkway from Central Park. As he approached, Kane made out who it was. Paul Kelly, the leader of the Five Points gang. Kane knew Paul Kelly's story quite well. He was an Italian immigrant whose actual name was Paolo Antonio Vaccarelli. He adopted the Irish moniker to fit in with the New York City boxing world. He was a good boxer, Kane recalled hearing. Good enough to earn the funds to invest in small athletic clubs, where he would recruit young men into his gang. The clubs became a front for his burgeoning criminal empire. It was said he had up to fifteen hundred men under his command. The only men in New York with equal influence in the underworld were Monk Eastman with his two-thousand-strong crew and Big Tim Sullivan, the long-standing leader of the Tammany Party. Kelly was not a brute like Eastman. He dressed well and was comfortable in some of the best restaurants and parlors in the city. Kane saw him as a man of his time. He had the intellect to charm the gilded set, and the muscle and money to keep the police at bay. If he were on the proper side of the law, Kane thought that he might admire him, but since he was not, he detested him more than any other man in New York. Kelly was as sharp and well-spoken as a Fifth Avenue banker and had the intellect to make his fortune legally, yet he had chosen the path of violence and corruption. He spoke three languages and was comfortable in the company of the highest social circles, but he was also known to have killed men and stuffed them into whiskey barrels. As he stepped onto the sidewalk, Kane decided he would make sure Kelly would pay for this disrespect. Hopefully with his life.

Kelly remained seated as Kane approached him without any prompting from the gunmen. He heard the cocking of their pistols as he stood over Kelly. The gang leader raised a hand, signaling "at ease" to his men, then leaned back on the bench.

"Have a seat, Mr. Kane. Or is it Captain?"

"I'll stand."

Kelly smiled and spread both arms across the back of the bench, crossing his legs. He was dressed as impeccably as Kane himself.

"Okay then. Business. Mr. Kane, are you aware that there is a price on your head? It's up to two hundred dollars. A big payday. My two associates here would kill you for a good steak dinner."

Kane squared his feet and straightened his back. "Why haven't they?"

"Well, you see, there is this myth going around about you. Some of my men believe that you can't be killed, that you are someone who is better left alone. People think that you're one of the most powerful men in New York. It started when you took Ward Boss Costello. He died in transit, you know. I guess you do. No matter. This myth, this story about you has grown since then. Many of my men believe that they would end up on a prison ship to Australia should you cross their paths. People think you have some very important people behind you. They think President Roosevelt himself is backing you, both of you with the Rough Rider connection and all. These people have noticed the damage that has been done to Tammany since the night you took Costello. They saw you walking around the docks a few years back, right before Van Wyck had his stock certificates stolen. They see a lot, these people. They know Roosevelt appointed that dago cop, Petrosino, to chief of detectives years back. The president of the United States is your friend and has ties to Petrosino? All the arrests? The barrel murders solved so quickly, all those loose ends? That fucking rat cop. That disgrace to his people. He gets funds for the investigation so quickly and easily. I have friends in the department; no one approved his budget on the Barrel Murders case. Yet, there he was— Petrisino, that little Italian, paying informants. Greasing the palms, feeding cheese to the rats. Big Tim Sullivan himself puts out the word to stay away from you. You must see how some may be wary of approaching you. How you have become a man to be feared in certain circles. Yes, many of my men think you're untouchable. Are you untouchable, Mr. Kane? If I raised my hand and my associates here opened fire, would the bullets bounce off?"

"You haven't laid a hand on me. Perhaps these people are correct. It seems that a lot of your associates think a lot of things, but it's a bit late in the evening to listen to your gangland gossip."

Kane was impressed that Kelly managed to piece together a good amount of what he and Jacob had been working on the last couple of years. They did strike up a relationship with Petrosino. They did help provide information and financial support during the investigation into the Barrel Murders. In fact, they tried to recruit Petrosino into the Volunteers, but he was too fiercely independent and aligned with the structure of law enforcement to pledge allegiance to any organization other than the NYPD. Kane knew Kelly was looking for a reaction. A reaction that would never come.

Kelly smiled at the retort.

"No, I'm sure you're not. Mr. Kane, let me explain myself. I'm sure you know who I am, but I'm afraid that you don't fully realize how much you need me."

"Need you?" Kane's response was dripping with condescension.

"Oh yes. You need me. I hold the price on your head. I set the bounty. Two hundred is a lot of money to a lot of people, but I haven't made the call yet. You see, my men are trained well. I say when the contract is ready. You have no say in this. You are only the gladiator in the ring. Winning your small victories. I'm the emperor holding my hand up. Thumbs-up you live, thumbs-down ... well, I think you know."

"This is nonsense. Get on with whatever business you have in mind or start the fighting."

Kelly laughed out loud. "Mr. Kane, everything I've heard about you is true. You're going to fight us?" Riley and Ellison laughed behind Kane.

Kelly continued. "Well, maybe you have a chance. A war hero and all. I've heard you're quite a boxer yourself. Maybe you take a bullet and keep fighting. Maybe two or three bullets. I've seen it before. Lesser men than you have escaped similar situations. Okay, let's say you get away. But you must remember, I have fifteen hundred men under my command. I go thumbs-down, and all of them are after you. It could be next week or a year from now, but someone is going to come up behind you and stick a knife in your neck. Not even the great Woodbury Kane can survive that. A knife in the neck. No. I don't think so."

"Why don't you dispense with the theatrics and get to the point?"

"Yes. You see, I don't believe in myths or conspiracies. I think you are nothing more than a rich prig playing cops and robbers. You think you can make New York, the world, a better place, and with all your money and influence, you can drive out the lowlifes like myself. All the while, you sit in your club with the very men who are paying me to steer votes their way. Half the members of the Metropolitan Club have passed money to me through intermediaries. Those men are far more corrupt than I can ever dream to be. They've raised armies against their own workers. No, there is no myth—it's a lie, a charade. You are ashamed of your status. Ashamed to stand with these corrupt men. These robber barons. So you think you can make the world a better place from the comfort of your country clubs and mansions? Well, Mr. Kane, you're as arrogant as the men in your club. Those bribers and union bashers. I could kill you on this street tonight, and it wouldn't make a bit of a difference to the people of New York, because the people of New York don't give one damn about you … but they love me. Why would that be? An immigrant over a Harvard man? I'll tell you why. I put bread on their tables. You? You don't do shit for any of them."

Kane had no interest in giving Kelly's pop analysis any credence. It was the same rationalization that every criminal had used for hundreds of years. He smirked and ignored the remarks, having no interest in debating with a gangster.

"You said you wanted to discuss business?"

"Yes, I do. Monk Eastman was arrested today. The fool beat up and robbed a student in plain sight of two Pinkerton agents then opened fire on them. They brought him in about four this afternoon. I'm sure he is expected to sleep off his drunk and walk out the door a few hours from now. I made some inquiries to friendly officials, and I'm assured he will go to trial quickly. I want you to use your influence to make sure he is found guilty, and when he is sentenced, I want him to go away for a good long time."

"So Monk goes to jail and you rule the city without any competition."

"Well, there's the police."

It was meant as a joke and taken as such. Kelly was the strong arm of Tammany Hall. Between the two organizations, they had the majority of the police department under contract. Kelly's only true concern from the police would be Detective Petrosino. Kane wondered when the detective would have his late-night meeting.

Kelly attempted to close the deal. "You see? We have mutual interests. You stay alive and continue to play your little hero game, and I expand my business." He stood up, signaling the end of the discussion. "My people tell me that Monk will go on trial in a week or so. I want him found guilty within two weeks. You get this done, or you only have two weeks and a day to live."

"And the sentencing?"

"I don't care. As long as he stays in the can until they hand it down. Then, like I said, a long time."

Kane stared hard at Kelly. "That would be fine with me. It would give me the opportunity to discard one piece of trash and go after another one."

It was the first time a man had dared challenge Kelly, in or out of the ring, in a very long time.

He stood and stepped up to Kane. They were nose to nose when Kelly spoke.

"I'll be waiting for you, pretty boy. I'm at the New Brighton Athletic Club most days. Not as swank as your club, but the company's better."

He brushed past Kane and started down Fifth Avenue. His men fell in behind him. Kane took a seat and immediately started thinking strategy.

Chapter 40

J acob Riis sat in the lounge chair and placed his wine glass on a doily on the side table. He had been summoned urgently by Woodbury Kane for an emergency meeting. The residence took up the entire floor of the hotel. Hotel living was a common arrangement among New York's wealthier set. Living in a home with concierge and room service was a luxury not afforded to many. Certainly not to Riis. The room was decorated a bit too opulently for Riis's taste, but the wine was excellent, as was the company.

"So, Woody, what is the urgent nature of your call? I go away for the week tomorrow, as you know. I'm thinking this could have waited until next week. I do hope you have a good reason for the kerfuffle."

Kane poured himself a whiskey straight up, sat down across the table from him, and crossed his legs. He took a thoughtful sip then placed the tumbler on the table.

"Paul Kelly threatened my life this morning."

Riis popped up in his seat then rested himself on the edge of it.

"Paul Kelly? How? What? I mean, when did this happen?"

Kane chuckled. He opened his hands wide, as if he were trying to gently calm a jumpy polo pony. "It's okay, Jacob. It's okay."

"Paul Kelly? It's okay, you say? Was he alone?"

Kane was as relaxed as a man sitting at the theatre.

"No. He had his men, Riley and Ellison, with him. They pulled Brownings on me outside the club. We talked for a bit."

"You're telling me that Razor Riley and Biff Ellison pulled guns on you and took you to Paul Kelly, who threatened your life .... and you think that is okay?"

"Yes, of course. It wasn't a threat. It was a proposition."

"A proposition?"

"Yes. Did you know that Monk Eastman was arrested yesterday?"

"No."

"Well, apparently he assaulted a young man, and two Pinkertons caught him in the act. They brought him in to police custody yesterday afternoon."

"So he's out by now." Riis smirked.

"No, he's not. I sent a note to a friend this morning. He'll be held until trial. That was Kelly's first request. He also wants me to make sure he is sentenced for a good long time."

Despite Riis's shock, he caught up to Kane's strategy in an instant. "Divide and conquer. Is that your idea? Go along with Kelly to get Eastman out of the picture, then we can concentrate on Kelly alone." Riis was silent for a moment, thinking. "Why you? Why now?"

"Costello. There's a price on my head because of it. Kelly claims he put up the bounty himself, but the call for my head likely came from Big Tim Sullivan. He was friends with Costello before he moved to the top spot. I'm convinced that Sullivan put up the bounty; he's slippery enough to keep his fingerprints off it, though. Kelly is trying to use the price on my head as leverage."

"I told you. I told you. What did I say? You and Teddy acting like I was crazy. Damn it, Woody. No one can know who we are. No one!"

"No, Jacob. It is not at all like that. Kelly thinks I'm a vigilante with some kind of wealthy man's guilt. The funny thing is that the street toughs and henchmen he surrounds himself with seem to know more than he does."

"What does that mean?"

"He told me some of the stories that are going around. That I have ties to Detective Petrosino; that I helped with the Barrel Murders."

"But you do. We do. How can you not be concerned about this?"

"Kelly is too stupid to see the truth in it. He's a goon. Not much more than the brawlers he spends his days with. He knows nothing of you or Teddy, certainly not about Morgan or Rockefeller. He thinks he can pick me up in the street and scare me into doing his dirty work. He's a thug in a nice suit. Nothing more."

Riis thought that this was finally the time to raise a delicate matter that had hung over their relationship and some of their operations for years. He sat back in his seat and took a sip of his wine.

"Woody, there are times when your class status blinds you from the hard facts of life for the working or lower classes. It is quite possible that Kelly or anyone in his class can be very intelligent. The unfortunate can be educated and well-mannered. These people are the heart of New York. I agree that Kelly is nothing more than a street tough in a nice suit, but he can be a formidable opponent."

Kane finished his drink in a long gulp.

"I know, Jacob. I know I can come off as a fop or a dandy. I know that I have an elitist viewpoint about many things. I admire your attitude toward the lower classes, your passion for raising people up from the shadows. I have come to terms with my faults. I can be very closed-minded. I'm aware of this. I must say that your friendship has helped me become a better person, but I'm not going to change much more than I have already. I like the way I live and with the luxuries that I have. I'm not going to give it up. I do think that, unlike most of my contemporaries, my mind has been expanded enough to *not* take my status for granted. I feel that my extraordinary life enables me to help others in my own way. I plan to continue to use my position to do the things I feel are right for this city. Right now, in this moment, what would be best for the city I love is to send Monk Eastman away for as long as possible and to put together a plan to eliminate Paul Kelly."

Riis responded with respect and admiration. "Well said, my friend. I have never doubted your passion for doing the right thing." He paused. "What exactly do you mean by *eliminate*?"

"I think we will have to kill him. It is not a choice. Once he starts thinking he can get me to do his bidding, he will not go away. I've thought about this all day. It is the only answer."

204   J o h n   N u c k e l

They both realized they were crossing the ultimate line. Kane had known for some time that this day would come. Their efforts had forced Tammany to shift from the criminal to the political. There was plenty to do on that front, no doubt, but they found themselves more involved in the underbelly of the city every day. To Kane's mind, the only way to deal with this level of criminality would be to answer violence with violence. They have entered a world where the currency was no longer payoffs to local police; in this arena, debts were settled and alliances were broken with murder and executions.

Riis laid his head back on the chair, took a deep breath, and closed his eyes. He felt the need to raise an objection, although he knew they had no choice.

"Is this whom we have become? We're killers now? Judge, jury, and executioner?"

"Jacob. We have been serving as judge and jury for quite sometime. I'm afraid the last step is a necessary one for our survival. Kelly will come for me eventually. Once he thinks I'm of no use to him, he will carry out his threat. Riley or Ellison will pull the trigger."

"I suppose you're right, Woody. I suppose you're right."

Woody looked at him, and in their silence they made a pact to never speak of the morality of this decision again. They crossed the threshold together.

"Kelly is a smart man; I don't underestimate him. We have to put together a solid plan of attack."

"You won't get much help from the police."

Kane smiled broadly. "Who needs the police when I have one of the great men of New York at my disposal. That is why I called you here, my friend. I have an idea."

"At your disposal?'

Kane laughed and stood to get himself another whiskey. Riis sipped his wine and tried once again to figure out if his friend was brave or crazy. He had been under the barrel of the guns of three of the most notorious killers New York City has ever known not twenty-four hours ago, and here he was chuckling like a child on a playground. Riis could never figure out if Woodbury Kane was a madman or a hero. He came to the same conclusion, as always—he was all of it and much more.

Woodbury Kane and Jacob Riis spent the next two hours determining the fates of Paul Kelly and Monk Eastman.

Chapter 41

October 1904
Monk Eastman sentenced to ten years at Sing Sing Prison.

November 1905

Razor Riley and Biff Ellison walked into the new Brighton Athletic Club with pistols drawn. They'd left Kelly and the Five Points gang in a dispute over their payout to join the Gopher gang not a year earlier. It was later speculated that they were making a play for their own territory. Kelly and his bodyguards were not prepared for the gunfight that ensued. Riley and Ellison opened fire and immediately killed Kelly's bodyguard. Riley shot the hat off Kelly's head, and Ellison missed his chance to kill the crime lord when the lights were suddenly turned off. He fired into the darkness and put a slug through the sleeve of Kelly's jacket. Riley was hit in the gut, and he and Ellison retreated into the dark night.

Kelly got away unharmed.

Like many evenings, the athletic club had been filled with a fair share of the social set slumming downtown to experience the debauchery of the Bowery. The brazen disregard of the rule of law and the complaints from men of influence prompted Police Commissioner McAdoo to close down the club. Tammany turned their backs on Kelly. Big Tim Sullivan was more interested in politics than payoffs by this time, and he left Kelly to fend for himself. Without Tammany's support, Kelly soon lost hold of his position. So much of his power was tied to Tammany that once the political bosses pulled away their support, he became just another thug.

His time in the limelight had gone in the blaze of gunfire. Many speculated he would have rather gone down in a firefight than to relocate to Upper Harlem, where he became a union representative. His empire was split into many factions, and Kelly was no longer the king of the New York crime world.

Biff Ellison had the insight to start paying off local police many years earlier. Although there were many eyewitnesses who identified him as one of the shooters, he wasn't arrested until 1911. Riley was found a few weeks after the shooting in the basement of his Chinatown hideout. He was dying of pneumonia brought on by an infection from the untreated gunshot wound when police arrived on the scene. Riley, a well-known piker with the reputation of a man who never had more than a sawbuck in his pocket, was found with two thousand dollars in a money belt underneath his jacket. The first officer on the scene wrote down Riley's last words: "Et Omnia Recta."

Chapter 42

J acob Riis stood over the grave of Woodbury Kane. He still hadn't
come to grips with the shock of his sudden death. As soon as Razor
Riley was found by the police, Kane had taken off on a duck hunt. He
returned early because of what he called "a slight cold," and the next day
he died from heart paralysis. Riis was at the funeral. His presence was
justified as a journalist, but he thought it better to not be at the burial in
Newport. No one knew of their friendship and certainly not of their
alliance. He waited patiently at the gravesite. He had been there for a few
hours and had said his words. The cemetery was deserted and snow had
started to fall, layering a fresh coating on the packed snow around the
grave, but still he waited.

Jacob Riis was waiting for the president of the United States to arrive.

He heard a horse approaching and turned around to see Teddy atop a
shiny black stallion. He was dressed in his full Rough Riders uniform. He
was in his parade regalia, complete with the sash and side-brimmed hat.
Jacob could see the reflection of the tombstones in his freshly shined,
knee-high boots. As he came closer, Riis could hear the sound of his
medals clinking and the clamor of his sword bouncing against his saddle.
Teddy stopped the horse ten yards from the tombstone and tied off his
mount on a barren tree branch.

As he walked past Jacob he put a hand on his shoulder and continued toward the grave. He stood at attention and saluted. Then he put his lips to his gloved hand and kissed. He walked the last two steps and placed the kissed fingertips on the top of the tombstone. Then, President Theodore Roosevelt got on his knees in the snow and lowered his head. Jacob could hear him mumbling a silent prayer or a tribute.

He joined Teddy and lowered his head once again and said a silent prayer for Woodbury Kane and his family. He also prayed for Teddy, that he would have the strength to continue to lead this nation. He prayed for the safe conclusion of the operations that the Volunteers had begun, for the safety of all involved. He selfishly said a silent prayer for himself. He asked the Lord to give him the strength to continue this work. To provide the will to carry on. For days now, he had struggled with the thought of doing this himself. He believed deeply in their cause and in the operations currently in progress, but he felt weak in a way he hadn't in many years. He felt as if his will, his drive, had been taken away with the death of Woodbury Kane.

Roosevelt stood and turned to Riis. His eyes were red, and his booming voice withered and dry.

"How are you, my friend?"

He stepped up and took Jacob in a big bear hug, and for a moment, Riis felt Teddy's spirit lift him. Teddy then let go and took a step back.

"I was addressing Congress on the day of his funeral."

It was the first time Riis had heard Teddy try to explain an absence, or anything, in fact. Teddy was not an excuse maker.

"I know. I read the notes of the speech. Very compelling."

"You read it?'

"Of course, Teddy. I read everything of yours."

Roosevelt seemed genuinely shocked. "You read my speeches? Why would you want to spend your time on such things?'

"Teddy, they will be history someday. I keep copies for my library."

"That's very kind of you, Jacob."

The president took off his gloves and rubbed both his hands over his face.

"He was a great man. Uncanny, isn't it?"

"What?"

"I watched him run up San Juan Hill, standing tall. No leaning, no ducking. Bullets flew past his head, and he didn't blink or cower once. He comes home from a hunt and dies in his luxury suite. Death is rarely just. Certainly not for men like Woody."

There was a heaviness to his words. Riis was well aware that Teddy had felt the devastation of sudden deaths in a way that no man should have to face. Twenty-one years earlier his wife and mother had died on the same day. Riis did not know him then, but his reaction to that tragic day was well-known. Teddy had left New York and headed out to the Montana territories. He worked as a sheriff for a time and tried his hand at ranching. Most New York society thought they had seen and heard the last of him. Riis was an early admirer of Teddy. Having read many of the man's papers, he was aware of his pugnacious wit and spirit. Riis had felt that Teddy had been the right man for this time in America. His theory at the time was that it would take a man of a certain social standing to put a damper on the excesses of the gilded age. To run down the robber barons.

Teddy did return eventually and became the police commissioner. Shortly afterward, he contacted the journalist to tour the Five Points. Teddy wanted Riis to show him how the other half lived. He also wanted to find out how his men, the New York police, allowed these conditions to persist. They roamed those filthy streets many late nights. Riis witnessed Teddy cuff a sleeping policeman across the face. It was a remarkable sight to see the chief of police, a man of great wealth and stature walking the streets with prostitutes and petty thieves. Riis had known then that this was a remarkable man. He knew before Teddy himself that he would be president one day—he had been a force that could not be stopped.

Riis looked at Teddy, and it seemed this great force had been slowed to a halt. He feared that Teddy may run away again. As president, he couldn't take off to Montana, certainly, but he could back off, slow down his drive for reform. He feared Teddy Roosevelt may become an ordinary man. He could see how deeply affected he was. For the first time since Riis had known him, there seemed to be an air of defeat about him. A sight that Jacob would have never imagined in a thousand years. He tried to reassure him.

"Woody lived a full life."

The president didn't respond. He stared over Riis's shoulder at nothing at all.

"We've done great things. Tammany is not much more than a fading political machine. Monk Eastman, Paul Kelly, both reduced to nothing. Great things, Teddy. We've done great things."

Teddy squeezed Jacob's shoulder, looked him in the eye, and suddenly he was back. He squeezed the shoulder tighter before letting go.

"Yes, we have. There is much more to do. We have to continue. Yes. Yes. Great work ahead of us."

Riis sighed with relief and smiled for the first time since Kane's passing.

Teddy walked toward his horse. Riis instinctively followed. Teddy, back in full fit, spoke as he walked.

"The supervision of any ongoing Volunteer operations will be your sole responsibility. I have to recuse myself from any future discussions."

"Teddy, we haven't mentioned a thing to you since you took office."

"Yes, I know, but it has felt like I've been involved every step of the way. Perhaps because I have been reading of your successes in the papers."

"You have been with us in spirit every day."

Teddy stopped at his horse. Riis briefly wondered where he had procured the horse and how he had arrived without an escort. Teddy read his thoughts. He patted the hind quarter of the stallion.

"The Secret Service lets me sneak out for a ride occasionally. I'm here for some speeches, so I snuck away. Great fun to ride again."

Riis knew his friend well. For Teddy, adventure, the outdoors was the tonic, the salve for his wounds. He had no doubt that Teddy would ride through the night. The great man stepped into the stirrup and mounted. Once comfortable, he looked down at Riis.

"You have to continue. Keep the pressure on the scoundrels, I say."

Riis looked up, knowing the rest of the conversation would take place with Teddy on horseback. He needed to be up there to push away his despair.

"I'm going to need some assistance. There is a lot to keep track of for one man."

"What of Morgan and Rockefeller? Are they still on board?"

"Yes, but they have become benefactors more than anything else."

"What about the executive committee? They are still members, are they not?"

"They would rather write a check and perhaps twist an arm at the club than be a part of the day-to-day operations. They're not suited for actual work."

Teddy laughed. "Yes, I know. Well, they don't care much for me, I'll say. As long as they see a financial interest for themselves, they'll continue to support you. Keep that in mind, always."

"I have and will."

"Do you know Giuseppe Petrosino?"

"Yes. We provided assistance with the Barrel Murders case. We actually tried to recruit him as a Volunteer, but he was not receptive. He seemed reluctant to work outside of the system."

"Well, he is a very good man. Dedicated. I've heard from him recently. He is not getting the cooperation from his own force that he needs. You know that I saw potential in him many years ago. I appointed him chief of detectives." He looked forward for a moment. "How many years now? I don't recall. I remember getting plenty of resistance for appointing an Italian. Even as a commissioner."

"I know he is very dedicated. He had a strong presence when we met him. Woody wanted to put him on the executive committee after the first meeting."

"He's taken on quite a task. The Morello Family. The Black Hand. Very dangerous group. He could use your help."

"I'm familiar with the group. Cold-blooded. Aren't they mostly street thugs? Throat slashers and the like?"

"Yes, I thought the same, but Giuseppe assured me they are expanding into counterfeiting and extortion, among other deeds. He sees them as the next big crime family if they are not stopped soon. I'll arrange for him to meet with you. You must take it from there."

"Yes. I will. Thank you, Teddy."

They shared a moment of silence.

Riis pondered out loud. "What do you think it was about Woody?"

"Woody?'

"Yes. What was it about him? There was so much about him that I didn't understand. You and I have clear ambitions. I'm a journalist, and you ... well, you're Teddy Roosevelt, but Woody? I don't know why he did the things that he did. Did you know he stared down Paul Kelly and his gunmen, then he turned the gunmen around to kill Kelly. Their own boss. He was remarkable. Yet nothing that he accomplished will ever be known. The world will know him as a man of the gilded age. A yachtsman, a womanizer, a drinker, and card player. We will have our legacies—you're part of history now and I've been published—there will be a record of our time on earth, but not him. Not Woodbury Kane."

Teddy shifted in the saddle, and the horse brayed slightly.

"He didn't want a record of his deeds. Our nation's history is made up of men like Woodbury Kane. Men who will never get any recognition, will never be in the history books. He's no different than the man who drove the first railroad spike, the cattleman who first crossed the Missouri River, or the foot soldier who died on the trail with Lewis and Clark. He was one of many men who gave their all without a notion of self-interest.

"I saw it in him when I observed him from a distance in the camp of the Rough Riders in the Cuban jungle. The day was as hot as a cast-iron skillet. There he was, this man of extraordinary wealth, doing dishes. Putting his best effort into the task. I've never seen as fine a job. He did what was right. *Et Omnia Recta*. He was a working man who happened to have great wealth. He was a soldier with the same force inside him as you and me."

"But still, he had a spirit within him that I can't define."

Roosevelt laughed.

"Jacob, my friend, perhaps you are too far removed from our evening forays in the Points. You have lost touch with the working man. I see men and women like Woody all the time. I've observed a nurse sit with a dying soldier through the night. Holding his hand. The dying soldier didn't know she was there. No one will know her name. I don't know it. I've seen extraordinary acts of courage and simple acts of compassion that will never be noted. Woody was one of many, thousands I'm sure, who dedicated themselves to a greater good. Most don't have his wealth or access to power, but they are the true Volunteers. Woody had the good sense to know this, and I would like to think he was representing these everyday people.

"He put a name to this desire to make things right when he created the Volunteers, but thousands can replace him. Perhaps you consider him extraordinary because he heard the call to serve his fellow man despite his great wealth. I don't see that as an extraordinary feat. No. He was one of many who have made this nation great. All of whom I hold in the highest regard. These are the people I serve. As for Woody, don't dare mourn him. He would thunder in your ear if he heard you now."

Riis chuckled. "I'm sure he would,"

Roosevelt sat taller in the saddle. "No. Don't mourn him. Celebrate his spirit; celebrate his drive."

Chapter 43

August 18, 2017
The Victory Grill Coffee Shop
55ᵗʰ Street and 10ᵗʰ Avenue
New York City

A nnie Falcone used the pen that came with the bill to reach down the side of her walking boot to scratch her ankle. Tony Falcone winced as he has done each time he witnessed this display for the past month.

"I wish you would stop doing that."

"I can't help it. It's hot. I sweat. It itches."

"Well, I hope you understand how unladylike it looks."

"Unladylike? Is that even a word. C'mon, Pop."

Annie had been staying with her father since she returned from the hospital. After the gunfight, she was whisked to the Martha's Vineyard Hospital's emergency room. After a brief triage, she was helicoptered to the city. There were two operations in a week at the hospital for special surgery, then she was released. The foot would heal—only one bone was broken. She was lucky, they said, though she didn't feel lucky for the throbbing pain that kept her awake over the following few weeks. The pain decreased gradually, and now it was manageable with Tylenol. Annie was anxious to get back to life—she had been staying with her dad during recovery. It was great to have his moral support; it was also great to have the elevator in his building. Her Brooklyn place was a third-floor walk-up.

As she scratched the itch with the Bic, she wondered when she would be able to run again in Prospect Park and take those steps two at a time like she used to. The doctor had said "soon," but it was hard for her to imagine putting much pressure on the foot.

The wound did provide Annie with something that was always in short supply in her life. It gave her time. Time to think about her future. She tried not to spend too much time thinking about Hank—he would always be Hank in her mind, not Pap. It had been a couple months now without any word from him, a good guy that got away. Probably too "high-level" for her, anyway. She figured he was probably in some bunker in DC or something like that. Annie convinced herself that her feelings for him were brought on by the heightened danger of the situation. There was no way she could fall for a guy so quickly under normal circumstances.

Her father didn't say a word about her future on the police force. When she did ask, he would tell her to concentrate on getting well. She was pretty sure that she was out. The shooting had been in the paper. Her dad hadn't shown her, but she'd found it online. The scene at the house, where she'd killed two men, was written up as a home invasion. Hank Suarez was named as the shooter and quickly exonerated. Self-defense. It was a line item compared to the coverage of Sheng's death. They'd made that fat bastard cop out to be a hero. Him and that wiseass chief. The FBI was all over the news praising the local policeman for acting quickly before they could arrive on the scene.

The story had gone down like this: the two local cops were sent to detain Sheng and his man until the Feds got to the scene. There was a gunfight. The chief emerged unscathed. He saved the fucking day.

Annie had heard of rogue cops tampering with a crime scene. You could drop a gun, plant some drugs, take some money. She was never involved in any of that bullshit, but she knew it went on occasionally. This job ... well, it was a work of art. It was amazing to her that no one questioned any of it. Hero cops and dead spies played pretty well, she guessed. She plopped the pen on the table and looked over at her father, who was staring at his apple pie. "Best damn pie in the city," he'd said when he ordered it.

"Pop, what's up? The pie okay?"

He looked up. "Honey, we have to talk."

From the timbre of the words, she knew what he was about to say.

"I'm out, right?"

"That's up to you, but it doesn't look good."

"I'm not surprised."

He laid down his fork. "We can't place you at the scene of either shooting."

"Yeah, I know."

"That means that there's only one way to account for your wound. You'll have to admit to being reckless with your firearm while off duty."

"I shot myself in the foot?"

"Yeah, I know. It's shitty. There's another way, though. You walk away from the force. Retire early, no mention of your wound."

"You mean the force hasn't been paying the hospital bills? Pop, c'mon. I don't want you spending that kind of money."

"Don't worry about that. This is part of the budget for the operation you were on. The Volunteers have plenty of money, believe me."

"The fucking Volunteers."

Annie looked at her father and saw the same look he'd had on his face at her mother's funeral. "Honey, I'll never be able to explain how scared I was when I heard that you were wounded. I will always hate myself for putting you in harm's way." He reached his hands across the table, and she took them. She expected more words of regret, but suddenly he morphed back to being the chief of detectives, the executive member of the Volunteers—not a concerned father.

"I saw the tape of the break-in at the house. I read the action report from both men on the scene of the Sheng shooting. You were excellent. Your actions helped secure the national security of our country. I don't know how well it was explained to you how dangerous Sheng was, but consider a man like him tapping into the electrical grid of the entire East Coast. That was what he had on those laptops. Our forensic guys say he was days away from shutting down every bank in the northeast. They're sure if he'd had more time, he would have crashed the financial markets. Days away, honey, and you helped stop it. The woman who helped save our country from a financial meltdown can't walk in to her captain and say

she shot herself in the foot. Besides, would Annie Oakley ever do that?"
He smiled broadly.

"Oh God. They told you about that?'

He patted her hands then released them. "It was the smart play. The
shooter was about to put one through our man's lung to get to Sheng. You
saved him."

"How is he? Our man?"

"Oh, him. He's fine. Sheng missed from two inches away. Just powder
burns."

They were silent as they each took in a forkful of pie.

"You weren't kidding about the pie."

"What did I tell ya? This is an old cops' place. I used to come here years
ago. It's been a while. Listen, I'm beat to shit about all of this. I always
hoped you would follow in my footsteps and have a great career with the
NYPD."

Annie took a slug of her coffee.

"Bullshit, Pop. You wanted me to follow in Mom's footsteps. You
didn't want me working with a gun in my hand."

"I guess you're right, but it goes to show: what the hell do I know?
Turns out you're pretty damn good with a gun."

"Don't be upset ... but I have something else I want to do. I've been
thinking about it for a while, and after this past couple of months, I think
I'm ready to go through with it."

Tony sat up straight. "What is it?"

"I want to open a bake shop. Well, not exactly. I want to have a bakery
with a café in front. Thing is, I want to bake."

Tears came to Tony's eyes as fast as if they were brought on by a
hypnotist's finger snap. She handed him her paper napkin, and all she
could think to say was, "Pop."

Annie knew. She knew how much he missed her mom, his wife. How
he longed to see her. She knew the smell of baking would heal his weary
soul. She knew she was saving him as clearly as she had saved Hank with
her behind-the-back shot. She also knew she would have a hard time
keeping her dad out of the kitchen, and that would be just fine.

She took another bite of the pie and thought about the ingredients that made up the recipe and what she might tweak. Tony stopped weeping as quickly as he started, embarrassed by the outburst.

"That would be great, honey." He tried to be stoic, but his voice cracked on "honey."

With those simple words, Annie knew she had found her purpose. She realized in that moment she wasn't meant to be a cop or even a baker. She felt a profound sense of accomplishment, even though she hadn't baked one cupcake yet. She was meant to help others. That was her calling. Being a cop or baking—neither was her calling. They were the pathways to her goal that enabled her to protect, to bring comfort, to help.

Annie continued with her thought. "I have a location. I did a lot of research over the years. More seriously over the last couple of months. You remember my friend who works for the Ritz? I asked her to bring a cake to her catering manager last week."

"The one that you didn't share?"

"Yeah, Pop. I'll make another for you, okay? Anyway, she tells me the guy flipped. Wanted to place an order right then. She had to tell him that I don't have a shop yet. Still, it's a good lead. I think it will work."

Tony smiled with the same look as when she'd won a basketball trophy or came home with a perfect report card. "I'm sure it will work. I believe in you. Always have."

"Thanks. There is one thing. I talked to the bank about the spot I have in mind. I need an enormous amount of money to show for collateral. Money I don't have."

"I spoke to Frank about your job status."

Annie bristled at the mention of McGinley's name. She hadn't said a word to her father about how she felt about him since she'd returned, but her expression was probably pretty easy to read.

"Listen, hon. I know how many of these operations begin. It's not uncommon for the man running the operation to keep some of the Volunteers in the dark. I'm sure you think he screwed you or lied to you in some way, but that's the nature of this business. I've held back information on every operation that I've headed. It's the way this works. There must be deniability, and to achieve that, people are only told what they need to know. Remember that this was my recommendation, and I was right that you were strong and capable enough to handle this. If you're pissed off at anyone, you should be pissed at me."

"That may all be true, but it doesn't mean I have to like him."

"Agreed. That's fine. You made a commitment to the group, so it's our responsibility to make sure you are made whole. You're helping us by walking away from the job. You should be compensated."

"I don't want to ask him for anything."

Tony knew this was the time for him to push her. He wasn't going to stand there holding the doorknob and listen to her pitch a fit. Not after everything they'd been through.

"Annie, let go of your anger and be clearheaded. This is your life. I can put up the money if you like, but as an organization, we are committed to helping those who help us. Remember, you volunteered, and you're agreeing now to change your life for us. We take care of our own."

"All right. How does this work? Can you approve the loan or co-sign?"

"No. This is Frank's operation. He's already asked me how we should go about compensating you. He's the man to talk to."

"Fuck. Do I have to meet with him again?"

"I'm afraid so. You're in luck. He should be pulling up any minute." Tony looked at his watch. "We have a meeting in five minutes."

"Shit."

Chapter 44

A black BMW with tinted windows pulled up to the curb. Tony looked out the coffee shop window and turned back to Annie. "That's him. I'll wait here. His driver will take you home. Frank and I are having lunch."

Annie took a deep breath and slid out of the booth. She stood and saw Frank McGinley stepping out of the passenger side. She looked down at her father.

"Pie before lunch, Pop? You better watch that gut."

Tony smiled up at her. "Hey, looks like I'm going to be eating a lot of pie soon. I need the practice. Annie smiled and turned, but Tony said, "Take care of yourself. I can't lose you too." He hesitated for a beat and reached his hand out to her. She took it by the fingertips. "I love you."

Annie was taken back since he hadn't said those words to her in many years. He was always affectionate but never overly. If this was to be the new way, she didn't mind it at all.

"I love you, Pop."

The heat outside hit Annie like a wet towel. The air had weight to it, and the sky to the west over McGinley's shoulder was dark and ominous. The air conditioning in the coffee shop almost allowed her to forget it was August in Manhattan. She felt the sweat under her boot start up again.

McGinley was dressed in slacks, a shirt, and Ray-Bans. He managed to look cool despite the temperature. She hadn't seen him since they'd first met in the bar where she'd signed on for the operation—when she'd volunteered and he'd lied to her.

They met halfway between the car and the coffee shop doorway. He stepped off to the side, signaling that he wanted to speak away from prying ears. Annie imagined that he had held thousands of meetings in doorways or alleys. He leaned against a shaded wall on the side of the building. Annie limped over and rested her back against the brick wall. They stood side by side facing 55th Street.

"You did a hell of a job. My man on the scene was very impressed, and he doesn't impress easily."

Annie wasn't in the mood for chatter. She wanted to punch him in the face, but out of respect for her father, she didn't say a word. McGinley continued.

"Every operation has its difficulties. We were under extreme pressure on this one because of Sheng's hacking capabilities and time constraints. I had to be more discreet than on previous operations. I've gotten quite a bit of pushback from my men on the job——the two men you met. I'm sure you have your complaints, but I couldn't see any other way to go forward. So that is it. We move on. I'm assuming your father told you what was at stake. How close we came to disaster. Considering all that, the outcome could not have been better, and for that, we are very grateful."

Annie clenched her fingers into tight fists. "So that's it? We move on?"

Frank ignored her anger and changed the subject. "Have you decided if you're going to leave the department?"

"Do I have a choice?'

"No, you don't. It would be too messy otherwise. We'll help you in your transition."

"You got it all figured out, don't you? You knew the danger I would be under, but didn't tell me. You also knew I could never go back to being a cop. Not after the big news story you created. You ask me if I've decided to go back to the force? Don't bullshit me, man.'

He turned, and she got a good look at the scars running under his jawline, including the roadmap of scar tissue beneath his eyes.

"Okay. No bullshit. This was what you signed up for when you volunteered. It is dangerous work. You're very good at it. I'm hoping we can use you in the future, but I'm not going to stand here and listen to you bitch about how unfair I was to you. If you don't like it, tough shit. We will move on without you." He lowered his voice back to the mellow tone he had before his outburst. "Now, how can we help you with your next step?"

Annie knew it was futile to continue arguing. It was shit-or-get-off-the-pot time.

"I want to open a bake shop. I have a location picked out on the Upper West Side. I already have an interested customer at a hotel. I think it will work."

"I'm sure it will. I know your cooking skills well. Do you know how many times Tony has brought something you baked to a meeting? My favorite is the Irish bread. My mom made it better, of course, but yours is close."

"Your memory must be playing tricks on you because that is my mom's recipe, and no one makes bread like she did."

McGinley raised his hands in an *I surrender* gesture.

"That may be the case. You have the talent, that's for sure. The rest is marketing. I know a lot of people in the restaurant business. We can help you."

"I'll need a pretty big bank balance to get the loans I need. Startup costs are steep. Equipment, mortgages, it's a lot up front. I put together the business plan. I can make it work, but I need a big infusion of capital for starters."

"I can take care of that. I do know some people in banking. If you're looking for investors, we can do it that way. Financing won't be a problem."

"I don't want any partners."

"Okay then. The executive committee will set up an escrow account. You can use that as your financing resource. If you want to remain independent, you'll have to pay off any loans from the account. I'll have something written up. I'll have a lawyer friend contact you. Send him the business plan."

"I don't want to owe you anything long-term. This is just seed money."

"Agreed. I don't want a piece of a bakery; I do want to protect the assets of the Volunteers, so I expect to be paid back."

"With interest."

"If you wish. I'm not concerned. With your work ethic and talent, I'm sure this will work out for everyone."

He turned and started around the corner toward the entrance to the Victory Grill. Annie walked a few steps behind him and spoke.

"This doesn't change what I think of you. I'd still like to shake the hand of whoever did that to your face."

She heard rolling thunder in the distance, across the Hudson, over in Jersey.

Frank walked the last two steps without turning. He put his right hand on the door and turned around, pulling off his glasses with his left. His scarred face looked worse in the bright sunlight. He smiled, and it raised goosebumps on Annie's forearms.

"You can't shake her hand. I killed her."

He walked through the door.

Chapter 45

Annie got in the car and took a second to compose herself. She wouldn't soon forget that smile and the words that went with it. She shuddered. *What the hell have I gotten into?* She shook her head and looked at her walking boot, her itchy leg about to drive her mad. She was about to tell the driver her address, when he spoke.

"Annie."

She knew his voice. She looked over and saw Hank. She didn't know what to do; the shock was so great. He was as handsome as she remembered.

"Hank.'

"Yes. It's me."

They both chuckled uncomfortably.

"How? I mean, I don't—"

"Yeah, I know it's a shock. I wanted to see you as soon as you got back but I had to wait."

"Had to wait? You have been here? I don't understand."

Hank took a breath. It was clear he had been rehearsing what he was about to say. He reached out his hand to her and she took it.

"I've been in New York since the shooting. I knew you were fine. They told me right away. I couldn't come to you, though. I've been holed up in Frank's townhouse this whole time. We have to wait until we think that my identity as Hank Suarez is foolproof." He rubbed a hand through his hair. "It's just a waiting game now. We're waiting to be sure that, since my name was in the paper, there will be no alarms raised in the intelligence community. Here or abroad. So far, nothing."

Annie was still shocked. "This whole time?'

"Yeah, I know. It killed me. I haven't seen my father yet either."

Annie blurted out what was on her mind since that day. "You saved me. You wouldn't leave that car without me. They would have killed me right there. You saved me."

"*You* saved *me*. A couple of times." He paused. "Maybe we saved each other."

She smiled. "Why are you here now?'

"I told Frank that I needed to see you. I couldn't wait anymore. I have a place in the Caribbean no one knows about. Frank thinks I'll have to lie low another month, maybe two. Come with me now. I have a plane waiting at McArthur Airport. We can be on the beach in four or five hours."

She didn't take even a second to think before blurting out an answer. "I'm opening a bakery. I can't go anywhere. I have to stay here. In New York."

Hank put out his other hand, and she took both of them..

"I don't want you to give up anything for me. I'll be in New York also once my identity is cleared. I want to be in New York with you. I'm forty years old, and nothing like this has ever happened to me." He shook his head. "I know I must sound like a schoolboy with a crush, but I just can't stop thinking about that night at my house when the moon rose up and shone on your face. Something happened to my heart then. The moment the moonlight hit your face I knew that I would never stop thinking about you. It's crazy, I know, but I mean, why can't we take a shot at this?"

Annie didn't know what to say. It was if he knew everything she'd been wanting to hear since that very same day. He didn't give her a chance to respond. He plowed ahead.

"I can't give up this life, though. I'm on the executive committee of the Volunteers. There will be times when we may be in danger because of it. I may have to go away for long periods of time. It won't be a normal life, but I know that it won't be any life unless I'm with you."

She still didn't answer. He pressed on.

"I have to go soon. I shouldn't be out on the street. I promised Frank five minutes tops. Come with me. Come now."

Annie looked into this eyes. She turned toward the Victory Grill and saw her father in the window, talking to McGinley. She knew he couldn't see her through the tinted window, but she held up her hand, anyway. Just then, he turned his head briefly to look outside, then turned back to McGinley and took a bite of his pie.

Annie looked at Hank, squeezed his hands, and smiled. Releasing his hands, she adjusted herself to face forward. She looked out at what was ahead of her.

"Drive."

Acknowledgements

Thanks to my early readers: Glenn Burgos, Kevin Nuckel, and Stephen Nuckel. After your thumbs-up, I was off to the races. Thanks to Randy Reis for suggesting the title. The referrals and guidance from Susan Shapiro and Charles Salzberg opened doors and emails. You've had a bigger impact than you might imagine. Thank you.

Janet Fix did an incredible job editing—so good, in fact, that I joined her publishing company, *thewordverve*. Here's to many successes in the future.

A heartfelt thanks to Larry Kirshbaum for sitting with me in the diner and sharing your insights. The last two thousand words written came straight out of your notepad. Thanks for the honesty.

None of this happens without the fabulous Vicki Wellington. You are the light of my life.

About the Author

John Nuckel lives in New York City with his wife and two children. He is a longtime "student of the city." When he's not writing, he's often researching in one of Manhattan's libraries or museums.

www.johnnuckel.com

John's Other Novels
Rector Street Series:
The Vig
Grit
Blind Trust

John's Short Stories
The Garden
The Victory Grill

Made in the USA
Middletown, DE
17 April 2022

64398928R00129